Praise for the Novels
of Ralph Cotton

"Cotton writes with the authentic ring of a silver dollar, a storyteller in the best tradition of the Old West."
—Matt Braun, Golden Spur Award–winning author
of *One Last Town* and *You Know My Name*

"Evokes a sense of outlawry . . . distinctive."
—*Lexington Herald-Leader*

"Disarming realism . . . solidly crafted."
—*Publishers Weekly*

"Authentic Old West detail and dialogue fill his
books." —*Wild West Magazine*

"The sort of story we all hope to find within us: the
bloodstained, gun-smoked, grease-stained yarn that
yanks a reader right out of today."—Terry Johnston

FAST GUNS OUT OF TEXAS

Ralph Cotton

A SIGNET BOOK

SIGNET
Published by New American Library, a division of
Penguin Group (USA) Inc., 375 Hudson Street,
New York, New York 10014, USA
Penguin Group (Canada), 90 Eglinton Avenue East, Suite 700, Toronto,
Ontario M4P 2Y3, Canada (a division of Pearson Penguin Canada Inc.)
Penguin Books Ltd., 80 Strand, London WC2R 0RL, England
Penguin Ireland, 25 St. Stephen's Green, Dublin 2,
Ireland (a division of Penguin Books Ltd.)
Penguin Group (Australia), 250 Camberwell Road, Camberwell, Victoria 3124,
Australia (a division of Pearson Australia Group Pty. Ltd.)
Penguin Books India Pvt. Ltd., 11 Community Centre, Panchsheel Park,
New Delhi - 110 017, India
Penguin Group (NZ), 67 Apollo Drive, Mairangi Bay,
Auckland 1311, New Zealand (a division of Pearson New Zealand Ltd.)
Penguin Books (South Africa) (Pty.) Ltd., 24 Sturdee Avenue,
Rosebank, Johannesburg 2196, South Africa

Penguin Books Ltd., Registered Offices:
80 Strand, London WC2R 0RL, England

First published by Signet, an imprint of New American Library,
a division of Penguin Group (USA) Inc.

First Printing, March 2007
10 9 8 7 6 5 4 3 2 1

For Mary Lynn . . . *of course*

PART 1

Chapter 1

On his way into town Cray Dawson had taken note of the long boardwalk crowded with prospectors, miners, teamsters, and a varied assortment of businessmen leading into the barbershop. He'd studied the gathering curiously as he rode closer, keeping his biscuit-colored barb at a walk, leading his pack mule on a rope behind him.

In a bustling dirt-street gold town like Crabtown, Montana, Dawson would ordinarily have given such a gathering a passing look and ridden on to a hotel or saloon. But as his horse and mule made their way past the barbershop, something caught Dawson's eye that caused him to give the crowded boardwalk a double take. Stopping the barb and the mule abruptly in the middle of the street, he stared almost in disbelief at the hastily painted sign reading SEE FAST LARRY SHAWL DEAD IN HIS COFFIN, 50 CENTS. Beneath the hand-painted words someone had added in thick pencil lead: WHILE HE LASTS.

"Oh no . . ." Dawson murmured, reality sinking in quickly, something inside reminding him that this should come as no great surprise, given the kind of life Lawrence Shaw had chosen for himself. Still, he felt stunned for a second at the thought of his lifelong friend lying dead in this town so far away from home—home for both of them being Somos Santos, Texas.

For just a fleeting second Dawson caught sight of the two of them years ago, tough young ranch hands, mounted on tough cow ponies, running down strays beneath the hot Texas sun. But that vision left as quickly as it came to him and he swallowed a tight knot in his throat and said to himself, "Jesus, Shaw, they didn't even spell your name right."

Coaxing the horse and mule over to the barbershop, Dawson stepped down from his saddle and spun the barb's reins and tied the mule's lead rope to a hitch rail. Stepping up onto the boardwalk near the crowded barbershop door he noted the smell of leather and sweat, of deep earth, witch hazel, and whiskey.

The rank bittersweet scent of civilization took a second of readjustment after weeks of living alone on the trail. So did the sound of a human voice when an old man wearing a flop hat called out through a tangle of ashy red beard, "Hey, mister, how about waiting your turn like everybody else here!"

Dawson felt eyes shift to him and take note of the tied-down Colt at his hip. Beside the old man a cautioning voice said, "Hush up, Reardon. We don't want no trouble!"

"To hell with trouble!" said the old man. "Wearing a big sidearm doesn't give all these bummers the right to shoulder their way past the whole world!"

Dawson agreed, but before he could tell the old man that he'd had no intention of cutting into the line a familiar voice called out from the open barbershop door, "Let this man through! This is Mr. Crayton Dawson, best friend of the deceased! He doesn't have to pay, *or* stand in line . . . give him room!"

Dawson saw the old man's expression soften. "Begging your pardon," he murmured almost in awe. "No offense intended. Any friend of Fast Larry . . ."

"None taken," said Dawson. As he turned from the old man and looked curiously at the moon face staring at him from the doorway, he said, "*Caldwell?* Jedson Caldwell?" as if he had trouble believing his eyes.

"At your service, Mr. Dawson," said the young dark-haired man in the doorway, not dwelling on the matter as he motioned Dawson inside. He wore a flat-crowned straw sombrero and a black pin-striped suit a size too small for him. The fingers of his black gloves had been snipped off in the manner of a stevedore's hand wear. "I must say," he added in a lowered tone as Dawson entered the shop, "we weren't expecting to see you here in Crabtown."

"I'm only passing through, on my way north of

here to do some digging," Dawson responded. He glanced at a slow-moving line of men who filed somberly past a pine coffin set atop a long wooden table against the far wall. He saw hats slip respectfully from their heads as they murmured among themselves.

"I would never have considered you the kind of man for prospecting," Caldwell replied. "Some time back I heard you were the law in Somos Santos?"

"I was. Now I'm prospecting a claim," said Dawson, as if to discourage any further discussion of his term as sheriff in Somos Santos. He stared at the long pine box, seeing on the floor beneath it a thin puddle of water where melting ice packed in sawdust dripped from inside the coffin and had spread in a wide circle. Wet dirty boot prints left a muddy path to the open side door. "I thought you headed for New Orleans."

"Victor, hold them back for a moment," Caldwell said, avoiding the subject of New Orleans. He spoke to the stocky young man who stood at the front collecting money from the sightseers. "Mr. Dawson will want a private viewing, I'm sure."

"*Cray* Dawson?" young Victor Earles asked in a hushed tone of voice, his eyes widening in excitement. "*The* Cray Dawson? The one who sided with Fast Larry against the Talberts? God Almighty, I've seen more big gunmen the past three days than I've seen in my whole—"

"Victor . . . ?" said Caldwell, giving the excited

young man a stern look, causing him to cut his words short.

"Sorry, Mr. Caldwell," Victor said sheepishly. He turned and planted a thick hand firmly on a miner's chest, stopping him from entering the barbershop. As Caldwell motioned Dawson toward the wooden coffin, Victor said harshly to the miner and the line of men behind him, "Quit pushing, damn it! Everybody will get their turn! The man's *dead*, he ain't going nowhere!"

"He's ripening awfully fast, though," a voice said from the line.

As stragglers moved away from the pine coffin and followed the grimy wet boot prints out the rear door, Caldwell gave Dawson a look and said regarding Victor Earles, "He means no disrespect toward Shaw. He's just young, and, well . . . not very bright, I'm afraid. He is a good apprentice, though, learning the barbering trade quite well."

"He the one painted the sign out front?" Dawson asked. He and Caldwell both took off their hats as they stepped up to the pine coffin. A scent of pine and paraffin wax loomed above the open coffin blanketing an encroaching smell of rancid death.

"Yes, as a matter of fact," said Caldwell. "Why?"

"He spelled Shaw's name wrong," said Dawson, avoiding looking down at the closed eyes and stoic face of his old friend for a second longer.

"That figures . . ." Caldwell said, letting out an exasperated breath. "I should have checked it sooner." As he spoke he kept a close watch on Dawson's face, wanting to see his expression as he gazed at the body.

"Just thought I ought to mention it," said Dawson, his eyes turning down toward the heavily waxed and rouged face lying in endless repose.

Caldwell watched intently, seeing Dawson's eyes search the dead face, then drift down to the hands lying folded on the abdomen. Dawson took a deep breath. He shut his eyes tightly for a second, then opened them and studied the face closer. "The damage was severe," Caldwell whispered, as if to keep from awakening a sleeping man. It came to Dawson that Caldwell could have shouted the information; it would have made no difference. Nothing would disturb this kind of sleep. "I only hope I did him justice," Caldwell concluded.

Dawson nodded his approval, looking closely at bluish green circles the size of chickpeas on the corpse's hands, face, and throat. "Shotgun, was it?"

"Yes, shotgun," Caldwell whispered. "An old hermit prospector found him before the creatures got to him. Brought him to me. I went right to work . . . filled the wounds with wax." He paused, then added, "I threw in that suit for him. It came from a dead judge's baggage. Thought I owed him a nice adios, after what we all three went through together."

"That was good of you, Caldwell," said Dawson. Now it was Dawson's turn to study Jedson Caldwell's face as the young undertaker spoke to him and stared down at the waxy face of the dead man.

"I would have telegraphed you in Somos Santos," said Caldwell, "had I thought you were still there."

"Would you have, sure enough?" Dawson said, nodding as Caldwell ran a palm across his perspiring forehead. "That would have been *real* kind of you, Caldwell." His voice took a slightly cynical tone. He raised his eyes, looked all around the empty room, then said in a lowered voice, "Now, do you want to tell me who this is lying here?"

"Huh? What? I don't know what you mean!" said Caldwell, also taking a quick look around. "It's Shaw! Who else could it be? Look at him!" He gestured with a hand toward the rough pine coffin.

"Hell, Caldwell, I *am* looking at him," said Dawson. "It's a good job you've done with all the coloring and wax filling. But I'm not buying it, not for a minute." He stared sharply at the undertaker.

Finally Caldwell gave in with a slight shrug. "All right, fair enough, you've caught me. May we talk about it out back?"

"By all means," said Dawson, staring at him curiously and sweeping his hand toward the rear door.

"Victor, start letting them in again," Caldwell said over his shoulder as the two walked to the rear door and out to a deserted alley running behind the main street of Crabtown.

"I don't know what you're trying to pull, but I'm not falling for it," Dawson said in a half growl while the undertaker closed the door behind them. He had to admit to himself that he was relieved to see that the body lying in the pine coffin was not his friend Lawrence Shaw.

"Okay, you've seen through it," said Caldwell, raising his hands chest high. "Before I say anything, let me ask you this . . . does it look like Lawrence Shaw?"

"I saw it wasn't him right away," Dawson replied, after only considering it for a second.

"Yes, of course *you* did," said Caldwell, "after a long close look. But you two were good friends. Would someone less familiar think it was him?"

Dawson just looked at him for a moment, then said, "You mean someone who'd only seen a picture of Shaw? Someone who had only seen him a time or two in passing, or from across a crowded saloon?"

"Yes, someone like that," said Caldwell, in an even tone, letting his hands down a little.

Getting the picture more clearly, Dawson said, "The wax and makeup are thick, but I suppose most folks would be fooled. The resemblance is awfully close."

"The wax and rouge and lip coloring are about right for a man chewed up by a shotgun blast," said Caldwell.

"You're the undertaker," said Dawson. "I can't argue with your professional practices." He nodded toward the rear door and asked, "Who is that anyway?"

"That is an unsavory fellow known as Stiff-leg Charlie Hyatt," said Caldwell in a near whisper, looking around to make sure no one was close by listening. "This was all Shaw's idea. There was no *hermit prospector*. Shaw found Stiff-leg on the trail and brought him here over a week ago. The body's holding up quite well, don't you think, in spite of the heat?"

"Well enough, I suppose," Dawson commented, not wanting to mention the smell rising from the coffin.

"The secret is, I have a tub of ice water I keep him in overnight. A teamster rides up and brings down ice from the high canyons. The suit is split in half, and sewn together into one piece. But you can't tell, can you?" Without waiting for Dawson to answer, he said eagerly, "All I have to do is lift it off him like it's a blanket and roll him into the tub. It's something I invented to make the dead easier to handle."

"What about Shaw and Stiff-leg Charlie?" Dawson asked to keep the undertaker focused.

"Yes," said Caldwell, continuing, "Shaw told me he found Stiff-leg lying against a rock, on his way here from Willow Creek. It looked like an ambush . . . a robbery perhaps." Lowering his tone he added, "Shaw found him with a bullet through his heart. He gave the body a blast of buckshot to justify my using so much wax and coloring. There was a close enough resemblance, but he asked if I could make it even more so." The undertaker offered a thin smile. "What could I say? I welcomed the challenge."

"My goodness," said Dawson, "Shaw wants out of gunfighting so bad he's faked his own death."

"Yes, and I decided there were worse things he

could do to get himself out of gunfighting . . . if you get my meaning," said the undertaker with a solemn look. "That's why I went along with this. He had suicide written in his eyes."

"Suicide . . ." Dawson pondered it for a silent moment, then dismissed it. "I thought you told Shaw and me that you'd quit this profession," he said, recalling their last conversation, three years earlier. "You were headed to New Orleans after our shootout with the Talbert Gang."

Jedson Caldwell sighed, realizing this was the second time Dawson had brought up New Orleans. "I did go to New Orleans," he said. He knew the matter would have to be addressed. "I spent six weeks at a barbering school there, learning a *new* profession." He gestured with a hand toward the rear door of his barbershop, noting the irony of his situation. He had traveled west years ago as an undertaker only to find that barbers had firm control of his profession and weren't about to give it up. "I decided if I couldn't beat them, perhaps I should join them. I'm now a bona fide groom to both the *living* and the dead."

Looking off and all around the rugged hilly country surrounding the town, Dawson said, "I wouldn't get too comfortable here. Crabtown looks like the kind of place that could be gone before your next breakfast."

"I keep that in mind constantly," said Caldwell. "Crabtown is a growing place, has been since sixty-four. But it might only be here as long as the gold holds out, times being what they are." He nodded toward the distant foothills. "The big findings are coming from up in Black's Cut right now."

"Black's Cut is where I'm headed," said Dawson. "I have a claim I bought from an old miner named Jimmy Deebs in Somos Santos. Thought I'd give it a try. If I don't find gold, at least I'll find myself some peace and quiet."

"Peace and quiet? Not at Black's Cut." Caldwell winced and shook his head. "Black's Cut is a good place to stay away from unless you're a friend of Giddis Black or Hyde Landry, which you are not, I'm going to venture."

"That's right, I've never heard of the men," said Dawson. "But I've got a claim, so I intend to work it."

"I saw your mule is already loaded with supplies," said Caldwell. "You might have done better to wait and buy everything from Black's Mining Supply, or from the Black and Landry Mercantile. Black might have settled for that."

Dawson stared at him. "So, I take it Giddis Black is the top dog in Black's Cut?"

"Oh yes," said Caldwell. "The name Black's Cut comes from Giddis Black and his thugs getting a cut of everything going in or out of Black's Cut. He was one of the first there, so I suppose he thinks he's entitled to a share of everybody's holdings. His partner Landry is worse than him, but stays out of sight most times. Black is the one who runs things day to day."

Dawson nodded. "Fair enough. I'll give Black his

cut, if I pull out enough gold to make it worth my stay." He shrugged and changed the subject. "What about you? What made you decide on Crabtown?"

"Why *not* Crabtown?" Caldwell said wryly, gesturing with a hand. But he considered it for a second and said, "The fact is, ever since our fight with the Talbert Gang, I haven't been able to settle down and stick in one place for very long anyway. Crabtown is just another stop on the high trail." He shrugged.

Dawson noticed the difference in the man as he listened to him speak. Caldwell had been meek, full of fear and self-doubt, when they had first met. Dawson had taught him to use a gun, enough to defend himself if the need arose. The need did arise, the day Caldwell stood with Dawson and Shaw against the Talbert Gang. Caldwell had killed a gunman named Gladso Furlin and saved Dawson's and Shaw's life in doing so. Immediately after the shooting Caldwell headed for New Orleans.

"Where is Shaw now?" Dawson asked, looking closer at Caldwell. He noted how the once weak and delicate hands had taken on an aura of confidence and appeared stronger somehow. Caldwell's once pleasant, innocent face now had a hardened edge to it, a look of calm certainty in the dark eyes that had not been there before.

"Who knows? Up there somewhere," said Caldwell. "Poor fellow. He helped me carry Stiff-leg Charlie inside. Then he rode off into the night. Since the day I laid the corpse out for viewing, there's been three hardcases ride in, as if to make sure Shaw is really dead. So far no one has questioned it . . . until you, that is."

"I see," said Dawson, "and you're keeping the body as long as you can to make sure everybody gets the news."

"Correct," said Caldwell, "the longer the better. Of course the money is good too." He grinned. "I'm afraid my barbering skills on the *living* still leave much to be desired." He sighed. "I'm afraid my heart isn't in it anymore." He stepped in closer and said, "The time I spent with you and Shaw taught me that a man can hold his head up and walk proud, do *what* he wants *when he wants* and beg no one's pardon while he does it."

"Careful, Caldwell," said Dawson, "you're sounding like a lot of young gunmen I came across sheriffing in Somos Santos."

"Aw, there, you see?" said the undertaker, wagging a finger for emphasis. "You were a sheriff . . . you had that opportunity and you acted on it."

"Believe me, if it hadn't been forced on me I never would have pinned on a badge," Dawson said in reflection.

"Be that as it may," said Caldwell, "you at least had the choice. I'll never have those kinds of choices as an undertaker. I'll have even less as a barber."

"You'll have a good secure future without all the heartache," said Dawson. "A barber and an undertaker might not get rich, but he'll never go hungry, is what I've always heard."

"There are all sorts of *hunger*, Dawson," Caldwell

pointed out. "Do not judge the depth or validity of my hunger unless you have experienced it."

"You're right," said Dawson, seeing a sadness in the undertaker's eyes. "I don't know your hunger, but I know how it is to need something and know you may never have it. I reckon it could be about the same."

He thought about Rosa, the woman he had loved—worshipped—even though she had been the wife of his friend Lawrence Shaw. His mind brought forth the passing thought of how she had died at the hands of Baron Talbert and his gang, and how he, Shaw, and this man standing before him, had brought down the gang in a fury of blood. Yet, at the end of it, what had his vengeance accomplished? His life was still hollow and empty without her. *Jesus . . .* who was he to judge, advise men on their lives, their hungers, their aspirations?

"How about pointing us toward a saloon here where I can buy you a drink and wash some trail out of my mouth?" he asked, hoping to change the conversation.

Caldwell started to answer, but his attention went to the doorway where Victor stepped back as two guns pointed at his belly. "That's all right, Victor! Please, let them in!" Caldwell said quickly, seeing from the look on Victor's face that the young man might lunge forward in spite of the guns.

"Obliged," said a low powerful voice from behind the two gunmen. Caldwell and Dawson watched as a tall poker-faced man stepped into the barbershop, the other two gunmen lowering their Colts and flanking him. A worn and battered marshal's badge appeared on his vest as he slowly opened his frayed riding duster. "I'm Federal Marshal Edgar Thornton. I'm not here sightseeing, this is official business. Maybe I should have gone straight to your sheriff."

"Our sheriff, Dan Foley, is out of town this morning, Marshal Thornton," said Caldwell. "But that's no problem. Take your time. I'm Jedson Caldwell, the barber here in Crabtown. Sheriff Foley would want me to accommodate the law." He cleared his throat and deciding to take a chance asked, "Is it possible that you might *positively* identify the body, for town records and the like?"

"I'll see what I can do," said the marshal, reaching inside his brush-scarred riding duster.

Chapter 2

Dawson and Caldwell stood quietly back by the wall and watched as Thornton and his two deputies walked to the coffin. The three gazed first at the unfolded newspaper page Thornton had taken from his duster pocket, then down at the body in the pine coffin. After a moment, Thornton folded the newspaper, shoved it back inside his duster, and said to Caldwell as he turned toward the side door, "For my money that's Shaw all right, Barber."

"In that case, Marshal," said Caldwell, hurrying over as he took a sheet of paper from his own pocket, "will you please attest to his identity in writing, make it legal so to speak? I'm sure Sheriff Foley would be obliged."

"An affidavit, huh?" The three men stopped. Thornton stared at the barber as if trying to read his intention. But then he shrugged, seeing Caldwell hold out a pen and a small dip bottle toward him. "Well, sure, as hospitable as you've been, why not?

Besides, anything for Sheriff Foley. You give him my regards." He took the pen in his gloved hand and scrawled his name across the bottom of the affidavit while Caldwell held it across the back of his hand for support.

"I certainly will. This is most helpful of you, Marshal," said the barber, examining and blowing on the wet ink signature.

"We'll be on our way now," said Thornton. "Just wanted a look-see to make sure Shaw's really dead. "We're hunting a group of ragged-assed sneak thieves who've stepped up to being murderers—killed a couple of Ute horse traders down near Elkhorn. We lost their trail yesterday. Hope to pick it up again today."

"If I might ask, Marshal," Caldwell said, stepping alongside the marshal, almost as if to follow him out the door, "was Lawrence Shaw wanted by the law?"

The two young deputies stepped in between him and Thornton. "No, you *may not* ask," one replied in a threatening manner.

"Stand down, Ragsdale," said Thornton, stopping at the door and giving the deputy a harsh stare of reprimand. "The barber was kind enough to allow us in at no charge. Let's show some manners." He turned his attention back to Caldwell. "Excuse my newly appointed deputies for being rude, Mr. Caldwell. I'm afraid they haven't been wearing a badge long enough to realize that good manners are a part of the job." He gave a tired smile from behind a thick mustache. "Allow me to introduce deputies Porter

Ragsdale and Clifford Nutt." He gestured toward the deputies with a gloved hand. The two only leered at Caldwell. Then Thornton said, "There were no charges against the late Lawrence Shaw." He patted the folded newspaper page inside his duster. "This is a picture of Shaw from a newspaper article in Hide City. Since we were in these parts I *did* have some questions about a couple of scrapes he'd been in the past year." He gave a glance toward the pine coffin, then added, "I expect it makes no difference now. Dust to dust, is what I say."

"Worms to worms, is what I say," Deputy Ragsdale murmured under his breath, yet still loud enough to be heard. Beside him Deputy Nutt grinned and stared steadily at Cray Dawson.

"That's enough, Deputy," Thornton warned, giving both deputies a dark scowl. Turning back to Caldwell and Dawson before taking his leave, he said to Dawson as if just stricken by a realization, "You used to be a lawman yourself, did you not, sir?"

"Yes, I was a lawman," said Dawson. "I was a sheriff in—"

"Where are my manners?" Caldwell cut in. "Marshal Thornton, this is Cray Dawson, a friend of mine out of Texas."

"—Somos Santos," Dawson finished.

"So," said Thornton, giving Dawson an almost crafty smile, "a *lawman* out of Somos Santos, Texas. Shaw's hometown. Now I remember. Before you wore a badge, you rode with Shaw, hunted down the Talberts. Killed Blue Snake Terril himself."

"Yes, it's true I rode with Shaw for a while," Dawson said in a lowered voice, sounding hesitant to admit it.

"Another big gun?" Ragsdale asked, butting in.

"Nothing new about that," said Nutt, staring at Dawson as he spoke. "Every man packing a three-dollar pistol is a *big gun out of Texas* these days. They don't impress me none."

Dawson ignored him and said to Marshal Thornton, "I'd just as soon not say who I shot or who I didn't shoot that day. Now that Shaw is dead, I'd just as soon the whole matter be forgotten."

"I understand," said Thornton, looking Dawson up and down. "Even wearing a badge, I take it, you had your share of wolves snapping at you after riding with a fast gun like Shaw."

"In spades, Marshal," said Dawson. "I'm out of law work now. I'm expecting all that to change."

The two deputies just looked at him curiously as if having a hard time understanding his line of talk. But Thornton nodded and said, "I hope it works out that way for you, Mr. Dawson. No man ought to end up like this poor devil." He gestured his gloved hand toward the pine coffin. "God rest his miserable soul," he added in reverence. Then with a touch of his hat brim, he turned and walked out the side door. The two deputies followed, looking back as if suspicious of Dawson and Caldwell for some undisclosed wrongdoing.

"Well," said Dawson, letting out a breath as the side door closed behind Marshal Thornton and his deputies, "you took quite a chance asking him, but it paid off." He watched Caldwell fan the affidavit back and forth for a second, then fold it and put it away. "Once he put his name to it, Lawrence Shaw became *officially* dead."

Caldwell sighed. "Yes, and he'll be glad to hear it." Rubbing his beard stubble he said, "Now, about that drink we were talking about. I'm ready for it."

Looking toward Victor, who stood busily riffling through a fistful of dollars, dropping change into expectant hands, and pushing the customers forward, Dawson said, "Are you sure you shouldn't be staying here, keeping an eye on your enterprise?"

"I could use a drink and conversation more than I can use the money right now," said Caldwell, already motioning Dawson to the rear door. "Besides, I want you to know that charging a fee was all Shaw's idea. He said it gave it the ring of reality it needed."

"He should know," said Dawson. They walked to the street and toward the Crabtown Palace Saloon a block away. Looking back along the boardwalk as more tough-looking characters stepped onto the boardwalk and walked to the front of the line, Dawson shook his head and said, "Now that you've got the identification of a federal marshal, maybe you need to bring this exhibition to a close and get Stiffleg into the ground. It looks like every undesirable in the territory has heard about it."

"I was just thinking the same thing," said Caldwell, also taking a quick look back at the line of sightseers and the faces of three new arrivals who stood with their horses at the hitch rail. "We've done what we set out to do. We should call an end to it while we're ahead."

As the two walked on toward the saloon, the three men at the hitch rail stood with their heads ducked from view and kept an eye on the side door of the barbershop until a young gunman wearing a fringed buckskin shirt and a battered bowler hat stepped out and walked toward them with a swagger, a look of arrogance on his face. "Here comes Peru now," said one of the men, a tough California outlaw named Rodney Dolan who liked being called Rex. "Looks like he ain't in no hurry to tell us whatever he found out."

"If he found out that really was Shaw he killed," said a young black horse thief named Elton Shears, "I expect he don't have to be in no hurry for nothing from now on."

"If we're riding with him, none of us will." A stocky young gunman named Hank Kuntz grinned.

Arriving between the horses, Madden Peru paced back and forth with a smug grin, looking from face to face. "I came within an inch of running smack into that marshal who's been dogging us!"

"He's here, in Crabtown?" asked Dolan, taking a quick look and seeing the marshal and his two deputies walk along the boardwalk a few yards, then step down, mount their horses, and ride away. He chuckled and said, "Our luck is still holding strong. He didn't even see us!"

"Don't look at them!" said Peru, keeping his head lowered. "Let them get the hell on out of town."

The four stood in silence, watching the marshal and his deputies until they were almost out of sight. Then Dolan said to Peru, "All right, they're gone. Now, what about the corpse? Is it Lawrence Shaw or not?"

"Oh, it's Shaw all right," said Peru, "bigger than life but deader than hell." He turned his eyes from one man to the next, making sure everybody heard him.

The three only stared at him in rapt silence for a moment before Dolan said in an astonished tone, "My God! You mean—it's true! You've really killed Fast Larry Shaw?"

"Didn't you hear me, Dolan?" said Peru. "I told you, Shaw's deader than hell." Seeing a few heads turn toward them along the boardwalk, Peru took his horse's reins from around the hitch rail. "Come on," he said, stepping up into the saddle, "let's get off the street and go talk about this." He questioned himself about the wax-filled shotgun wounds he'd seen on the corpse's face, but he wasn't about to mention it to Dolan and the others.

"Yeah," said Dolan, also unhitching his horse and climbing into his saddle. The others followed suit. "We need to figure out where this puts us, killing the *fastest gun alive*."

"Where it puts *us*?" said Peru, giving him a look. "You mean where it puts *me*. Let's not forget who it was did the killing."

"I ain't forgetting it, Peru." Dolan gave his companion a look of thinly veiled envy and turned his horse to the dirt street. "I doubt you'll let any of us forget who did the killing."

Inside the Crabtown Palace Saloon, Caldwell and Dawson walked past the few drinkers at the bar and up the stairs to a room at the far end of a long narrow hallway. Before Caldwell even knocked, the door swung open a few inches and Dawson saw a weathered face stare out at them. "Sheriff, this is a friend of both Shaw and myself. We can trust him," Caldwell said quietly, seeing the pair of suspicious eyes giving Dawson the once-over.

The door opened farther. The sheriff turned his eyes from Dawson and he said to Caldwell, "I saw them riding in and ducked in here before they saw me. What did Thornton have to say?"

"The marshal didn't have much to say," said Caldwell, stepping into the room. "They were in a hurry, on the trail of some killers." He gave a gesture toward the open window. "I told them you're out of town for the day. It all worked out nicely for us."

"Oh? How so?" asked the sheriff, looking again at Dawson as he spoke. He walked across the floor to the open window that faced down upon the street.

"I asked him to identify the body, and he did, *officially*," said Caldwell, pulling out the signed affidavit and showing it to the sheriff.

"My, my," said Foley. He glanced at the paper, handed it back, and shook his head as he leaned slightly and looked out at a rise of dust on the trail out of town. "There was a time you wouldn't have put nothing like that over on Thornton. He's been a dogged lawman all his life. Not much ever got past him." The sheriff continued staring out the window a moment longer, his expression turning to one of sad contemplation. "Like myself, I expect he's gotten too old."

Giving Dawson a look, Caldwell cleared his throat and said tactfully, "I don't think it's that at all, Sheriff Foley. I like to think it's because I did such a skillful job preparing the corpse."

The sheriff ran his fingers back through his thin white hair and turned facing them, his attention going back to Dawson. "You must be Dawson."

"Yes, I am," said Dawson, giving the old sheriff a questioning look.

Sheriff Foley shrugged a thin shoulder. "He said you're Shaw's *friend*. Only friend I ever heard Lawrence Shaw mention was the man who rode with him to hunt down his wife's killers. So I just figured . . ."

"You figured right, Sheriff," said Dawson, touching his hat brim.

"And this is Sheriff Daniel Foley," said Caldwell, cutting in to make an introduction. "I'm certain you've heard of him?" he asked, hoping Dawson would realize how important it might be for an aging lawman like Foley to have his name recognized by a man like Cray Dawson.

"You can bet I have," said Dawson; but upon seeing a look of doubt in the old sheriff's eyes he added quickly as proof, "You're a Texan like myself. I expect every young saddle buck or trail waddie from Rio Bravo to Indian Nations has heard of Dan Foley."

"Aw, I never done nothing, just did my duty," said Foley, averting his eyes modestly for a moment. But both Dawson and Caldwell could tell Dawson had said the right thing.

After a pause, Dawson asked, "How many other people know about this?" He looked back and forth between them.

"Just us three," said Caldwell. "There's a young widow, Madeline Mercer, who lives near here that I wanted to tell, but Shaw wouldn't hear of it. She and Shaw were . . ." His words trailed, then came back, saying, "Well, you know how it is with Shaw and women." Caldwell raised a finger for emphasis and added quickly, "Not that I'm judging him, you understand."

"I understand," said Dawson, recalling how women in every town he and Shaw had traveled through together had thrown themselves at the man known as the fastest gun alive. "How is she taking his *death?*" he asked.

Caldwell and the sheriff looked at one another, and then Caldwell said, "To be honest, we have not gone to check on her yet. She came to town in a buggy day before yesterday, visited his body in private for a moment, then left."

"With no doubts, no questions about it being Shaw's body?" Dawson asked.

"None," said Caldwell. "She will be leaving the territory as soon as she has sold and settled her late husband's cattle and land holdings here. I doubt if we'll be hearing from her again. Her dead husband, Bradley Mercer, owned a chunk of New York and New Jersey. Don't know what brought him here in the first place."

"Good, she's leaving, then," said Dawson, letting the rest of the story pass. "It sounds like Shaw and you two have everything worked out."

Caldwell and the sheriff looked at one another again, nodding. "All that's left is to nail down the coffin lid and get the body into the ground," said Caldwell. "A few days from now, Lawrence Shaw will be just a name carved on a pine grave marker. Lives will go on—"

Before he'd finished speaking, loud angry voices resounded up from the street, interrupting him. No sooner had the voices settled than Victor shouted from the boardwalk out in front of the barbershop, "Mr. Caldwell! Sheriff Foley! Come quick!" Before his words ended the angry voices started again.

Looking down through the open window, Sheriff Foley noted two young gunmen facing one another from a distance of thirty feet between them. "Gunfight," he said flatly but with urgency in his voice. "Well, gentlemen," he added, hiking his gun belt, "looks like it's time for me to get back to work."

"I've got you covered, Sheriff," Caldwell said, the two of them turning toward the door. To Dawson he said over his shoulder, "Come by the shop this evening, dinner's on me."

Chapter 3

Dawson followed Caldwell and the sheriff down the stairs and toward the front door of the saloon. On their way, the bartender, who had scurried from behind the bar and now stood at the bottom of the stairs, pitched Caldwell a sawed-off shotgun as the two hurried past him. Keeping the shotgun pointed at the floor, Caldwell stayed close to the sheriff's back, shoving through the drinkers who had hurried over from the bar and stood staring out above the batwing doors.

"Go for your gun, Hill, you line-jumping son of a bitch!" shouted one young gunman to the other young man facing him.

"I'm giving *you* the first move, Prince," the young man replied coolly. "You're going to need it. Nobody pushes me from behind."

Before Davey Prince could respond, Sheriff Foley came running from the saloon, Caldwell right beside him. "Hill! Prince! Don't neither one of yas make a move!" he shouted with ironlike authority in his voice.

"Stay out of this, Sheriff!" shouted Prince. "This is a fair fight! He tried stepping in front of me in line! I don't have to take that off of no man!"

Caldwell shot a glance toward Victor, who stood on the boardwalk. Victor gave a nod, letting him know that Prince wasn't lying. Bobby Hill had stepped in front of him. But it was not something Caldwell wanted to comment on right then. He stood with the shotgun up and ready, moving the barrel back and forth slowly between the two while Foley tried talking them down.

"I don't give a tinker's damn who got pushed or who got stepped in front of!" said the sheriff, his big Colt already out, cocked and ready. As he spoke he moved forward slowly, getting himself almost but not quite between the two. "Anybody draws a gun and starts firing amid all these folks is going to go down with a belly load of buckshot and bullets! I'm not having it!" His voice had grown louder and more harsh as he spoke. But then he deliberately lowered it almost to a growl as he finished with "Do you *boys* understand me?"

Dawson stopped a few feet back, giving the sheriff and Caldwell plenty of room to handle the situation. Sizing the two young men, Dawson pegged them both as nothing more than a couple of hotheaded ranch boys in their early to mid teens. Fighting over their place in line, he told himself, like ordinary schoolboys would do given a different place and time. But being young didn't make them any less dangerous with a gun, not here on the raw edge of the high frontier.

"He pushed me from behind, Sheriff," said Hill without taking his eyes off Prince. His right hand poised an inch from his gun butt—ready to shake hands with the devil, Dawson told himself, watching intently.

"Bobby Hill," said Sheriff Foley, still in a lowered tone, "you're getting too old for me to have to run to your pa and tell him . . . so's he can take a layer of hide off your rear end." He paused, then added, "You want your ma hearing how you died in the street?"

"I ain't planning on dying, Sheriff," said the young man, looking determined.

"Then you better plan on hanging," Sheriff Foley said with resolve. "Either way, it'll make a lasting impression on your ma . . . your pa too, for that matter."

Dawson saw the slightest waver in Hill's demeanor. Foley saw it too. As if the young man had envisioned his family gathered around his grave, his hackles seemed to ease down, not much but just enough. Seeing it, Foley turned his eyes to Davey Prince. But the young man saw what was going on and he said before the sheriff got the chance, "I've got no ma, no pa either. So you can save your breath, Sheriff." He stared fixedly at Bobby Hill and said, "I'll put his blood in the dirt. Nobody steps in front of me."

"Good Lord, Davey, look at you!" said Foley, taking a whole other approach, Dawson noticed, seeing that this young man had decided he had less to lose and wasn't at all afraid of dying. "I was just telling some folks the other day what a good man you've turned into. You ride and rope with the best of them. Now I've got to tell them I was wrong, that you're just one of them hotheaded fools that don't give a bead of sweat for nobody."

"It ain't working, Sheriff," Prince said flatly.

"Okay then, try this on," said Foley. "I believe Bobby is cooled down enough so I can deal with him like a man. So, he ain't going to draw unless he has to. Can I count on that, Bobby?"

After a second of pause, Hill said, "Yeah, Sheriff, you've got my word."

"There now, Prince," said the sheriff. "You go for that gun, you're drawing on me and the barber, nobody else. And we *never* stepped in front of you."

"Damn it." A nerve twitched in Prince's jaw as he considered it. "This ain't fair, Sheriff Foley," he said finally.

"That's right, it ain't," said the sheriff. "All the more reason you ought not to die over it." He said to Hill without taking his eye off Davey Prince, "Bobby, raise your gun hand and stick it inside your shirt, like if you was getting a photograph taken, Napolean style."

"You're taking his side," said Prince, watching Hill's hand come up slowly and rest between his shirt buttons.

"I know you're real mad about it right now, Davey," said the sheriff. "But in about ten seconds it won't matter anymore."

"Huh?" Prince looked less confident.

"Bobby is out of the fight now," said Foley, with cold deliberation. "It's just you against us. Caldwell, you ready to drop him?"

"Ready, Sheriff," said Caldwell, tightening the shotgun to his shoulder.

"Damn it to hell," said Prince, seeing things were only going to get worse for him, "this is not right, everybody jumping in this way."

"Talking's over, Davey," Foley said, his voice taking on an urgency designed to put more pressure on the young gunman. "Get your hand in your shirt or you're dead! Caldwell?"

"I've got him, Sheriff," Caldwell said in a firm somber tone, his shotgun poised intently.

"Wait, damn it!" said Prince.

Watching, even Dawson himself let out a tense breath. He thought at first that Foley was only bluffing, but now he was beginning to wonder. Continuing to watch the sheriff, Dawson saw Prince raise his gun hand, slip it inside his shirt, and give Bobby Hill a look of disgust. Caldwell walked up close and jerked Prince's Colt from his holster.

"You made a wise decision today, Bobby," Foley said, walking in and quickly taking Hill's Colt from his holster. He stuck it down into his waistband. Turning toward Prince and seeing that Caldwell had disarmed him he said, "We're taking both of yas to jail, let you cool down some before we turn you loose."

Dawson stood back and watched the onlookers along the boardwalk while Caldwell and Foley took the two young men to jail. Caldwell called back over his shoulder, "Come back to the shop as soon as you get settled in, Dawson. You've got a free bath, shave, and haircut coming. If not from me, then from Victor."

"Obliged," Dawson replied, idly raising a hand to the rough beard stubble along his jawline. "I'll take your offer. But dinner's on me this evening."

Caldwell gave him a nod of acknowledgment, nudging his prisoner along.

"Damn, Sheriff," Dawson heard Hill say, Foley walking him along by his forearm, "I did what I was told, I shouldn't be going to jail."

"That's right, you shouldn't," said Foley. "But since you wasn't smart enough *not* to go to jail this time, maybe you need to sit and think how to do it different next time."

"You mean, keep my mouth shut and not start trouble with nobody in the first place?"

"There, you see?" said Foley, nudging him on toward the jail. "You're getting smarter already."

Dawson smiled to himself, shook his head slightly, and walked to where he'd left his horse and mule standing at the hitch rail out in front of the barbershop. As he gathered the reins and the lead rope, a tall one-eyed man wearing a black linen suit and a handlebar mustache stepped down from the boardwalk and stared at Dawson from beneath a wide-brimmed hat. "Did I hear right a while ago? You're Cray Dawson—the hombre who helped Shaw kill off the Talbert Gang?"

Dawson weighed his words before replying, studying the man's face and demeanor, seeing the wide fierce scar running down through a blind white-clouded eye. "I am Cray Dawson," he said at length, offering nothing more about having ridden with Lawrence Shaw.

A slow flat smile formed beneath the waxed and sharply pointed mustache. "Yes, I did hear right, then. You are Cray Dawson." His right hand clutched his lapel near the protruding butt of a black-handled Remington resting in a holster across his flat stomach. "I'm Brue Holley. The man who would have killed your pal Shaw had somebody not beat me to him."

"I've heard of you, Brue Holley. You're a bounty hunter," Dawson said flatly, his hand relaxing close to the Colt on his hip.

"It's true I've been a bounty officer most of my grown-up life," said Holley, his smile still intact. "Have you got something against bounty officers?"

"Not at all," said Dawson. "I'm just letting you know what I heard about you." He remained civil but not overly talkative. "Shaw and I rode together after the Talbert Gang. Years before that we rode herd together. We were never what you call *pals*. But I had lots of respect for the man. Whether or not you would have killed him is something we'll never know." Without excusing himself, Dawson pulled on the reins on his horse and pack mule in order to walk away.

Holley chuckled. "To not be pals, you sure got the raw uglies about me saying I meant to kill him."

"All right, we *were* friends," Dawson said flatly, still pulling his animals away from the hitch rail without turning his back on Holley. "The fact remains Shaw is dead. I suppose you'll have to live with the question of what you might or might not have done. Looks like you'll never know."

"That's not necessarily true," said Holley, his smile going away, leaving a hard-edged stare in its place. "I understand you're just as fast as Shaw with a gun."

"You heard right," Dawson said without hesitation. He'd been caught by a threat like this too many times in the past to try to ignore it and hope it would go away. He dropped the reins to the dirt and stood squarely facing Brue Holley, his hand still poised near his Colt, but no longer relaxed. "Now what?" he added, every part of his demeanor making his intention clear.

"Whoa!" said Holley, seeing the look in Dawson's eyes turn hollow and deadly. "I'm not looking to throw down with you, Dawson. You've misread my meaning." He raised his hand a more friendly distance from his big Remington belly gun. "What I meant to do is offer you a proposition that serves both our interests."

"You said you came to town to kill my friend, Shaw," said Dawson. "I can't think of anything you and I might do for one another."

"I see we've gotten off to a bad start, Dawson," said Holley, trying to keep the conversation civil. "But I dare to differ with you. I'm sure we share an interest in common." He tried offering another thin sterile smile that didn't work. "Hell, let your bark down, Dawson. I'm not interested in shooting it out with you. I want the son of a bitch who was fast enough to take Shaw down. If you're out to avenge your friend's death the way any man would, that makes us both hunting the same game."

Dawson knew he had to be careful what he said next. He didn't want to act as if Shaw's death meant nothing to him. A sharp-eyed bounty hunter like Brue Holley might see through this ruse and foil Shaw's attempt at carrying out his fake death. "I don't know that my friend Shaw would want me avenging him," said Dawson, "and even if I could outgun the man that killed him, I wouldn't have any idea where to start looking."

"That's where I come in," said Holley. "I'm a good detective. I can start by locating the person who found Shaw's body. Once I know where he found it I can start searching from there."

"Bad luck already," said Dawson. "Some drifting hermit found Shaw. He could be anywhere by now." Dawson feigned considering things for a moment as if he might have some interest in working with Holley. "If that's your part of the deal, what's mine? It doesn't take two men to search for whoever shot Shaw."

"That's right," said Holley, "but I figure odds are whoever did this had others with him. He'd need witnesses to back up his story. I find that man, I'll be needing some backup help. You keep his friends off me while I kill him. You get your vengeance, simple and sweet."

"And you get the reputation for killing the man who killed the fastest gun alive," said Dawson. He had to keep himself from shaking his head in disgust.

"Something like that," said Holley. "Only I figure Shaw quit being the fastest gun alive the minute his eyes closed. The man who killed him is now the fastest gun alive . . . until he faces me, that is." He smiled again, this time tweaking the sharp point of his mustache. "What do you say? Want to go with me, get that son of a bitch?"

Dawson stared for a moment as if actually giving the idea serious thought. Finally he said, "Obliged, but I work better alone. I better keep it that way."

"Ah!" said Holley. "So you are out for vengeance after all?"

"I didn't say that," Dawson replied, drawing on the reins again, to lead his horse and mule away. "Truth is, I came up here to work a claim. I just happened through Crabtown and saw the sign on the barbershop."

"You better throw in with me, Dawson," said Holley, seeing his proposition hadn't worked. "Look at all these gunmen flocking here just to see Shaw's body. Any one of them would jump at the opportunity I'm offering you.''

Dawson shook his head. "No, they wouldn't. These gunmen will want what you want, to kill the new fastest gun alive."

Holley walked along with Dawson for a few steps before stopping and watching him and his animals walk away. "If you change your mind before I head out tomorrow, come let me know," he called out. "I'm pitched just off the main trail a mile out."

Dawson raised a hand in acknowledgment, but walked on without looking back. Instead he looked at the crowd still lined and milling along the boardwalk, and at two more horsemen turning from the middle of the street, headed for the hitch rail. "Look at this," he murmured to himself as if speaking to his friend Shaw. "You would think the *president* was laying dead in there. . . ."

Chapter 4

At the Hotel Montana, Dawson unbuckled his saddlebags from behind the saddle, threw the bags over his shoulder, and slipped his Winchester from its saddle boot. He turned the horse's reins and the mule's lead rope over to a young man wearing a soft-billed service cap with the hotel's name embroidered across the front of the crown. "See that they both get well grained," he said, taking a silver coin from the pocket of his vest and pressing it into the young man's outstretched hand.

"Yes, sir," said the young man, closing his fingers over the coin almost with a snap. "Anything else you need here, you ask for me, Bennie Hitchins." He eyed the Winchester in Dawson's hand and the holstered Colt with rapt fascination.

"Obliged, Bennie," said Dawson. "I'm—"

"Oh, I know who you are, Mr. Dawson!" said the young man. "I heard Mr. Caldwell call you Fast Larry's friend. Then Victor told me you rode with Fast

Larry!" He grinned excitedly. "Anything you want, you just let me know." As he spoke he'd already begun backing away, leading both animals.

"Obliged again," Dawson repeated. He watched both man and animals disappear for a moment into the traffic along the dirt street. Only when he'd seen the three reappear and walk into the livery barn a block away did Dawson step onto the hotel boardwalk and into the large clapboard and brick hotel building.

Within minutes of having signed into the hotel and taken a room overlooking the busy street, Dawson lay scrubbed and soaking in one of three tubs in the Montana's private bathing house behind the hotel. When he'd finished, he changed into clean trail clothes he'd brought from his saddlebags and turned his dirty clothes over to one of the many Chinese bathhouse attendants to be boiled, dried, ironed, and delivered back to his room the following afternoon.

While he had soaked in steaming sudsy bathwater, another Chinese attendant had dusted and brushed his hat. Still another had cleaned and saddle-soaped his boots. When he stepped out of the tub, knowing that Caldwell and Victor would both be too busy to give him the shave and haircut Caldwell had promised, Dawson shaved himself with a bone-handled razor he carried down from his saddlebags and ran a wooden comb back through his washed hair.

When he'd stepped into his shiny clean boots and placed his dusted Stetson atop his damp head, Dawson tipped the leader of the bath attendants and returned to his room to clean and inspect his Colt and his Winchester before meeting Caldwell for dinner.

From the open window above the busy street, Dawson looked down at the congested boardwalk out in front of the barbershop where the line had grown even longer than it had been when he rode into Crabtown. Just off the boardwalk, in front of a tall red-and-white-striped barber pole, a group of tough-looking men had begun to gather after they'd seen the body and left through the side door. Tall bottles of whiskey made their rounds from hand to hand.

Dawson shook his head as he watched, reloading his Colt and slipping it into his holster. "My, my. All this because one man was good at killing others. Shaw, you beat all I've ever seen. . . ." He gazed up along the line of foothills northwest of town as if Lawrence Shaw might be somewhere watching from some high distant location. "If you're smart you'll never be seen or heard from again."

It crossed Dawson's mind that maybe when Stiff-leg Charlie went into the ground, talk of who was the fastest gun alive would be buried with him. Yet something told him that wouldn't be the case. As he contemplated such a notion, his hand idly slipped the Colt back out of its holster in a way so smooth, quick, and natural that had someone been watching they would have a hard time catching sight of it.

He couldn't judge Shaw too harshly for faking his own death, Dawson thought as he twirled the Colt back and forth effortlessly, then let it spin down into his holster. He knew firsthand how hard it could be to be known as just a fast gun, let alone the fastest gun alive. After riding with Shaw he himself had gone through a period of time when it seemed that every gunman, saddle tramp, and liquored-up cowhand had convinced themselves that killing Cray Dawson would make them a *somebody* in a world full of nobodies.

I hope it works out for you . . . he heard himself telling Shaw. On the street below an empty bottle flew through the air and landed in the dirt. A gunshot barked sharply from among the crowd and the bottle exploded in a spray of broken glass. Dawson watched, yet his mind still dealt with the matter of Lawrence Shaw, of himself, and of the blind and mindless fate that propelled a man toward his destiny.

On the street one drinker pushed another as Dawson considered the events that had brought him and his friend Shaw back together after they'd ridden for so many years on separate trails. Below, a fistfight broke out; another bottle flew through the air; another shot exploded.

As the events of the past moved across his mind like vague images through a morning fog, he pictured himself and Rosa Shaw, the two of them together in Lawrence Shaw's bed, locked in a lovers' embrace. And yet as he pictured it, at the same time he pictured the terrible bloodletting that was to follow her death when he and her husband wreaked vengeance on the men who had killed her.

At the risk of his life Dawson had tried to clear the air with Shaw before they rode off in search of Rosa's killers. He tried to tell Shaw, but Shaw wouldn't allow it. Perhaps he'd already known, Dawson thought, watching the two men on the street rolling, punching, and kicking through the urine-soaked ground along the hitch rail where horses whinnied and reared and crow-hopped clear of them.

Yes, Shaw knew, Dawson told himself, the same as he'd told himself a thousand times before when his memory reached this part of its familiar reenactment. Shaw knew, yet he'd never allowed it to be discussed between them. Had they talked about it, and had Dawson admitted in no uncertain terms what had actually gone on between himself and Shaw's wife, Dawson realized there was a good possibility he would've been dead. Not faking death, he thought, glancing away from the muddy urine-stained combatants to the door of the barbershop, but truly dead, as dead as Stiff-leg Charlie.

But all of that was behind him, Dawson forced himself to realize, putting both the memories and their participants out of his mind. He watched the fighters on the street unlock from one another, back off, and take a new stand, one grabbing his muddy empty holster, the other fumbling with the mud-slick handle of a big Star revolver. But before he could get the gun cleared and raised, Sheriff Foley sailed in out of nowhere.

With the agility of a man half his age, the aged sheriff knocked the armed man to the ground, at the same time yanking the Star from its holster and making a vicious swipe with the barrel across its owner's skull as he tried to raise himself to his knees and pull a hideout gun from inside his muddy shirt.

Good work again, Sheriff . . . Dawson winced slightly at the sight of iron gun barrel against human skull. But as he watched he saw the other man make a move toward his gun lying in the mud only to meet the hard hickory shotgun butt as Caldwell stepped in from the crowd and slammed it into his jaw. Mud flew from the man's hair before he hit the ground.

"Another nice job, Caldwell," Dawson murmured aloud. While the pie-faced undertaker turned barber stood with his shotgun at port arms, Foley walked into the crowd of toughs, jerked two bottles of whiskey from drunken hands, and backed away, the muddy Star in his waistband, his own Colt out, cocked and pointed, backed by Caldwell's scattergun.

Dawson shook his head slowly and couldn't help but ask himself, if Shaw were truly dead, was this the sort of man who would lay claim to his reputation? Quarterwise to the crowd, Brue Holley rode slowly along atop a big black-stocking silver-gray. He sat half turned in his saddle, observing Foley and the crowd with detached interest.

There's one to watch out for, Dawson reminded himself, seeing the bounty hunter right himself in his saddle and ride away, the tails of a black bearskin coat hanging far down the horse's flanks. Yet, even as Dawson cautioned himself, he took a deep breath and let it out, reminding himself that this life was behind him now. He'd left all this behind him in Somos Santos, Texas, in the top drawer of a battered oaken desk, in a piece of tin shaped into a star.

"Adios, fastest gun alive." He smiled to himself, picking up his hat and setting it atop his head. "Wherever you are."

Madden Peru, Rodney Dolan, Elton Shears, and Hank Kuntz stopped their horses midtrail, then spread out a few yards in four directions and sat staring at Brue Holley, who sat atop his big silver-gray blocking the trail. Holley made a menacing figure in his black bearskin coat, his wide-brimmed hat lowered on his forehead, a tall Spencer rifle standing in his gloved hand.

"What do you want, Holley?" Peru asked in a less than hospitable tone, recognizing the bounty hunter and not allowing himself to be intimidated by him.

"Well now," Holley replied, "ain't you the unsociable one today?"

"There's no reward on any of us," said Peru. "So you've got no right or reason to bring us any trouble."

"Right you are," said Holley, turning the big silver-gray and nudging it a step closer. "I'm not bringing any trouble to yas, although if I was to kill every one of you and wait a few days for your pasts to catch up to you, somebody up here would post a reward." He tweaked his mustache, staring hard at Peru even as he smiled.

Staring straight back at him without a smile, Peru

said to the others loud enough for Holley to hear, "When I say to, everybody unload on his ass. The world will thank us for it."

"Easy, now, Madden," said Holley, appearing undisturbed by Peru's comment. "Like I said, I ain't after yas. I just want to talk some, see if we can't help one another out for a change, instead of all the time going around with a mad-on."

Peru eased down a bit and said, "What's on your mind, bounty man?"

"I expect you already heard about somebody killing Fast Larry Shaw. I'm looking for the old prospector who brought his body to town. You boys prowl these foothills like coyotes. I figured you'd know who he is."

The four only stared at him with flat indiscernible expressions.

"Well, do yas?" Holley asked.

"We're waiting," said Peru.

"Waiting for what?" Holley asked, getting a little agitated by Peru's attitude.

"Waiting for you to tell us just how you can *help us out*," said Peru. "You've only told us how *we* can help *you*."

Holley growled under his breath, "Smart-aleck son of a bitch." But aloud he said, "I know you boys are going to keep doing what you do up here in God's country. Sooner or later somebody'll want to see you hang. When that time comes, instead of me killing you, I'll tip you off, let you know who's on your trail and how hard and fast you'll need to run." He squinted. "Make sense to yas?" His good eye scanned the four one at a time. "Rodney? *Cunts?* Nigger boy?"

"It's *Kuntz*, gawdamn you!" said Hank Kuntz, his hand almost instinctively going for his holstered pistol. Shears also bristled at Holley's insult, but he managed to keep his rage in check.

"Hank! Elton!" Rodney Dolan snapped quickly, taking the authority. "Don't let this old turd get to you."

"The thing is," Peru replied to Holley in a haughty tone, "none of us is going to be running from *anybody* from now on."

"Oh, really?" said the bounty hunter. "What does this mean, that you're all going on up into Canada, let the queen's red darlings get the honor of killing yas?"

Ignoring him, Peru said, "Besides, you don't need to track down any hermit prospector to try and figure out who it was killed Fast Larry . . . you're looking at him."

At first Holley only gave a dark chuckle and said, "Sure you did, Peru." But then, seeing the serious look on Peru's face, he said, "Hey, you're not joking with me, are you?"

"Do I look like I'm joking?" said Peru in a confident even tone, something different than Holley had ever seen from him.

Holley fell silent for a moment, studying each of the four faces in turn. "If I thought it was true, it would save me a lot of traipsing through the foothills," he said in a somber voice. "Of course it means I'd have to kill you and take what thunder you took from Shaw."

"You'd *try*," Peru said flatly.

Holley looked back and forth at the faces for a moment, his face a grim killing mask. It appeared to Peru that at any second, the bounty hunter would drop the rifle barrel and get off a left-handed shot while his right hand brought his Colt up into play, a move Holley had made famous. "Get ready, boys," he murmured under his breath.

But suddenly, instead of Holley making his trademark move, he burst out in a laugh that held the four young gunmen stunned for a moment until he collected himself and said, "Peru, you almost did it. You almost had me there for a minute." He chuckled as he backed his horse a step off the trail, toward a clump of trees where he'd been lying in wait. "The likes of a ragged-ass sneak thief like you killing Fast Larry Shaw? I'd have to be a damn fool to believe something like that."

"It's true," said Dolan, "we saw it with our own eyes. We're his witnesses!"

"Oh well, why didn't you say so?" said Holley, pulling farther out of pistol range toward the trees. "Now, that makes all the difference in the world. Nobody would believe Madden Peru. But hell, who would ever question an upstanding bunch like you three scarecrows?" He laughed again as he stepped his horse out of sight, calling back to them, "Good luck getting the world to believe this. You should have made a deal with me, boys. When things go wrong for you—and things will go wrong for yas— I might have helped. But now all I say is to hell with yas."

The four sat staring blankly until Holley rode out of sight. Finally, Peru said in a rejected tone, "That son of a bitch didn't believe me."

"Well," said Dolan, "you have to admit it is a stretch, thinking somebody like one of us killed a man like Fast Larry Shaw."

"But I killed him, damn it. You all saw me do it," Peru insisted. "What the hell is it going to take to convince folks I done it?" He looked at Dolan with a bemused expression.

"We go on and do what we planned to do," said Dolan. "To hell with Brue Holley. He's nothing but a short-shanked over-the-hill bounty dog anyway."

"You mean on into Crabtown?" asked Kuntz.

"Yeah, on into Crabtown," said Dolan. "Only you and Shears will wait for us outside the town limits, case it goes wrong and we end up in jail. You two will have to come break us out."

"I don't see why me and Shears can't ride in too," said Kuntz.

"We went over it, Kuntz," Dolan said with an exasperated breath. "You've got too bad a temper to stand up under questioning." He looked at Shears and said, "No offense, Elton, but you being a Negro . . . well, nobody is going to take your word for nothing."

"I hear you," said Shears. "No offense taken."

Dolan went on, saying, "We'll tell the sheriff there are two more witnesses if we need to . . . but only if we need to." He turned to Peru and asked, "Are you ready to go do it?"

"I've been ready," said Peru, gigging his horse as he turned it toward Crabtown.

Chapter 5

———

On a narrow mud-rutted side street, Dawson, Caldwell, and Sheriff Foley sat at a corner table in Clure's Drover's Restaurant, a small plank and tin roof structure just off Crabtown's main thoroughfare. They ate thick elk steaks roasted on an open grill out back and served with sliced potatoes under a blanket of thick steamy gravy and chopped prairie onions.

"Things have gotten steadily worse ever since word got out," said Sheriff Foley, the conversation having been about the riffraff arriving in town to see the body on display. "By now the news has made it to all the cattle trails, I expect."

"Yes, I'm certain of it," said Caldwell, having just swallowed a mouthful of gravy and potatoes. "To-morrow morning, we put the body in the ground and have done with it." As he spoke he raised a mug of dark beer as if in a toast.

Dawson took a drink of hot coffee and watched as the sheriff carved himself a large bite of steak and raised it to his mouth on a wooden-handled fork. "Sheriff, you and the barber here do good work together, if you don't mind me saying so."

Foley only nodded as he chewed hungrily on the tender savory meat.

"We don't mind you saying so at all," said Caldwell, with a smile. "I consider that quite a compliment coming from you." He gestured toward Foley. "This man has taught me a lot about upholding the law. He's the best I've ever seen."

"Ah," said Foley, waving the compliment away with his fork. "I just know my job, is all. I reckon I ought to by now. I've been serving in some legal capacity or other ever since this place was still called Last Chance Gulch . . . all the way back in sixty-four."

"Back when the four Georgians first struck gold?" Dawson asked.

Foley eyed him, impressed by his knowledge of the town's history. "I admire a man who scouts his trail before he rides it."

"I didn't want to come all this way for nothing," said Dawson.

Foley nodded. "To answer your question, yes, this is where the four Georgians first struck placer gold. Crabtown is named after one of the Georgians, fellow by the name of John Crab. But there's been more than placer gold struck here. There's also been quartz gold, lead, and silver struck all around. That's why there's always such a boom going on. This place is a hub of commerce. There's talk of changing the name again, to something more proper sounding. Some are mentioning taking the same name as a town in Minnesota . . . Saint Helena."

Caldwell grinned. "But some are saying Crabtown has never been a saint, so maybe they'll decide to drop the *Saint* part."

"Saint or no saint, I suppose Shaw couldn't have picked a better place to die," Dawson commented, his voice lowered enough to keep from being overheard in the quickly filling restaurant.

"Not if he wanted the word to get around and get around fast," said Caldwell, swigging his dark beer. "That's why he chose it." Looking Dawson over, he changed the subject by asking, "I trust you found the baths and services at the hotel satisfactory?"

Dawson carved himself a bite of steak, replying, "I've never been east, but I can't imagine New York having anything finer."

"Good, good." Caldwell beamed. Then his smile settled and he said, "I apologize for you not getting the haircut I promised. But if you'll stay a day longer I'll see to it you get—"

"No apology needed, Caldwell," said Dawson, cutting him off. "I understand how it is upholding the law." He looked back and forth between the two and said, "The fact is, I'm eager to get to Black's Cut, find my claim, and see what I've bought for myself."

"Black's Cut?" Foley asked, looking concerned. "Do you know anything about Black's Cut?"

Caldwell cut in, saying, "Don't worry, Sheriff. I've warned him about Black and Hyde Landry—not that

I think it's done any good." He gazed at Dawson, as if wanting a response.

"I listened well to what you told me," Dawson said earnestly, "and I appreciate it. I place a high value on good advice."

"Then there's no more to be said on the matter," Caldwell concluded. Then, giving Foley a glance, he said to Dawson, "Now that you've had your bath, a shave and haircut, and clean clothes, I hope you'll allow me to ask a favor of you."

"Ask away," said Dawson.

"Since you're leaving tomorrow and headed toward Black's Cut anyway, I hope you'll agree to stop by Widow Mercer's place and look in on her for us. I hate to think of that poor lonely woman, left alone in her grief for the second time in just as many years."

Dawson looked hesitant. "I don't know. I'm wanting to find my claim and get started."

"Oh, but it's right off the trail to Black's Cut, no more than two miles out of your way . . . three at the most," said Caldwell, not giving up. "It would mean so much to her. I wouldn't ask, but, well . . . you see how busy we are here."

Dawson considered it. "Three at the most, eh?"

"At the *very* most," said Caldwell. "Actually less, I'm certain."

"All right, I suppose I should," said Dawson, "as bust as you fellows are, and since Shaw and I are—" He caught himself, looked around quickly, then corrected himself, saying in a lowered voice, "That is, since we *were* friends, maybe it would look good if I did stop by and checked on her."

"That's the spirit," said Caldwell. "I'm much obliged. I can't tell you how much this will mean to her . . . to all of us for that matter."

"All right, it's done, then," said Dawson, returning to his steak. "How do I get to her place?"

Before Caldwell could answer, both he and Foley turned facing the two men walking toward them from across the busy restaurant floor. One of their voices had called out the sheriff's name, not in a demanding tone, but just loud enough to cause heads to turn.

"Yes, what can I do for you?" asked Foley, rising halfway from his chair, a napkin in his left hand blotting his lips, his right beneath the tabletop, holding his Colt cocked and ready. Dawson and Caldwell both half turned their chairs, facing the two.

"Begging your pardon, Sheriff, I'm Madden Peru. This is Rodney Dolan." The pair stopped four feet from the table, their hands respectfully away from their holstered Colts.

"You can just call me Rex," said Dolan, a little put out that Peru hadn't introduced him as Rex in the first place.

"I see," Foley replied. He looked the two over good, already getting an idea of the caliber of men who were addressing him. The name Madden Peru sounded familiar to him, but he wouldn't mention that right away. "All right, Mr. Peru . . . Mr. Dolan, what is it I can do for you today?"

Standing stiffly and sounding rehearsed, Peru said straightaway in a somber tone of voice, "I want to declare to you that I am the man who killed Lawrence Shaw. I killed him face-to-face in an act of self-defense, a deed that my friend—that is, Mr. Dolan here—will swear an oath to as my witness."

"Oh, he will?" Foley, Dawson, and Caldwell all three gave one another a look. "Well then . . ." Foley had been caught off guard by such an admission. After an appraising look at the two men, their side-arms, their demeanors, the sheriff summed them up as saddle tramps, trail thieves, lowlifes.

Seeing, but not understanding, the reaction they'd received, Peru added, "There are two other witnesses if one ain't enough. But I'd have to go round them up."

Recovering quickly from his surprise, and realizing what type of men stood before him, Foley said, "No, I reckon more witnesses won't be necessary." He sank back into his chair, laid his cocked Colt over in his lap, and let out a breath.

"So?" Peru looked a little offended at the sheriff's lack of interest. "What do we do now?" He stared at Foley in anticipation. "Do you have any questions? Want to hear how it all happened?"

"It was a hell of a thing to witness," said Dolan. "The two of them stood squared off. Shaw went for his gun and before he hardly got it out of his—"

"Hold on, fellows," said Sheriff Foley, cutting them off with his raised left hand. "We're all trying to have dinner here." He gestured with his hand all around the restaurant at the many faces turned toward Dolan.

"I thought you'd want to know how it happened," said Dolan, "me being a witness and all."

Caldwell cut in and asked Peru, "Are you saying Shaw had already gone for his gun and you *still* beat him to the draw?" As he asked he scrutinized Peru's shooting gear, a holster hanging limply on his hip, no tie-down, the dirty butt of his Colt lying half hidden below the leather edge. At the bottom of the holster, the gun barrel stuck out. The high rounded factory front sight was still attached, something a fast gun handler always took time to get rid of right away to keep it from snagging.

"Yeah, damn right that's what I'm saying," Peru replied, sounding indignant. "After I killed him I leaned him against a rock alongside the trail, gun in hand. Why? Are you casting doubts? You calling me a liar?"

To Dawson's surprise, Caldwell stood up slowly, his right hand poised calmly near his holster, and said to the frustrated Peru, "A liar would be one of the kinder names I'd have for you, sir." He looked Peru up and down and raised a calm hand toward Sheriff Foley to keep him from rising to his feet to back him. Foley sank back slowly into his chair. Caldwell continued to Peru, "If you told me you stole Shaw's horse, or a pair of his long johns he left hanging on a bush to dry, I *might* believe you. But don't disturb my dinner to purport that you killed a man whose chamber pot you're not fit to carry."

Dawson had never seen this side of Jedson Caldwell. He sat in silence, staring, knowing that the man facing Caldwell had already lost his bark and wanted a way off the spot he'd suddenly found himself in.

"Mister, I know who you are. You're just the town barber," said Peru, raising his gun hand slowly away from his gun and pointing at the impassive Caldwell. "I know you're the one has Shaw's body on display, and I know you and him were friends. So, I'm ignoring your remarks, for now anyway."

Beside Peru, Dolan gave the three diners a hard look and said, "Yeah, right now we've got bigger fish to fry." His harsh glare centered on Sheriff Foley. "So, tell me, Sheriff, what do I do now about being a witness to him killing Fast Larry Shaw?"

Foley took a sip of coffee and considered it for a moment, then said to Peru, "The next day or so I'll write both your names down when I'm in my office. Anybody asks, I'll tell them you said you killed Lawrence Shaw."

Peru looked agitated at not getting the sort of response he'd expected—respect, fear, praise, he didn't know, but this wasn't it. "That's all?" He tossed a hand. "I kill the fastest gun alive, something nobody has been able to do till now. All I get is you'll write down my name and tell anybody who asks that I *said* I killed him?"

"What else can I do for you?" Sheriff Foley asked, with a flat expression. "I had no time to hire a band."

Peru gave a tight, angry imitation of a grin. A nerve twitched in his jaw. Trying hard to maintain his self-control, he said, "Oh, now, that's funny, Sheriff . . . *real* funny."

Dawson lowered his face to keep the two men from seeing him smile at the sheriff's remark. "Gentlemen," he murmured. Shaking his head slowly he forked a bite of meat and raised it to his mouth. This was yet one more situation Caldwell the barber and Foley the sheriff had under control. He listened and watched and chewed his steak.

"This is some fine damn howdy-do!" Peru said in a raised voice, turning his attention to the other diners in the busy restaurant. "I kill the fastest gun alive! I come here to declare it and make a full admission to the deed, all of it in *self-defense*, of course, and *by Gawd!* I get snubbed, rebuffed, and rejected by the *gawddamned* legal authority!"

Sheriff Foley pointed a finger at him and said in a severe tone, "Keep up the cursing, fellow, you're also going to get yourself *arrested* by the legal authority."

"Hear that?" Peru shouted to the diners. "Now I'll be double-dog-damned if I'm not being threatened by *jail!*"

"Not anymore, you're not," said Sheriff Foley, coming up quickly and around the table, gun in hand, cocked and pointed. "You're under arrest. Raise your hands. I'd advise you to keep your mouth shut!"

Before either Peru or Dolan could make a move, the sheriff had them covered. To make matters worse for the two, Caldwell had also sprung straight up from his chair. But instead of drawing his Colt, the

barber snatched his sawed-off shotgun from somewhere beneath the table as if by magic and swung it
into play. Across the restaurant, chairs scooted out
of the line of fire. Diners leaped for cover.

"*Damn . . .*" Dolan whispered under his breath,
knowing they'd been bested. Raising his hands chest
high he said to Caldwell, "Don't shoot that scattergun, Barber. I'm not making any move. I've
warned him about his cussing, it's intolerable at
times."

"I *ain't* going to jail!" Peru shouted, but even as
he said it, Foley had spun him around, jerked his
right arm behind his back, then his left, and snapped
a pair of newly designed handcuffs on his wrists.

"You're going, fellow," said Foley, giving him a
nudge with his gun barrel. "It's up to you if you go
standing on your own or dragged by your collar."

Peru fell silent and walked toward the door, Foley
right behind him. Caldwell gave Dawson a knowing
look. "That's how *he* said the body was found, leaning against a rock." The two realized that in all prob-
ability Madden Peru had been the one who killed
Stiff-leg Charlie and left his body where Shaw had
found it. "What can we do about it now?" Caldwell said.

"That's how *who* found him?" Dolan asked, standing with his hands still raised. "I heard some old
hermit found him."

"Yes, the old hermit, that's who I meant," Caldwell
lied. He jiggled the shotgun. "Let's go."

"Me?" Dolan asked. "Why? I didn't cuss anybody.

I just came as a witness to Madden shooting Fast Larry."

"You're not under arrest," said Caldwell, stepping over and jerking his gun from its holster, "but I'm walking you outside, keeping an eye on you until your pal is behind bars. Now start walking."

As the barber followed Dolan toward the door, he said over his shoulder to the stunned diners, "Everybody back to your meal, folks . . . enjoy yourselves." He said over his shoulder to Dawson, "I apologize, but duty calls. Come by the office when you finish eating. I'll tell you how to get to the Mercer place."

Dawson nodded and watched Caldwell and the other man walk out the door.

Outside, being nudged along the busy street by Sheriff Foley's gun barrel, Peru said over his shoulder, "Man, I don't understand this at all! I come to tell the law what I done, and you two won't even believe me!"

"Look at yourself, Peru," said the sheriff, "then ask yourself, if you were *me* would you believe something like *you* killed Lawrence Shaw?"

"I like to think I'd give any man the benefit of the doubt, Sheriff," said Peru. "But I can swear on a Bible with no fear of eternal damnation that I killed Lawrence Shaw."

"Sure you did," said Foley. He realized this was Stiff-leg Charlie's killer. "But you'd best shut up about it for now. You're digging yourself a hole you don't even know you're digging."

"What does that mean?" Peru asked.

Realizing he couldn't explain anything more on the matter without revealing whose body lay in the pine coffin, Foley said, "If you can manage to keep your mouth shut overnight, I'll turn you loose come morning. Fair enough?"

Peru gave it some quick consideration. Something was wrong here, but for the life of him he had no idea what it could be. Shaking his head in bewilderment, he finally said, "I'm not saying another word the rest of the day, Sheriff. You can count on it."

"That's the first smart thing I've heard come out of your mouth," Foley said solemnly. The two walked on toward the jail at the far end of the street.

Peru kept his mouth shut all the way to his cell. But once the iron door clanged shut in his face, he couldn't resist blurting out, "Sheriff, I do have to say one thing."

"One more thing is going to get you one more day in jail," Foley warned him. "Are you sure what you've got to say is worth it?"

"I can't help it, Sheriff," Peru blurted out. "I really am the person who killed the man laying in that pine box across street, and I deserve everything coming to me for doing it."

Foley looked at him grimly for a moment. "I understand," he said. "Now shut up before I see to it you *get it*."

Chapter 6

———————

Dawson left Crabtown before the first purple fingers of dawn crept up over the horizon. He had finished his dinner alone the night before, and had not had the chance to socialize with either Caldwell or the sheriff. Right after dark the two had joined him at the bar in the crowded saloon. But no sooner had Caldwell told him how to get to the widow Mercer's spread—before they could even order themselves a drink—than a brawl erupted in the street between two groups of miners, and the barber and the sheriff left at a run.

As soon as the two ran from the saloon, Dawson had paid for his drink, finished it, and left unnoticed through the side door. When he rode out the next morning toward the foothills northwest of town, he'd seen a freight wagon someone had backed up and left at the side door of the barbershop. *Shaw's funeral hearse*, he'd surmised. *No, it's Stiff-leg Charlie's funeral hearse*, he'd corrected himself with a trace of a smile, thinking about Lawrence Shaw and his self-orchestrated demise as he'd ridden on.

At midmorning Dawson sat atop the biscuit-colored barb at the edge of a grassy cliff overhang. He spent a moment watching sunlight glimmer across the backs of cattle grazing on a long sloping hillside. At the bottom of the hillside a creak meandered out of sight. A thousand yards across the valley he saw the Mercer domain, a large cedar clapboard Victorian house perched on a short stretch of flatland, partially hidden in a breezy sway of towering pine.

"Jesus, Shaw," he murmured aloud to himself, coaxing his horse forward onto a thin rounding hillside trail, "you threw away more than most men can even dream of. . . ."

Two-thirds of the way around the hillside a large yellow hound loped up out of the brush lining the trail, and after only a token amount of bluster and barking fell in alongside the barb and led them to the house. At the open gate in a picket fence surrounding the house, the hound veered away, slipped beneath the pickets at a low spot he'd created for himself, and reappeared beside Dawson's horse at the front porch.

As Dawson stopped his barb a few feet from the house, the hound barked toward the front door until a white curtain stirred at a parlor window. "Obliged," Dawson said to the big hospitable hound.

A moment later the door opened a few cautious inches and a woman's voice called out, "If you're here looking for work, I'm sorry . . . but I no longer have need for any ranch hands."

"No, ma'am, I'm not here looking for work," said Dawson. Jigging the mule's lead rope as if to show his intent, he added, "I'm Cray Dawson. I'm here to . . ." He paused, then said, "Well, I'm here to see how you are doing. Jedson Caldwell asked me to stop by."

"Cray Dawson?" said the voice, the door grudgingly opening a few inches more. Caldwell's name seemed of little matter. "You're Lawrence's friend from Somos Santos?"

"Yes, ma'am, I am," said Dawson, his hat off and resting against his chest. "I just rode out from Crabtown, on my way up to work a claim." He jiggled the lead rope again and gestured toward the distant higher hill line. "I—I wanted to see you and express my condolences . . . tell you how sorry I am."

"Lawrence spoke so highly of you, Mr. Dawson. He called you his *best and lifelong friend.*" The voice revealed a painful forbearance. The door opened farther. The widow Mercer stepped out onto the porch. Dawson looked at her closely, his breath almost stopping in his chest as she turned sideways enough to lean a long shotgun against the front of the house. *Oh my, Caldwell, what have you done to me?* he said to himself.

"Please feel free to call me Cray, ma'am, if I may offer." He heard himself responding to her, yet he felt no importance in his words. His voice sounded distant to him, the meaning obscured by the soft radiant beauty of the woman facing him, her hands folding gently across her stomach. "Yes, we were friends. We grew up together. I'm awfully sorry to hear about his death."

With her nod of invitation, Dawson stepped down from his horse, spun the reins around a hitch rail, and tied the mule's lead rope close beside them. Even as he'd spoken he wondered if his words sounded believable, if his grief looked adequate for that of the deceased's *lifelong* friend. *Damn it, Shaw . . .* For the first time since he'd started going along with his friend's ruse, he felt ashamed, standing here deceiving this poor lovely grieving woman.

"I—I hadn't expected anyone to be so kind as to come console me," she said. "I know how busy Mr. Caldwell and the sheriff are these days."

Had this woman been drinking? If so, that was understandable, Dawson told himself. Having noted her struggle to keep her voice from surrendering to a flood of grief, he said softly, "Yes, ma'am, they are awfully busy." He saw a lingering redness in her eyes. From tears or alcohol? he asked himself. Perhaps both. He detected the slightest whiskey slur to her words.

"But it is so considerate of *you* to come. I know how much Lawrence would have appreciated—" Her words halted in her grief. She fought back a surge of emotion, pulled a delicate kerchief from the long sleeve of her gingham dress, and pressed it to one cheek and then the other as a new welling of tears began to spill.

Dawson stepped up onto the porch, hat in hand, not wanting to continue with this deception, but knowing of no way to stop betraying the widow Mercer without betraying his friend. Shaw had not asked him into this situation, yet Dawson felt a little angry at both Shaw and himself for having stumbled into it by chance and now finding himself involved. "Ma'am, if there is anything I can do, I want you to know—"

Now it was his words that failed, as the grief-stricken woman threw herself against him and sobbed with shameless abandon. "Please . . . hold me, Mr. Dawson," she pleaded in a crushed and broken voice. "I don't know how . . . much more . . . death and loneliness I can stand!"

"Yes, ma'am." Dawson's arms went around her instinctively. His hat fell from his hand to the porch floor. He clutched her to him as if to absorb the pain from her, feeling her tears through his shirt, warm on his chest. *Oh my goodness,* he thought, knowing this was wrong, being a party to deceiving her, yet knowing of no way to stop. "Yes, ma'am," he repeated, this time in a whisper, his hand rising, caressing her hair, soothing, condoling her. *Stop it!* he admonished himself. *Stop it now!*

But he didn't; he couldn't.

"First my husband, James," she sobbed. "Then, just when I thought I might . . . find happiness again . . . poor Lawrence, killed by some unknown assassin." She sobbed harder. "All this sorrow . . . I can't hold it inside. I have to let go of it or . . . I can't bear such grief."

"I know, I know, *please*," Dawson whispered, "you can let go. I'm here, I'll hold you, ma'am—" He continued stroking her hair, struggling hard with himself to keep from blurting out Shaw's illegitimate demise. "I'll hold you. . . ."

Dawson had been right about the whiskey. He caught a strong scent of it now as he continued holding her against him. When her sobbing had ceased, when she had gained control and spent what Dawson judged as a proper amount of time for a woman to stand with her arms wrapped around a man she'd never met, he cleared his throat quietly, as if making sure she was awake. "Ma'am," he whispered, lowering his head closer to her ear, "maybe you'd like to go inside?"

She raised her tear-streaked face to his. Her eyes searched Dawson's for any undisclosed purpose he might have intended. Seeing none, she paused, then said above a whisper, "Yes, of course. You must be weary after the ride from Crabtown. I'll prepare you a room."

"Uh, ma'am, that won't be . . ." Dawson felt her hand move down his forearm, take his gloved hand, and press it—a bit firmly, he thought—as she turned toward the open door.

He wanted to tell her that he had not planned on spending the night and wouldn't think of imposing on her. But he found no chance to say anything as she led him inside the coolness of a well-furnished parlor, saying over her shoulder to him, "I have an elk stew that I prepared earlier, in case I should feel more like eating." She sighed. "Life must go on, I've found."

"Yes, ma'am, you're right," Dawson said. "I know that's what Shaw would tell you if he were here."

"Yes," she said, stopping and turning to face him, with a familiarity he found almost unsettling, "I believe he would." Still holding his gloved hand, she gestured toward a short divan. "Please be seated, and may I offer you a drink, Mr. Dawson?" She only let go of his hand as he turned to seat himself.

"Yes, ma'am, obliged," he replied, unused to such bold behavior from a proper lady like the widow Mercer. "I would enjoy a drink." He settled himself quickly, reminding himself that he had no idea how a proper lady *should* act in a situation like this, especially one who had lost both a husband and a suitor in the space of a year.

Seeming to have gotten over her crushing wave of grief for the moment, the young widow said, as if able to read his mind, "Please do not think of me as some broken *vulnerable* woman, Mr. Dawson." She offered a coy smile and added in a knowing tone, "Of course, I realize there are men who are only attracted to broken vulnerable women." He saw the questioning look in her eyes.

"No, ma'am, I'm glad you're feeling better." He was unaccustomed to such candid behavior, and uncertain of how to respond. The woman had a way of moving him along in whatever direction she chose for him. He could see how Shaw and she might have hit it off. He could also see how Shaw must've felt that she was strong enough to deal with the news of his death and not let her in on his ruse. *She's tough as iron*, he told himself.

"Good, then," she said, as if seeing his revelation of her. Touching a hand to the side of her auburn hair, she said, "I'll get your drink, and even have one with you." She paused on her way from the parlor and looked back at him. "I hope you don't think me a terrible person." She smiled and said without giving him a chance to answer, "I won't be a moment."

"No, ma'am, not terrible at all," he murmured to himself as she left the room. But that was not completely true. While he did not consider her a *terrible* person, clearly she had been drinking, allowing that to be the reason for what appeared to him as a bit *forward behavior.* He heard her footsteps go into the next room and stop, followed by the tinkle of glass as she poured two drink glasses of whiskey and returned with them on a tray beside a tall half-filled decanter.

"I am by nature a *progressive* thinking woman, Mr. Dawson," she said, reentering the parlor with the conversation still going. "It is something my late husband said he admired most in me." She bowed slightly and set the tray on a low parlor table in front of the divan. She smiled as she picked up both glasses and handed one to him. "And I'm certain I needn't tell you, dear Lawrence felt the same."

"Yes, ma'am," Dawson replied, not knowing what else to say. He held his glass up toward her as she tipped hers slightly as if on the verge of making a toast.

But instead of making a toast, she stood with her glass raised and asked with candor, "Tell me, Mr. Dawson, or, because I feel I already know you, may I call you Cray?" She didn't wait for his answer, but continued, asking boldly, "How does a handsome Texan like you like his women?"

Well, now . . . He stared up at her for a moment, not allowing his surprise to show. It was clear enough to him where this conversation was headed. "Ma'am, I think I need to tell you, my intentions are to get on up around Black's Cut to work my claim. I don't want to say anything that might mislead you, or cause you any complications. I know you have been through an awful lot, and I—"

"Yes, that much is understood," she said, cutting him short somewhat impatiently. Was it impatience or eagerness? he asked himself. While he'd spoken the young widow took a fair drink of whiskey and set the glass down on the tray. She moved around the table and sat down beside him on the divan, loosening a long pearl-tipped hairpin from her hair and shaking out her long silky hair. "But haven't we both already agreed, *'Life must go on'?*" she asked, her breath quickening, her hand reaching for the top button of her gingham dress and loosening it as she stared intently into Dawson's eyes.

"Yes, ma'am, we did," said Dawson, relaxing, no longer trying as hard to resist the heat her passion evoked in him.

His mind quickly sorted what information he'd gathered from her over the past few minutes. Madeline Mercer had a way of seeing to it her bidding was met. Sympathy was the last thing she wanted; her actions had made that clear. Dawson knew he had no right to question the validity of her grief. Yet her tears had put her right into his arms on the front porch; from there it had only been a short step to her parlor, *and from there to this,* he told himself, seeing her fingers at work on the rest of the buttons down the front of her dress.

"I think Lawrence would just have to understand, don't you, Cray?" she asked in a breathy whisper.

Without having to remind himself of where Shaw might be or what he might be up to this very moment, and of what little regard he'd given this woman when he'd made his plan, Dawson replied, "Yes, ma'am, I think he'd have to."

Chapter 7

Rodney Dolan rode up to a ragged tent riddled with bullet holes sitting on a narrow back trail leading into Crabtown. He stepped down from his horse and hitched it beside his partners' horses, spinning the reins around an iron bar tied down between two cedar posts. On the front of the sagging tent a crudely painted sign read SNAKE EYES SALOON & GAMING PARLOR—REAL LIVE WOMEN! Alongside the tent a line of drunken miners stood relieving themselves into a muddy ditch. Dolan spat and walked into the open tent flap.

At the far end of a makeshift bar—three beer-soaked planks resting on two empty whiskey barrels—Shears and Kuntz gestured him toward them, Kuntz wagging a whiskey bottle back and forth like a railroad lantern.

"Where the hell is he?" Shears asked, looking past the approaching Dolan as he walked across the packed dirt floor toward them.

"He *still* couldn't keep his mouth shut," Dolan said, shaking his head in exasperation. "The sheriff added another day." He snatched the bottle from Kuntz's hand, threw back a swig of red-rye, and ran a hand across his mouth.

"Jesus, Rod—I mean, *Rex*," Shears said, correcting himself quickly, "it's been four days! What does he keep saying to cause all this?" He took the bottle from Dolan, poured himself a shot glass full of whiskey, then shoved the bottle to Kuntz.

"I don't know." Dolan shook his head again. "I expect if we're going to wait for him to keep his mouth shut, we could be in this shit-hole for a *long* time."

"Are we going to have to bust him out?" Kuntz asked seriously.

"Bust him out?" Dolan gave him a flat stare. "Do you want to be known for setting free an *idiot*? I don't. Besides, what makes you think we ought to be riding with a man who can't keep his mouth shut? Boys, this is the outlaw trail we're on. This is a dog-eat-dog life we've chosen. A man needs to know who he can count on and who he can't. I'm seeing a side of Madden Peru I don't like much. Can't keep his *mouth shut*? What the hell is wrong with this fool?"

"I wouldn't go so far as call the man a *fool* or an *idiot*," said Shears, a bit indignantly. "We've been through some tight situations together."

"Yeah," Dolan said cynically, "having some sod-buster firing a shotgun at us in the darkness whilst we ride off on his horse? Is that the sort of tight situation you're talking about? 'Cause if it is, I've got a girl cousin in Ohio could take his place most any time . . . and she'd not say a word if somebody drove a nail in her forehead."

"What's got you so struck down on Peru?" Kuntz asked, passing him the bottle after filling his shot glass.

Letting out a tense breath, Dolan calmed down some and said, "Hell, I don't know." He stepped up against the bar and took a clean shot glass the bartender placed in front of him. "I can't get over how little respect he was shown by the sheriff and the barber."

"A man kills the *fastest gun*, he right then becomes the *fastest gun*," said Shears, looking puzzled by the whole affair. "It's always been that way, it's always going to be that way. Before guns, it was whoever swung the fastest sword—chopped somebody in half. Whoever threw the fastest rock, bashed somebody's head in." He shrugged in bewilderment. "What's gone wrong here?"

Dolan stared at the plank bar top in brooding contemplation, his hand wrapped tightly around his whiskey glass. "If you coulda just seen the look on the sheriff's face . . . the barber's too. They looked at Peru and me both like we were nothing but ragged-assed trash! I know what went through their minds— I saw it in their eyes. They thought, *hell, there's no way this tramp could have killed Fast Larry Shaw*. To tell you the truth, I have a hard time believing it myself. Are we mistaken about how this all happened? Or about how fast Peru is? Am I missing something here?"

Kuntz shrugged, considering it, and said, "No, he's

fast sure enough. And he killed Shaw, deader than hell. That much is true. We all three saw him do it. Shaw caught us stealing his string of horses alongside the trail whilst he took himself a little siesta. Remember how Peru turned facing him?"

"Maybe Shaw was blind drunk," Dolan speculated.

"Huh-uh, Shaw wasn't drunk," Shears reminded him. "Peru is just fast."

"Yeah," said Kuntz. "Shaw went for his gun. None of us three was fast enough to stop him, I'll admit it."

"But Peru stopped him," said Shears. "Stopped him cold! One shot through the heart before Shaw even cleared leather. Let's not forget it."

"Maybe he got lucky," said Dolan, still doubting Peru now that things hadn't turned out the way they had all expected.

"Lucky?" said Kuntz. "I wish to hell I had that kind of luck going for me. Peru is fast as lightning, there's no way around it."

"Don't forget he killed those two Ute horse traders when they came gunning for him," Shears put in.

"They both had rifles," said Dolan. "It ain't quite the same as outdrawing and burning a man down face-to-face, with a six-shooter, the way he did Shaw." He paused, then added, "Yeah, there's no denying Peru is fast. But why did he let that sheriff and the barber dog him down, haul him off to the jail? His trouble is getting people to take him serious."

"I don't know why he let that happen," said Shears, shaking his head. "I guess it all caught him by surprise, things not going the way he thought they would."

"All right, then," said Kuntz, tired of all the speculation, "if we ain't going to bust him out, and he
can't shut up long enough to get out on his own,
what are we going to do, just leave him there to rot
'cause of his big mouth?"

"I say we only give him one more day," said
Dolan. "I'll visit him again in the morning. If he ain't
getting out then, that'll do it for me. I've got no more
time to waste on the man, fast gun or not."

When Sheriff Foley awakened before daylight, he
stood up from his bed against the back wall of the
jail, lit an oil lamp, and walked toward the potbellied
stove where he had banked a bed of coals the night
before. On his way past Madden Peru's cell he saw
the young outlaw sitting on the side of his cot, staring contemplatively, his hands folded beneath his
chin as if he was in prayer. "Trouble sleeping, Peru?"
Foley asked, seeing the glint of the oil lamp in his
dark eyes. "Or just an early riser like me?"

Without replying to the question, Peru said, "Sheriff, can I ask you a question?"

"Yep, so long as it's not more of your railing about
how wrongly you've been treated," Foley replied.

"Naw, nothing like that," said Peru. "When the
barber was here yesterday, he said a man like Lawrence Shaw had respect everywhere he went. Said it
had nothing to do with being a fast gun. Said that
Shaw would have gotten respect even if he'd never
fired a gun. Do you believe that?"

"Yes, I do," said Foley, setting the oil lamp down.

He picked up a short poker and stirred up the bed of glowing coals until a flame began licking up. "I've seen it in many a man."

"How does a fellow get that way?" Peru asked, almost humbly.

"Hmm. I don't know." Foley thought about it some more as he reached down into a wood pile beside the stove, picked up a handful of kindling, and laid it into the growing flames. "It's too easy to just say some fellows are born with it and some ain't," he offered at length. "These days there's all sorts of speculation as to why a person does what he does. Folks of learning say it all has to do with how a fellow's raised . . . the kind of man his pa was, even his grandpa . . . the kind of character that's been instilled in him . . . all such as that."

"Makes respect sound like something handed down," said Peru, seeming to consider the sheriff's words closely.

"I reckon it sounds like it," said Foley, "but there's more to it." He shoved some small lengths of firewood into the flames and closed the iron stove door. "Why do you ask?" He picked up the coffeepot from atop the stove and shook it slightly.

"I never knew my pa," said Peru, applying Foley's words to himself, "so I reckon I don't know what I got from him, respectwise, or any other wise." He sighed in a despondent manner. "I reckon I never got much of anything from anybody . . . nothing fit to have anyway."

Foley had stepped over, coffeepot in hand, to a

wooden water bucket sitting against the wall beside the stove. He'd taken a dipper from a peg on the wall and started to dip water into the pot to wash out last night's grinds. But upon hearing Peru's words, Foley stopped and looked over at him through the dim circle of lamplight. "Been doing some soul-searching, have yas?" he asked.

"So what if I have? Anything wrong with it?" Peru came back quickly, sounding defensive.

"No, nothing at all wrong with it," said Foley. He busied himself cleaning the coffeepot and filling it with fresh water. "Jail's one of the best places I know of for a man to take a good look at himself." He stepped over and set the pot atop the stove. He felt the heat rise slowly, seeing a flick of red orange through a door vent. "I believe a jail cell gets more conversions than a church pew, the truth be known." He gave Peru a guarded look. "That is, if *conversion* is what a man's really looking for."

"I've been nothing all my life," Peru said, speaking as though it would have made little difference whether or not the sheriff was there. "I've been kicked from one spot to the next since the day I was born. I always felt like if I ever did one thing right, maybe it would cut me from the herd and send me running on my own . . . set me free so to speak, make me a *somebody*." Finally he looked at the sheriff as if to see if his words were understood.

"I'm listening, Peru," Foley said quietly.

"Somehow I got good with a gun," the young outlaw continued. "I don't know how it come about. I didn't practice it that much—hell, I barely could afford bullets." He shrugged. "But one day there I was, fast as a rattlesnake, didn't even know it at first. It took a couple of my pards telling me before I realized it myself."

He paused as if to ponder his next words as he spoke them. "Now here I am. I've killed the fastest gun alive, but it's gained me no more respect than if I'd kicked a can down the street." He gave the sheriff a fixed gaze. "I feel like you know something I need to know, Sheriff."

"Well, I see you've learned a more polite way of discussing things." The sheriff stared back at him, stalling. This was the same line of talk that had kept Peru in jail twice as long as he should have been. Only now it was different. This was not the same ranting, accusing, cursing young man Foley had shoved into the cell. This was a man running things through his mind, looking for answers about himself, knowing something was missing inside him.

Standing and walking to the door of his cell, Peru clutched the iron bars intently with both hands. "Talk to me, Sheriff," he said, not loud, not abrasive and demanding, but almost pleading. *The new fastest gun alive, looking to a lawman for answers,* Foley thought. "Tell me what I need to do. I want to be respected, just like Shaw was, like you, the barber, hell, like anybody . . . except the kind of two-bit saddle-tramp I am."

Foley knew he could not tell Peru the truth, that he'd killed the wrong man. But instead of pushing the young man's question aside, he said, "Maybe some men gain respect over a long period of time, the way they carry and conduct themselves, the way they treat others."

"In my case all they know is what they see," said Peru with a bitterness in his voice. "I've never carried or conducted myself with any respect. What would have been the reason?"

Foley studied Peru's eyes as he continued, trying to be kinder to Peru than he'd been so far. "In your case, let's say you chose a faster way. You wanted the respect another man earned. You wanted one bullet to give you what he had, but it won't do it. Killing the fastest gun alive makes you faster than him . . . but it won't give you the respect he earned his whole life. You'll have to work for that, if you've got the character to do it."

"I don't want to be how I am anymore," Peru offered. "I'm sick of it."

"Oh?" Foley put his hand to the side of the coffeepot, judging it. "Then there's something for you to think about while we wait for some fresh coffee." He gave a thin, tired smile.

"The coffee sounds good, anyway." Peru slumped against the bars as if realizing the sheriff was right and wondering to himself if he *did* have the character to make something better of himself.

Chapter 8

No sooner had the sun risen above Crabtown than the dirt street began to come alive with the sound of horses' hooves, hammers and nails, and creaking freight wagons. As the sheriff and his prisoner sipped on their third cup of coffee, Jedson Caldwell arrived at the door with a pair of boots wrapped in a bundle of fresh laundry under his arm. Stepping inside the sheriff's office, Caldwell looked all around, seeing Foley and Peru apparently involved in conversation. Peru sat on the edge of his cot inside his cell; Foley sat at his battered oak sheriff's desk, one boot propped up on an open drawer.

"Pardon my interruption, but it's time for breakfast, Sheriff," Caldwell said. "I told the cook to save you plenty of hoecakes."

"Obliged, Jedson." Foley stood from his chair stiffly and picked up his hat from the edge of the desk. Looking at the bundle of clothes and boots under Caldwell's arm he asked, "What have you got there?"

"Shaw's old duds," Caldwell replied. "The China-man brought them to me on my way here, all boiled and washed, boots cleaned and shined." He laid the bundle on the sheriff's desk, looked at it for a moment, then sighed for Peru's sake and said, "Don't know what I'll do with them now. Didn't need them for Shaw. The dead judge's suit worked out well."

"Do you ever cut hair anymore?" the sheriff asked, stepping toward the door.

"Victor is filling in for me this morning." Caldwell smiled.

"He's doing a good job, is he?" Foley asked, adjusting his hat onto his head.

"No complaints so far," said Caldwell. As he spoke he looked over at Peru behind the bars and asked, "Is he getting out today?"

"He's settled down a lot," said Foley, not mentioning that he and Peru had been talking, not wanting to reveal anything Peru had said to him. Instead he stared at the quiet prisoner and asked him, "What about it, Peru? Do you think you can keep a civil tongue if I turn you loose this morning? That is, after I bring you some breakfast back, of course."

"Yes, sir, Sheriff, I can," Peru replied; then he sipped his coffee, looking at the two from over the edge of his cup.

"There you have it," said Sheriff Foley. He smiled and touched his fingertip to his hat brim, seeing the surprised look on the barber's face. "Coffee's strong and hot, enjoy it." He nodded toward the steaming coffeepot as he walked out and closed the door behind himself.

"Well then," said Caldwell, gazing at Peru, "looks like when your friend Dolan comes by today, we'll be setting you free."

"Yeah, I suppose," said Peru, not sounding too enthused at the prospect. He stood up, watching closely as Caldwell unrolled the bundle of clean clothes. "Did I hear you say you've got Shaw's clothes there?"

"Yes, that's right," said Caldwell. He unrolled the trousers and looked at the shiny boots before standing them on the sheriff's desk. As the clothes unrolled a folded hat flopped open onto the desk. "I had the laundry wash and clean everything, thinking I would need them."

"You've got his boots and hat too?" Peru asked.

"Yep, boots and hat too," said Caldwell. "Never know when somebody might need them." He held up a shirt, looked at it, and shook his head. "Lot of the bloodstain came out, but here's the bullet hole where you shot him dead. It wouldn't have been satisfactory for a funeral shirt anyway, the shape it's in." He shook the woolen shirt a little and laid it on the oak desk, bullet hole facing up.

"No, I suppose it wouldn't," Peru said, trying not to look too ashamed of himself. He watched in silence for a moment, until the front door opened and Rodney Dolan stepped inside.

"No guns!" Caldwell said firmly, his hand wrapping around the butt of his Colt, ready to bring it up from the holster.

"Whoa! My mistake!" said Dolan, his hands rising chest high. He backed out the door, loosened his gun belt, hung it on a peg on the front wall, then stepped back inside.

Across the street, sitting inside the restaurant looking out the window, Sheriff Foley saw what had happened and smiled to himself.

Stepping back inside the sheriff's office, Dolan still held his hands chest high and said, "There, no harm done, Barber. I'm just here to see my pard, same as yesterday, if that's all right with yas."

Caldwell nodded, his hand still on his gun butt. "Go on, you can talk to him. But don't cross the line." He nodded at a black-painted line four feet from the iron-barred cell door.

"Wouldn't think of it, Barber," said Dolan, walking over to Peru's cell. At the line on the floor he stopped and spread his hands in anticipation, stared through the bars at Peru, and said, "Well?"

"Howdy, Rex," Peru replied.

Dolan looked perplexed and taken aback. *"Howdy, Rex?* Is that all you've got to say?"

"What do you want me to say?" Peru asked, making eye signals to let Dolan know he didn't want to say too much under Caldwell's scrutiny. "I'm still stuck here! I'm not getting out!"

"What? This is crazy!" said Dolan, swinging around toward Caldwell. As soon as he'd turned facing Caldwell, Peru waved both hands and shook his head, pleading with Caldwell to go along with him and not to let him out of his cell. "What the hell has he done now?" Dolan demanded.

Caldwell shook his head. "You'll have to take it up with the sheriff when he gets back," he said, not lying, but not telling the truth either. "If I were to guess, I'd bet it's something he said." The barber gave a slight smile as Dolan turned back to Peru.

"Jesus, Madden! Are you a lunatic?" said Dolan. "I've never seen anybody who won't shut his mouth long enough to get freed from jail!"

"I couldn't help myself," Peru said, seeing Dolan had fallen for it. "The sheriff keeps me stirred up, making remarks, treating me like I'm lying about killing Fast Larry."

Lowering his voice just between the two of them, Dolan held a hand on his chest as if it were a gun, and whispered as he rolled his eyes slightly, "Ain't it time me and the boys, *you know . . . ?*"

"No, nothing like that," Peru said in a whisper himself, shaking his head vigorously. "Not yet anyway," he added, to make it sound real.

"Not yet? Why, *not yet?*" Dolan whispered in a rasping voice.

Peru looked all around quickly, searching his mind for something to say. When nothing else came to him, he whispered in reply, "The sheriff hasn't brought me my breakfast yet."

Breakfast! Peru's words caused him to actually stagger back a step. Dolan gave his jailed partner a strange, bewildered stare. *"Jesus,"* he said finally.

Caldwell watched the stunned outlaw turn and walk out the front door, both fists clenched at his sides. When he looked out the window and saw Dolan walking away, fastening his gun belt back around his waist, he said to Peru, "What was that about? Are you starting to like living behind bars?"

"Obliged for not telling him otherwise," said Peru, ignoring Caldwell's question. He gestured a nod at the clothes and boots on the table. "What are you going to do with all that?"

"I'll find a use for it," said Caldwell. "Sooner or later, somebody will haul a body in off the wilds buck naked. I'll need clothes for it."

"Can I have them?" Peru asked bluntly.

"You want the clothes of the man you killed?" asked Caldwell. "What for? You've got your own clothes and boots."

"I'll trade mine for them," Peru offered quickly. "What do you say?"

Caldwell thought about it, then said, "First the sheriff said you can leave, but you won't leave. Now you're wanting to change clothes with a dead man? What are you thinking?"

"Just the trousers, boots, and hat," said Peru. "The shirt's ruined."

Out in front of the jail, Dolan turned his horse in the street and rode straight to the Snake Eyes Saloon. He hitched the horse at the iron rail and walked straight through the open tent flap to the plank bar, hardly giving a glance toward Shears and Kuntz, who stood awaiting his return. Shears looked toward the front of the tent as if Madden Peru might come walking in. "Where's Madden?" he asked.

"Where do you think? Still in jail," Dolan growled. He snatched a bottle of rye from the plain bar top, filled a shot, and tossed it back in one gulp. He picked up a cork, stuffed it down into the bottle, and shoved the bottle down into his coat pocket. "Let's ride!" he said in an angry rasp.

"Wait! What about Peru?" Shears asked.

"He couldn't keep his mouth shut, *again*," said Dolan, turning toward the open front of the sagging tent. "I'm through with him."

"What about busting him out?" asked Kuntz. He hurried to keep up as Dolan walked away across the packed dirt floor, kicking a skinny cat that crossed his path. The cat let out a screech, landed, and darted away.

"I offered us to break him out," Dolan said. "He said he was waiting for *breakfast!*"

Kuntz and Shears followed Dolan from the tent to the horses, Shears looking off along the busy street running into Crabtown as if Peru might yet appear.

At noon, Peru stepped out of his cell wearing his own fringed rawhide shirt, but the loose-fitting clothes and boots he thought had belonged to Lawrence Shaw. He recognized the clothes, having last seen them on Stiff-leg Charlie the day he'd shot him. Thinking back, had he realized the man he'd just shot was Lawrence Shaw, he would have kept the gun and holster. But the shooting rig hadn't struck him as anything special, so he'd sold gun and holster at a trading post for four dollars.

It wasn't the sort of shooting rig he'd expect a big name gunman like Shaw to wear, he reminded himself as he picked up the Montana-crowned hat from the desk and placed it atop his head. He noted that it sat tighter than the battered bowler he'd grown used to. But now that he'd thought about it, a big gunman like Shaw didn't have to wear anything new and showy, just something that fit his hand and got the job done. "Now then, Sheriff," he said, "if I can trouble you for my gun belt, I'll be on my way."

"Right away," said Foley, liking the politer manner he'd seen Peru take on since his arrival. The sheriff walked around behind his desk, unlocked and opened a lower drawer, and laid Peru's rolled-up gun belt on the desk. Peru's range Colt stood in a weathered slim-jim holster.

Before picking up the gun belt, Peru drew the Colt and turned it back and forth in his hand, looking it over good. He checked it, saw that it was still loaded, then laid it on the desk. Foley and Caldwell watched him unroll the gun belt, put it on, and stoop as he wrapped the rawhide tie-down around his thigh. "Obliged for trading me the clothes, Barber," he said as he tied the rawhide, then straightened up and adjusted the holster.

"You're welcome," said Caldwell. "I can't say I understand your purpose in wanting them." He looked at the worn and battered bowler hat lying on the desk, the worn-down boots Peru left standing in the cell. "Although, maybe they do have a little more life in them than what you were wearing."

"Yeah, that's what I thought," said Peru, but without sounding like he meant it. He picked the Colt up from the desk and spun it backward and down into his holster slick and expertly, his quickness catching both the sheriff's and the barber's attention.

The two watched as Peru drew the Colt fast and effortlessly, as if the act were simply a reflex, like the quick deadly strike of a snake. "The money, Sheriff, if you please," he said, the Colt slipping quickly into his holster.

"Huh? Oh yes, your money," said Foley, caught up in watching the fast silent action of gunmetal and human skill at work. He reached in the drawer again, came up with a brown envelope, and emptied a thin folded stack of bills and a small mound of coins, both silver and gold, onto his desk. "Feel free to count it if you like, young man," he told Peru.

"I'm not going to, Sheriff. I trust you both," Peru answered. He gave a thin trace of a smile, shoved the bills into his rawhide shirt pocket, scooped the coins into his hand and into his trouser pocket, except for one coin he held in his right palm. He asked Caldwell, "The fellow sitting with you two at the restaurant that evening?"

"Yes, what about him?" Caldwell replied.

"He was Shaw's pal, Dawson, out of Somos Santos, Texas, wasn't he?" he asked.

"Yes, that was Cray Dawson," Caldwell said a bit

guardedly, wondering where this was headed. "He has left Crabtown already. Why do you ask?"

"He's real fast too, I expect, riding with Shaw like he did?" Peru asked without answering him.

"He is fast," said Caldwell, "but he's no gunfighter. If you're thinking anything about—"

"Where did he go?" Peru asked, cutting him off.

"Back to Somos Santos, I'm sure," Caldwell lied, giving Foley a quick glance.

"If you're thinking about working up a gunfight with Cray Dawson you'd be making a big mistake," Foley cut in.

"You're saying he's faster than Fast Larry Shaw, the man whose hat and boots I'm wearing?" Peru asked.

Foley and Caldwell just looked at one another. What could they say? "Peru, I've seen some good in you the past couple days," said Foley. "Don't go doing something that—"

"Relax, Sheriff," said Peru, his tone and demeanor still sociable, "I'm not looking for trouble with Dawson. If he's not out to 'venge his pal Shaw, I've got no fight with him." He turned to Caldwell. "I am curious how fast he is, though."

"I'm not a good person to judge who's fast and who's not," said Caldwell. "I've seen lots of fast guns. After a while their speed all looks about the same."

"No kidding?" Peru asked.

"No kidding," Caldwell replied.

"Tell me something, Barber, and tell me the truth,"

he said, his eyes fixed coolly on Caldwell's. He held his right hand waist high and flipped the gold coin up, not far, only a few inches. Foley and Caldwell watched the coin fall. Peru stood relaxed, as if he would let it fall to the floor. Yet as the coin dropped back to waist-level, suddenly his Colt barrel appeared beneath it, bounced it back up a few inches. It fell again, this time landing in his right palm, his Colt having disappeared back into his holster. "Is that *fast?*" His eyes seemed to have not left Caldwell's face. "Or is that about the same as everybody else?"

Caldwell and Foley stood as if stunned. "I hope you've learned something here, Peru," the sheriff said finally, neither he nor Caldwell commenting on what they'd just witnessed.

"I have, Sheriff," said the young gunman, sincerely. "I've learned to give some thought to character. Some men have it. Some never will. I'm obliged that you slowed me down and taught me that." He touched his fingertips to the brim of his newly acquired hat, turned, walked out the door, and closed it behind himself.

The two stood watching the closed door for a moment. Finally, Foley said, "I don't know if I've ever seen a gun slip a holster that fast in my life."

"I do know . . . and I can tell you straight up, I *never have*," said Caldwell, as if still in awe.

Chapter 9

———

Two days out of Crabtown, headed southwest along a ridgeline overlooking Little Mexican Creek, Rodney Dolan ducked low in his saddle at the sight of three riders crossing the wide shallow water. Reining his horse quickly away from the edge he said to the others, "Everybody stay! It's that damn marshal!"

"Whoa!" said Kuntz, veering his horse so quickly that a short spray of loose dirt spilled off the edge and rained down.

"Damn!" Dolan said, sarcastically. "Why don't you just call out to them? Tell them we're up here, you fool!"

"Sorry, Rex," said Kuntz. "I reckon this horse cuts too sharp for his own good sometimes." As he spoke he patted his horse's withers.

"Give him a crack of a pistol butt twixt his eyes, next time," Dolan growled. "We'll be lucky if Thornton and his law dogs didn't see that."

Shears stepped from his saddle, handed Kuntz his

reins, and moved close to the edge in a crouch. He peered down and watched the three horsemen continue across the shallow creek without looking up. "I don't think they saw anything." He crept back to his horse, took his reins from Kuntz, and remounted. "Think they picked up our trail, or just happened to be riding in this direction?"

"I don't know," said Dolan, "but unless they're sleep-riding they know there's three riders on the trail ahead of them."

"Maybe we can shake them when we get to some flatter ground."

"We could get back down to the Mexican and ride in it until we find a place where we won't leave any prints," Shears offered.

"Ha!" Dolan scoffed. "Good luck shaking an old dog like Thornton once he's gotten this close. We was lucky in Crabtown, but we can't keep ducking and hiding forever." He stared at the two for a moment, then said, "I don't think we're going to see much peace until we get rid of Thornton and his men once and for all."

"Us three against them three," said Kuntz. He shook his head slowly. "That's bad odds."

"The odds might be bad now, but they damn sure ain't going to get no better." Dolan looked along the path they'd taken up the hillside from the creek, knowing that soon the marshal and his men would be riding along this same edge. "What we need is to find some good high cover, lay up, and pick their eyes out," said Dolan.

"Cover is fine," said Shears. "But I don't like standing off three lawmen up here, without a place to put a horse into a run if we have to get away in a hurry."

"Neither do I," Kuntz agreed, looking warily back along the narrow trail.

"This ain't something we can spend all day jawing about," said Dolan. He gazed toward a tall wall of rock farther along the trail. "Follow me," he ordered, jerking his horse around on the trail.

Two hundred feet below, Thornton's hand still rested on his Colt as he stepped his big dun up out of Little Mexican Creek. The spill of dirt was all he'd needed. Things would be coming to a head pretty soon. He had spotted Dolan, Shears, and Kuntz during the night through his field lens. These were three of the men he'd been trailing. Where was the fourth?

When the dirt and loose rock had spilled down from the cliff above, he'd seen Ragsdale and Nutt start to turn their attention upward instinctively; but he'd stopped them, saying quickly and quietly, "Don't look up, you'll tip them off!"

Now, out of sight in the shade of the cliff along the inner edge of the creek, Nutt said, "Maybe that wasn't them at all." He looked back and forth anxiously between the two. "Some critter might have caused that dirt slide, do you think?"

"Damn, Clifford, look at you!" said Ragsdale with a dark chuckle. "You're not going into a nervous frenzy on us, are you?"

"I asked a simple damn question is all, Porter!" Nutt snapped in an angry trembling voice. "I ain't nervous about a gawdamn thing!"

Raising a quieting gloved hand toward the two, Thornton gazed sidelong up the rocky cliff side. As if thinking aloud, he said, "They saw us. They know we're onto them now. But they don't know that we *know* they saw us," he added. "Maybe that's all the advantage we need."

"What are you talking about, Marshal?" Ragsdale asked, sounding a little nervous himself.

"They'll be waiting for us up there, you can count on it," said Thornton. He looked back cautiously along the trail they'd been tracking the three men on. "I wonder what happened to the fourth man. We don't want him closing in behind us."

"This could be a trap! I don't like riding into a trap," Nutt said, sounding more rattled by the minute.

"Nobody *does*, Clifford," Thornton said, trying to calm the frightened man. "And we're not going to if we can keep from it."

At the base of a steep rock wall, Dolan slid his horse to a halt and looked up. "This is it, boys. Up there is where we make our stand." Eighty feet up, a short scrub pine clung to a thin ledge. He looked both ways along the trail. In either direction lay a long clear stretch that would provide no protection once the lawmen were on the trail beneath them. He gave a cruel grin. "They won't have a chance to get out of rifle range even on horseback, us lying up among the rock."

"Yeah, but how the hell do we get up there?" Kuntz asked, looking dubious at the jagged wall of rock streaked with patches of dirt and sparse clinging vegetation.

"We *climb*," Dolan said flatly. "And we better do it pretty damn quick, if we want this to be a surprise attack. They'll be rounding the trail most any time now." He looked back, checking for the lawmen's dust.

Shears slid down from his saddle and pulled his horse along by its reins toward a break in a line of thick brush alongside the trail. "I wish Peru was here. We're going to need some good shooting to get this done."

Dolan and Kuntz followed the black horse thief onto a steep elk path leading up to the first narrow ledge that widened back beneath the rock wall. They tied their horses to a weathered downfall pine beneath the overhanging cliff, jerked their rifles from their saddle boots, and hurried upward. Gripping rock, roots, and at times climbing hand over hand until they reached the next broken ledge, the three collapsed for a moment, their breath heaving in their chests.

"If I didn't . . . want to kill this law dog before . . . I sure want to kill him now," Dolan gasped in a breathless halting tone, "making me . . . do all this." He waved his rifle in both directions. "Get spread out! One that way . . . one the other," he demanded. "Don't shoot . . . until I give the order. We'll wait until . . . they're right beneath us. Then we'll pour it on them!"

Dolan watched the two hurry away in opposite directions and take up positions overlooking the thin trail below. Satisfied they had wisely taken advantage, he lay back and breathed deep, catching his breath, waiting, estimating it would only be a matter of minutes before the three lawmen rode into sight.

But when an hour had passed with no sign of dust rising along the trail, Dolan grew restless, peeped up over a rock as if to make sure the lawmen had not slipped past them, then looked in both directions along the long length of trail. Perfect cover for a perfect ambush, he told himself. Now where were the lawmen?

Almost before the question slipped across his mind, as Dolan backed away from the cliff edge, Thornton's voice boomed down to him from the top of the rock wall another sixty feet up. "You horse thieves down there. We've got you covered. Drop your guns and raise your hands."

"Damned if we will!" Dolan shouted in surprise, swinging his rifle up against his shoulder. Even as he fired, rifle shots from above pounded the ground around his feet, keeping him from running closer to the wall and out of their line of fire.

"You're not going anywhere, horse thief," Thornton shouted down to him, sounding confident from his higher position.

"Shoot them, boys!" Dolan shouted defiantly to Shears and Kuntz. "Don't go down easy!" As he shouted he scrambled over the edge of the cliff, rifle in hand, with bullets whizzing past him. Turning, firing up at the lawmen, he noted the blood on the back of his glove where it had run down from under his duster sleeve. "What the—" He turned his hand back and forth, then felt the warm blood running down his chest. "Ah, hell, I'm shot."

The heavy firing from the high ridgeline lulled for a moment. Thornton called down, "Have you boys had enough? We can rain fire upon your worthless asses for as long as it takes."

"Go to hell, up there!" Dolan heard Kuntz call out from his position in the rocks. He heard a shot resound from Kuntz's rifle.

"Thataboy, Hank, damn their hides," Dolan said to himself. He jerked his glove from his hand and ran it inside his duster. He sighed as he felt the source of the blood flow, a numb two-inch-wide hole where the bullet had exited his right breast. Taking a sweat-crusted bandanna from around his neck, he wadded it up along with his bloody glove and shoved both inside his duster and jammed them into the wound to slow the bleeding.

"Come down and fight, you cowardly sons a bitches!" Dolan heard Kuntz shout. He heard him fire another shot. Then he heard a heavy volley of fire and realized the three rifles had turned their attention in Kuntz's direction.

Catching a glimpse of someone moving on his right

along the outer edge of the trail, Dolan swung his rifle barrel in that direction and saw Shears throw up his free hand and say, "Don't shoot! It's me!"

"What are you doing here?" Dolan shouted as the three rifles fired steadily. "Didn't I tell yas to stay in position!"

"That was when *we* was going to ambush *them!*" Shears responded, crouching down beside them. "I figured now that they's ambushing us I better get out of there!" He stared down along the trail in both directions while rifle fire from the high ridgeline pounded Kuntz's position. "There ain't no way to get out of here without getting shot to pieces."

"See," said Dolan, "I was right. This is one *fine* spot for an ambush."

"I wish Peru was here," Shears said. "We could use a good gun hand."

"To hell with Peru," said Dolan. "He made his bed, he can lie in it."

Shears gave him a puzzled look and jacked a fresh round into his rifle chamber. As Dolan had spoken he'd adjusted the wadded-up glove and bandanna inside his duster. Seeing the blood on his hand when Dolan pulled it from inside his duster, Shears said, "Jesus, Rex! You're shot!"

"Tell me something I didn't already know," Dolan said with a wince, starting to feel the effects of his wound and the loss of blood.

Noting Dolan's condition, Shears said, "Hell, man, you're dying on me!"

"No, I'm not, damn it," said Dolan. "Don't count

me out long as I can fire a gun." His eyes swam a bit as he spoke. Shears heard a dazed slur in his voice.

"Have you lost your mind? Hell, you already *counted out* of it!" said Shears. "I'm giving us up. Peru is the one they want anyway, for killing those Ute horse traders. Hell, even that was self-defense!"

"You're not giving us up, so shut up and start shooting, darkie!" Dolan warned him.

"*Darkie?*" said Shears, looking stunned at first, but then offended. "I *know* you've lost your mind now!" Laying his rifle beside Dolan, he stood up and stepped over onto the trail. Hands held high, he walked forward shouting at the ridgeline above the rifle fire, "Hey, we're through here! We're giving up, all right?"

The rifle fire that had been firing steadily on Kuntz's position stopped. Thornton called down to him, "Stay right there." Thornton looked down, back and forth, seeing Kuntz's body lying stretched out alongside the trail in a dark puddle of blood. Unable to see Dolan off the edge of the trail, he called out, "Where's the third man?"

"He's right back there, shot bad," said Shears, thumbing back over his shoulder.

"The fourth man?" Thornton called out.

"He's gone," said Shears, lying for Peru. "He's been gone ever since we saw yas there the other day in Crabtown. He got scared and run."

"Hear that, Clifford?" Ragsdale said to Nutt, giving Thornton a sidelong look of contempt. "They was there under our noses."

Thornton ignored the deputy's remark and called down to Shears, "Which one of yas killed those horse traders south of here?"

"He killed them, Marshal. But it was self-defense. Those traders threw down on him first. Anyway, those horse traders worked with us, bought all our stolen livestock . . . seven stole some with us themselves."

"That's enough out of you!" Dolan shouted from over the edge. Managing to lay his rifle down over a rock, he took a blurry-eyed aim. "I ain't sitting here listening to you talk to these damn law dogs!"

"Dolan here is shot bad," Shears called out, hearing Dolan's voice growing thicker and weaker. "Will you get down here and give him some help now that we've given ourselves up?"

"I told you to shut up, Injun!" said Dolan, getting delirious from the loss of blood.

Injun? Shears started to turn and look back at him, calling out, "Rex, we're going to be all right. They're coming down to help us. Just settle down and throw out your rifle—" His words stopped short as Dolan's rifle exploded.

"Well, there you have it," said Thornton. He raised his field lens to his eye for a better look, staring down at Shears, who'd fallen to the ground, then struggled up onto his knees. He watched as Shears swung his head back and forth like an injured bull, a long string of blood dangling from his lips. At the edge of the trail Dolan crawled forward, leaving a trail of blood. He collapsed reaching out toward Shears's body.

Thornton let go of a tense sigh and lowered his field lens. "He was so concerned about his pards, he ended up killing the one who tried to save him."

"I expect our next stop is back to Crabtown, pick up the fourth man's trail?" asked Nutt, standing, rifle in hand.

"No," said Thornton, "we're through here."

"But the fourth man killed those horse traders," Nutt insisted.

"Like as not this one was lying to save himself," Thornton said. "If the horse traders were really working with them, then good riddance to them."

"I don't understand—" Nutt started to protest. But Thornton cut him short.

"You don't have to understand," Thornton snapped. "You just have to do what I tell you." He nodded toward the bodies of the outlaws. "Gather them up. We're headed home."

Chapter 10

━━━◆━━━

At the bar inside the Crabtown Palace Saloon, Madden Peru stood alone, looking down at his left boot propped on the brass bar rail along the floor. He wondered why one of his newly acquired boots showed no wear across its top, but had been terribly worn down unevenly on the inside of its sole. Peculiar, he thought, the things you find out about a man after you've killed him. He'd never known until now that Shaw had anything wrong with his leg. Of course he'd never seen Shaw except for that one time, the time when he'd shot him dead through the heart.

Peru raised his glass of whiskey and downed it in a gulp. There were lots of other things he didn't know about Shaw—things he'd *never* know now. He ran a hand across his mouth and considered the matter, wondering if he and Shaw might have been friends had they met under different circumstances— him not being out to steal the man's horse, that is.

At the far end of the bar, Jedson Caldwell gave

Peru a nod and got one in return. The story of Peru being the man who killed the fastest gun alive had traveled like wildfire across Crabtown, and beyond. Caldwell had mentioned it to Victor Earles, knowing that soon enough the story would have spread from the diners at the restaurant who'd heard Peru make his claim the night Sheriff Foley arrested him. He couldn't have kept the story quiet if he'd tried. Besides, Caldwell reasoned, him and Victor being the town's barber and assistant, it was almost their *duty* to pass along any such news that came to them.

This was the second night after Peru's release from jail, Caldwell reminded himself, watching as two local miners approached Peru, bought him a drink, and struck up a conversation. Caldwell looked on, glass in hand, surprised and satisfied at the way Peru conducted himself. "Obliged," he'd heard Peru tell the miners, accepting the drink, acknowledging in a lowered nonboisterous tone that yes, he was the man who had killed Fast Larry Shaw.

"We both saw Shaw shoot down two hired gunmen at Willow Creek," one miner said. "We never saw anything so fast in our lives, right, Orville?"

"Right you are," said the other miner, raising his drink to his lips. Before sipping he said to Peru, "We've been all over the West. How come we never heard of you before, mister, fast as you are?"

Caldwell, hearing the conversation clear enough without eavesdropping, looked down and studied the whiskey glass in his hand.

Peru shrugged, drank his shot glass empty, and

set it on the bar top. "It's a big country, I reckon," he said, not knowing how else to answer such a question.

"How did Shaw take it," the other miner asked, excitement glinting in his eyes, "the minute that bullet hit his heart? I mean did he just drop dead or carry on some? Could you tell he knew he was dying?"

Peru just stared at the miner for a moment, feeling as if personal ground was being trod upon. "Mister, we both threw down. . . . I killed him before he killed me. That's all a drink buys you." He touched his fingers to his hat brim, turned from the bar, and walked toward the batwing doors.

Way to handle it, Peru, Caldwell said to himself, raising his glass with a trace of a private smile. He could not have found a better person for the role of killing Shaw if he'd tried. He hadn't planned on things turning out this way, but after seeing how Peru handled himself, and how skillfully he handled a gun, Caldwell and the sheriff both had decided they could breathe a little easier.

Yet, no sooner had Caldwell thought about being able to breathe easier than he heard the voice from the middle of the empty street, "Madden Peru, this is John Bob Selman, I come to call you out!"

Caldwell saw Peru stop at the doors and look out over them. Grabbing his shotgun from against the bar, Caldwell started toward the door, saying, "Let me handle this, Peru. I'm the law when the sheriff's not around."

But Peru raised a hand toward him, stopping him in his tracks. "This ain't about the law, Barber. This is me and him. Anyway, I know this ole boy. Likely he's just liquored up and full of Chinese dope."

"Anything that threatens the peace in Crabtown *is* about the law," said Caldwell. But he'd stopped and lowered his shotgun, letting Peru know that his had been more an offer of help.

Peru read his eye and said, "Obliged, but I knew this would come, soon as word got out. If I didn't want it, I should have kept killing Shaw a secret." As he spoke, he slipped his Colt effortlessly from his holster, checked it, and spun it back into place, making certain it stayed loose. "I'd be lying if I said otherwise." The miners, the few other early evening drinkers, Caldwell, and the bartender all hurried to the doors and the large dirty window for a look as Peru stepped out on the boardwalk and left the doors swinging behind him.

"John Bob Selman," Peru said flatly, stepping off the boardwalk and into the empty street, "I haven't seen you since we both tried our hand at *legal* droving." Behind Selman the street lay empty, the townsfolk having taken cover after seeing John Bob walk intently toward the saloon while he checked his gun.

"Don't even talk to me about *legal* steers," said Selman. "I hate them from the point on their horns to the smell on their ass." He opened and closed his right hand as if to loosen it up. "I heard all the way in Rustler's Hole that you outgunned Fast Larry Shaw."

"You heard true sure enough, John Bob," said Peru, standing comfortably, as if he'd done this a hundred times throughout his life. "Now what is this about you calling me out?" He gave Selman a pointed gaze and said in a quiet tone, "Have you been sucking the Chinaman's pipe on your way over here?"

"Naw!" John Bob glanced around and added with a twitch in his cheek, "I didn't know there was any dope up here in Crabtown."

"Oh yeah, lots of it," said Peru. He liked standing here, feeling in charge, knowing the risk but willing to take it. He reminded himself to savor this cool evening wind on his neck, and the hushed silence surrounding the street. If he lived, this was what he lived *for*, he realized. "But sucking dope ain't what's on your mind now, is it?" He took a short step forward and stopped. "What was all that about you calling me out?"

Cutting a hungry glance past the Chinese letters on either side of the Chinese laundry's doors, Selman swallowed dryly and said, "That's right, Peru, I'm here to take from you what you took from Fast Larry Shaw."

"I didn't know you even knew Shaw, John Bob," said Peru, giving a slight grin.

"I didn't," said Selman, "but that makes no never mind to me. How come you never said nothing about being a gun hawk? All that time, you never said a word."

"It never come up," Peru said with a shrug, keeping his gun hand loose and ready. "But now here you are, the first one, and you come all the way from Rustler's Hole just to see me?" He offered a slight grin. "I'm more than just a little honored, John Bob." He took on an air of resolve. "Let's get right to it— what do you say?"

"Suits me." Selman's eyes went longingly to the Chinese laundry again for just a second. Looking back at Peru, he said, "Good stuff, is it, over there? I mean, you know, for afterward?"

"Afterward?" Peru said, bemused. "John Bob, what is it you think you came here to do, have a night on the town? If we throw down, there ain't no *afterward* for you. Everything is going to be *was* from then on. I'm going to kill you blood-running dead. You understand?"

Selman cut a glance again toward the Chinese laundry, then back to Peru. "You should have said something, all that time, Peru!" His voice turned shaky and harsh. "Damn you for not doing that!"

"I apologize, John Bob, if that helps," said Peru. "The truth is I never realized how fast I'd gotten until lately. Three, four years ago, I doubt I could have taken Fast Larry Shaw." He paused as if to let the words sink in and give his next words more emphasis. "But now I *did*." He took another short step. "Now I'll kill you, too. Ready?"

"Not so fast." Selman fought himself to keep from taking a step back. He licked his dry lips, thinking of how soft and cool he would be right now, wrapped in a tingling sweet opium embrace. "Maybe

I was a little too quick to anger. But you should have said something." Before Peru could reply, he jerked his head toward the Chinese laundry. "So, is it . . . good stuff, that is?"

"I never use it," said Peru, "but "I've heard it's *real* good."

"*Real* good!" Selman grinned. "Damn . . ." He gazed steadily at the laundry doors for a moment.

"But let's get this shooting done, what do you say?" said Peru.

"Huh?" Selman turned his eyes back to him as he'd blanked out for a moment.

"You? Me? A shoot-out? Remember?" Peru reminded him.

"Oh. Yeah." Selman licked his dry lips again, paused for a moment, then said, "I don't want to kill you, Peru, not really. I just was upset, you never saying nothing about being so fast."

"But now I've apologized for it," said Peru. "So, are we square with one another?"

"If we're not, I'll let you know later," said Selman, taking another short step backward, his eyes still drifting toward the laundry. He started to turn, and so did Peru. At the batwing doors, Caldwell stepped out, his shotgun hanging in his hand. But then Selman stopped and chastised himself. "No, damn it!" he cursed. "I came here to do something! I ain't quitting until it's done!" His hand poised near his holstered Colt.

While Peru and Selman had talked, Sheriff Foley had returned to town, seen the empty street, and

slipped down from his horse and moved up on the
two men from the side, staying in the afternoon shadows. He'd felt relieved seeing Selman start to turn
away; but now that the young gunman grew angry
and turned back facing Peru, the sheriff moved
quick.

"Both of yas get your hands in the air!" Foley
shouted at Selman, seeing the gunman's hand ready
to make a move.

"Sheriff, stay back!" said Peru, raising his hands
as Foley had ordered, yet knowing he still had things
under control.

But Foley would have none of it. "You both heard
me," he shouted at Selman. He advanced hoping to
draw Selman's attention away from shooting Peru.
Seeing things ready to fly out of control, Caldwell
brought the shotgun up.

Sheriff . . . ? Selman misunderstood. He glared at
Peru and shouted, "This is how you do it? Three
agin one? You and your law dog pal?" He went for
his gun in spite of the odds.

Even with his hands chest high in the air, Peru got
his Colt out and fired before Caldwell had either a
chance or a reason to raise his shotgun and fire.
Peru's bullet hammered Selman in the chest, sent him
backward to the ground. But a wild shot from Selman's Colt exploded sidelong, a blue-orange streak
splitting the afternoon light.

Caldwell saw the shot hit Sheriff Foley, causing
him to jackknife and drop to his knees, both hands

clutching his stomach. "Oh no!" Caldwell leaped from the boardwalk and ran toward the downed sheriff.

John Bob Selman's Colt rose from the dirt and managed to fire one more shot before he died. The shot sliced through Caldwell's shoulder and caused him to stagger to a halt, but only long enough to swing the shotgun and fire a blast of nail heads into the dying gunman.

Within seconds both Caldwell and Peru had knelt down over the fallen lawman. Peru held the sheriff's head in his lap, owing to Caldwell's wounded shoulder. "I—I made a bad . . . mistake not trusting you . . . Peru," Foley said in a tight pain-filled voice. "You had it . . . settled."

"Take it easy, Sheriff," said Peru, wiping his hand back over the sheriff's sweaty forehead. "You're going to be all right."

Foley shook his head weakly. "No . . . I'm not." He nodded toward Caldwell, who held a hand pressed to his bleeding shoulder, dark blood having already soaked through his black linen suit coat. "You . . . look after Jedson. I'm heading home . . ." He let out a breath, his eyelids slipped down halfway closed.

"Sheriff! Sheriff Foley!" Peru shook him vigorously, as if to bring him back to consciousness.

Caldwell, having seen more death than the young gunman, said in a resolved tone, "He's gone, Peru." Looking all around as townsfolk ventured out and drew nearer, he said with his eyes glistening wet, "Get him up off the street. Don't let them see him like this."

Two days later, looking out the dust-covered window of the sheriff's office, Peru said over his shoulder in grim reflection, "If I hadn't come here declaring I killed Lawrence Shaw, none of this would have happened."

"I can't argue with that," said Caldwell, struggling with tying a clean black necktie one-handed, left-handed at that, his right arm in a sling. "But the same can be said about any one action being the cause of the *next* thing that happens, be the next thing good or bad."

"What?" Peru turned, giving him a puzzled look.

"I'm simply saying, if you want to dwell on circumstance, everything we do causes the next thing that happens. Much of what happens next is out of our control. All we can judge ourselves by is our *intent* at that particular time." He continued struggling with the necktie as he asked, "Did you come here with the intention of setting off a string of acts that would lead to Sheriff Foley's death?"

"Don't talk crazy. Of course I didn't. I liked that ole lawman," Peru said.

"All right, then don't reach back into the past and find a way to make yourself guilty. You can only judge your *intentions*." He stopped struggling with his necktie and raised a half-gloved finger for emphasis.

"I never attended some fancy barber school, or some high-thinking undertaker school," said Peru, stepping forward and shoving Caldwell's hand aside. He took the necktie between his thumbs and fingers, adjusted its length, and tied it into a looping bow. "But I know right and wrong, and I feel I did wrong in coming here." He gave an extra tug on the necktie as if to make sure it didn't come loose. "To tell you the truth, walking around in Shaw's boots and clothes had caused me some strange thoughts. I feel bad about killing him. Even though it was self-defense," he added pointedly.

"In that case . . ." Caldwell picked up a dusty hand mirror and inspected Peru's tying abilities. He nodded his approval, saying, "You'll have to do whatever you feel is right to divest yourself of this guilt . . . the guilt of killing Shaw . . . the guilt of causing Sheriff Foley's death." He couldn't tell Peru that even his *guilt* was built on a false premise. *Shaw's boots . . . ? Ha*, thought Caldwell, *if he only knew*.

"I don't know how to get rid of guilt. I never had any before. Killing Shaw made me a somebody, but being a somebody makes me have to think about things different. I wasn't guilty of *nothing* when I was a horse thie—" He caught himself in time to stop and say, "A *nobody*, that is." He rubbed his temples. "Jesus," he asked with a troubled look, "what do people do to stop themselves feeling guilty?"

"Religious folk, those who believe in a higher presence, pray, and get forgiven," said Caldwell. He shrugged his good shoulder a bit stiffly. "Others of us, like myself, learn to rationalize our actions, try to improve . . . better ourselves morally, so to speak."

"You don't believe in God?" Peru asked, surprised.

"Oh yes!" said Caldwell. "I believe in God! But like most people I believe in God as a way to hedge my bet on eternity." He grinned, winked, and reached for his freshly brushed bowler hat. "I believe in God just in case he exists. Nobody wants to be caught short come judgment day."

"You're not much help, Barber," said Peru. "I didn't come here to get Sheriff Foley killed. But it worked out that way, owing to the kind of person I am. Had I come here on a better and more honorable purpose, I expect my actions would have caused better things to have happened around me."

"Whoa! I'm impressed at such a level of higher thought," said Caldwell. He placed his bowler atop his head and tapped it down snugly. "All this, from wearing a dead man's boots?" He looked down at Stiff-leg Charlie's boots on Peru's feet, the left boot as smooth as brand-new on top. As he stared down he wondered if there would ever be a point when Peru could know the truth. Judging from the changes he'd witnessed Peru going through he wondered if in this case honesty was really the best policy.

"I don't know where it's coming from," said Peru. "But I know Sheriff Foley was a good man, and I believe he tried to help me be a better man. I feel responsible for him going into the ground today, and I don't know of any way to make up for it." As he spoke he reached out, opened the door for the injured barber, and followed him out onto the boardwalk.

"I could have opened the door for myself. I'm not completely helpless, you know," Caldwell said, stepping down off the boardwalk.

Beside him, Peru said, "Sheriff Foley told me to look after you, Barber. I intend to do it."

"I understood him to mean *right then*," said Caldwell, walking along toward the barbershop, where Victor Earles stood beside a minister in front of a large gathering of townsfolk, "to look after me and my bleeding shoulder."

"Yeah, I know," said Peru. "But I think he meant more than that. I think he meant *look after you* until you're back able to keep the law here in Crabtown. So that's what I'm doing."

"That could take a while," said Caldwell, thinking things over as they walked. "I expect once the word gets out about Sheriff Foley's death, there'll be some riffraff who think they can ride into Crabtown and do as they please." As if struck by a sudden idea, Caldwell stopped in the street and said to Peru, "I'll tell you what can help you get rid of this guilt you're feeling." He looked Peru up and down as if appraising him all over again.

"Yeah? What's that?"

"The town wants me to be acting sheriff in spite of my wounded shoulder. I'll do it, but only if you'll be my officially sworn deputy."

Peru paused, giving him a peculiar look for a moment, before saying, "Pin on a badge? *Me?*" He looked around as if making sure no one heard them and said in a lowered voice, "I'm going to be level with you, I've come close to being an outlaw most of my life."

Caldwell gave him a wry smile. "You'd be surprised how many good lawmen have come in off that same trail." Seeing Peru start to waver toward the idea, he said as further inducement, "You wouldn't believe how much guilt you can get rid of pinning a star in front of your heart."

PART 2

Chapter 11

A month would pass before Cray Dawson and Madeline Mercer stood on her front porch in the first early rays of sunlight and said their good-byes. Much of their days and nights together had been spent wrapped in one another's arms, both of them having spent too many long nights alone before Dawson veered off his trail to Black's Cut to check on her—something that, as it turned out, he would always be obliged to Jedson Caldwell for asking him to do.

In the crisp Montana morning, Madeline Mercer had spread open the blanket she'd draped around her and enclosed Dawson inside, drawing him against her warm nakedness. She whispered, "Hurry back," and pressed her lips to his.

After they'd kissed long and deep, Dawson's lips left hers only by the slightest fraction, enough for him to reply against her cheek, "I'm not even sure I *can* leave."

"Then don't," the young widow whispered, her hand traveling down him beneath the blanket.

But Dawson had to go. He knew it, and so did she.

He longed for the warmth of her now, of her skin against him, of her mouth close to his. Leaving her might have been a mistake, he told himself, studying the low flames of his campfire on a ridge overlooking a dome of light above Black's Cut in the near distance. *I'll wait for you no matter how long it takes,* she had whispered the night before he'd left, the two of them beneath the warm quilt, still breathless from their passion. She'd smiled. *But please hurry back to me. . . .*

Yes, he told himself, now that he'd come to his destination. Leaving was a mistake. No matter what amount of gold he managed to scrape out of the hills around Black's Cut, he would not be satisfied until he made his way back to Madeline Mercer. Stirring a stick around in the coals of his fire, he thought about her, and chastised himself for a damn fool, out here in the chilled Montana night, the woman lying aching for him as much as he ached for her.

All right, enough! He stood up from the fire, a tin cup of coffee in hand, and walked over to check the animals, trying to take his mind off her. She said she would wait, and she would. He had to quit thinking so much about it. The best thing he could do for now was get to his claim, work it, establish its worth, and see what his prospecting venture had brought him.

He sipped the coffee and stared for a moment at the closing lights of Black's Cut. Yet, he could not put the woman out of his mind so easily. He thought about the irony of how the first and only love of his life had been Rosa, Lawrence Shaw's deceased wife.

After Rosa's death Dawson thought he would never be fortunate enough to love another woman; and for a long while it appeared he'd been right. Shaw, whether right or wrong, had taken up with Carmelita, Rosa's younger sister, shortly after returning home to visit his wife's grave.

When Shaw left Carmelita, as he, Dawson, and Carmelita herself knew he would, she and Dawson had taken up with one another and tried for a time to make a life together. But it didn't work out. How could it? he asked himself. Carmelita had fallen too much in love with her dead sister's husband; Dawson had been too long and too hopelessly in love with Rosa Shaw. The only thing that had drawn him to Carmelita had been her kinship to Rosa.

He shook his head thinking about it. Had Carmelita stayed with him, they would have soon begun destroying one another, instead of only making one another miserable, which they had done from the start. *So she left* . . . he told himself, as if relating the story to Madeline, the two of them snuggled under the covers in a glow of candlelight. It was something he would have to tell her, someday, after they had been together awhile longer, maybe even . . . *well, married*, he told himself.

Married . . . ? a voice asked inside his mind. *Yes, why not?* the same voice answered. He wasn't a rounder, at least not by choice. He wanted to settle down, have a wife, a family, like any other normal man. He sipped the coffee and wondered for a moment how Madeline would take it, hearing him tell her that the only three women who'd ever been in his life had stepped into it by having at some point stepped *out* of Lawrence Shaw's. *Rosa, Carmelita, and now you, Madeline* . . . he revealed to her in his mind, finishing the coffee and slinging the grinds from the cup.

But that was enough of that, he thought, walking back to the fire and setting the cup upside down on a clean flat rock. He wasn't a man to quit what he'd started. Tomorrow he'd arrive in Black's Cut, replenish his own supplies and pick up fresh grain for his horse and mule, and go find his claim. Madeline said she'd wait for his return before completing the sale of the Mercer spread and heading east. He believed her. He had to.

He thought about how Caldwell had warned him about Black's Cut and about Giddis Black, the man who ran the boomtown with an iron fist. He appreciated the barber's advice, but he wasn't overly concerned. He was just passing through, he reminded himself, picking up his blanket, shaking it out, and spreading it on the ground near the banked fire. His business lay up in the hills surrounding Black's Cut, where men found their fortunes in placer gold.

If there was one thing Giddis Black couldn't abide, it was a devious whore. He stood at the edge of the catwalk on the roof of Black's Best Chance Saloon &

Brothel, two floors above the mud street. He gazed idly up at the mountains northwest of the little boomtown bearing his name. Smoke from his cigar raced away in the chilled morning breeze. Let one whore get by with cunningness, he told himself, and soon every whore in the place would be testing him. He'd learned long ago that deviousness among a stable full of whores had a way of spreading like the plague.

Hearing the trapdoor on the roof squeak open, then close, twenty feet behind him where the catwalk began, he said without looking around, "Top of the morning, Palmer. What do you have for me?" Half turning he held out his hand and rubbed his thumb and fingers together in the universal sign of greed.

"Three good ones," said Sly "Devil" Palmer, running his hand inside his wool coat. He looked down and back and forth along the street, as if making sure no one was watching, something that apparently no longer concerned Black. "One is dust and stream nuggets. The other two are bills and coins." He handed Black a long leather wallet and two small leather pouches tied with drawstrings.

"Ahh," said Black, taking the three items, hefting them in his palm. "Dust and nuggets are always better," he said, grinning, raising an eyebrow toward the wallet, "but we turn nothing down." He eyed Palmer with partly feigned suspicion. "Did you give me a fair cut?"

"As fair as you deserve," said Palmer, the two of them used to one another's banter.

"Umm-hmm." Black nodded, dropping the three items into his long greatcoat pocket and smoothing down the pocket flap. "I'll count it this morning over coffee. Will you join me, or is sitting at a table another civilized act you've abandoned to the wilds?"

Palmer gave a dark grin. "Sure I'll drink some coffee with you this morning. If Landry shows up, what do I say about how much was there?" He nodded at the items bulging in Black's pocket. He said it knowing what Black's response would be.

"On second thought maybe you'd better go on about your business." He patted his coat pocket and added, "I'll explain the accounting, if Landry has any questions."

"Suits me," Palmer said. He touched his fingers to his battered hat brim. "I'll be taking my leave, unless we have other matters to discuss."

"Wait," said Black, "I'm afraid we do." He puffed on his cigar and let out a stream of smoke. "I'm going to need you and Willie to take Violet and Clarity out of town and see to it they never come back."

"You mean . . . ?" Palmer left his question hanging.

"Yes, that is exactly what I mean," said Black. A thin, tight smile formed between his drooping mustache and his narrow pointed goatee. "Violet has tested my patience to the limit." He pointed his smoking cigar at the lanky gunman and said, "Learn from this, Sly. . . . *Never* make a whore your favorite. She'll see it as a weakness and try to exploit you with her guile, and you'll end up killing her *every time.* Do you hear me?"

"Yeah, I do," said Palmer, nodding. Then he

stopped nodding. "It's a damn shame, though, as scarce as whores are right now."

"Be that as it may," said Black, "get them out of here. I never want to see them again. They've both seen too damn much while we were getting started here." He stared into Palmer's eyes. "What these whores know could hang us both."

"Yep, no denying, they were both right there at times and places where they shouldn't have been," Palmer agreed. He seemed to reminisce for a moment, picturing himself, Giddis Black, and the two whores. But his vision only lasted for a moment before he said, "How soon do you want it done?"

"Right away," said Black. "The sooner the better."

"Want me to take Giddis Junior?" Palmer asked.

"No, leave my son out of it," Black said firmly. "Take Willie along. Tell him to do it quietly."

"Chicken style, you mean?" Palmer grinned.

"Sure, chicken style, why not?" Black shrugged. "What do we care? If it makes Willie happy. Just get it done, *please*," he said, wanting to dismiss the matter. "I don't need too many details."

But Palmer enjoyed taunting him. "Chicken style is not only quieter. It's cheaper than bullets, too."

"All right, whatever you decide," said Black, sounding impatient with the conversation. "You handle this—tell Willie what to do. You're in charge." He rubbed his hands together, saying as he turned away from the gunman, "I wash my hands of it."

"Consider it done, Giddis," said Palmer. He touched his hat brim again.

This time as he turned and walked away, Black looked back at him with a dark confident glint in his eyes. "Good man . . ." he murmured as Palmer opened the trapdoor, stepped down inside the building, and lowered it behind him.

Sly Palmer walked down the steep stairs, then out onto the second-floor landing overlooking the bar and the row of empty gaming tables. He stood for a moment, his hands spread along the railing. At the center of the bar stood two old men, the first of the morning drinkers. At the far end of the bar he saw Violet O'Conner and Clarity Jones, the two women he and Black had been discussing.

Both women looked haggard and spent, having been up all night, dancing, drinking, and entertaining the late-night crowd between frequent trips up the stairs to one of the small bedrooms. Clarity stood at the bar, sipping a cup of hot coffee. Violet sat atop the bar, examining her sore feet in turn. Her dress was up over one knee, and her shoes were off.

Glancing up at the landing as she sipped her coffee, Clarity said under her breath, "Don't look up, but Sly Palmer is staring down at us like we're a couple of candy sticks."

Violet nodded, casting a sidelong glance herself. "Okay, I see him," she said. "*Looking* is all right, so long as he doesn't want to handle the goods. I'm done in. Besides, I don't like that two-at-a-time stuff anyway. All it does is make him feel like he's some kind of big randy stag."

"Well, you best be getting a friendly face on, girl-o.

Here he comes," Clarity said quietly with a trace of an English accent, speaking over the edge of her warm coffee cup.

"Oh, hell, I'll try," said Violet. She shoved her disheveled hair back with her hand. "Why can't all these pigs understand that every working girl needs her beauty rest now and then?"

"If they understood that," Clarity whispered, "they wouldn't be such pigs, now, would they, dearest?"

The two turned with charming smiles as Sly Palmer walked up closer. Palmer swept an arm around Violet and pulled her closer to the bar with him until he held both women in an embrace. "How's my favorite doves?" he asked, nuzzling the bare flesh above their low-cut dresses.

"Uhh, stop," said Violet, pretending to enjoy the rough beard stubble scraping her skin, "you'll get me all steamy!"

"Where have you *been* so long, Sly Palmer?" Clarity demanded in mock anger. "We haven't known what to do with ourselves!" She gave him a slight shove and a feigned frown.

"Well, ladies, I'm here now," said Palmer, "and I'm taking you both on a little wagon trip with me over to Helms. So get your coats and hats."

But Violet gave him a dubious look. "Helms? Why? What's at Helms?"

"Giddis has some new Chinese girls coming. He wants us to meet them at Helms."

That was good enough for Clarity. She slipped

down from the bar top and began stepping into her shoes. But Violet wasn't as compliant. "Why are *we* going? We never went to meet new girls before."

Palmer shrugged. "These Chinese girls are shy as fawns. Seeing Willie might scare them. Seeing you two will make them feel better. Giddis says he wants them cleaned up and made presentable before they get here."

"Willie's going?" Violet asked, her expression turning more concerned.

"Don't worry, he won't be in the wagon. I'll keep him settled down."

"I don't like him being near me," said Violet. "Does he have to come along?"

"Yep, he's coming," said Palmer with finality. "There's been hostiles killing and burning all along the trail from Helms and Crabtown. If we get them on our backs you'll be glad we have Willie on our side."

"Giddis wants us to do this?" Violet asked.

"If you don't believe me, ask him yourself," said Palmer, nodding up toward the landing just as Giddis Black stepped into sight and leaned on both arms on the railing.

Looking up, Violet and Clarity saw Black give a single nod, as if he'd overheard their conversation from his lofty perch. "All right," said Violet, knowing from the dark look in Black's eyes that he was in no mood to be questioned, "we'll get our coats."

"Good," said Palmer. "I'll go have Willie get the wagon ready."

As the two women walked to the coatrack in the rear of the saloon, Violet said in a lowered voice, "I don't like this. We better both watch our steps out there."

"We certainly will," said Clarity. "But I'm sure we'll be all right." Yet, as she took her coat from the rack and slipped it on, she palmed a pearl-handled straight razor she took from inside her dress and tucked it down into her coat pocket.

Chapter 12

At midmorning, Dawson met the wagon and the two men on horseback at a turn in the trail on his way to Black's Cut.

He touched his hat to the women and veered his horse and mule to one side, giving the party the right-of-way. As he did so, he noted nervous smiles on the women's faces, and unpleasant scowls on the faces of the men. But he gave it no mind until both wagon and horsemen had ridden past him.

But then, one of the riders, a monstrous man wearing a full and tangled beard, swerved his horse around and rode up on him fast from behind. On instinct Dawson spun his horse and brought his Colt up, cocked and ready, pointed arm's length at the big man's forehead. "Whoa, Willie, stop!" Dawson heard the other man shout. But it was Dawson's Colt, not the other man's command, that had already brought the big man's horse sliding to a halt.

At a distance of five feet, the big man growled,

staring into the darkness of the gun barrel. "Take that gun sight out of my face!" he said in a harsh tone.

Dawson kept the Colt fixed and steady, replying just as harshly, "Pull your *face* back out of my *gun sight.*"

Seeing this stranger meant business, Sly Palmer said as he turned his horse and gigged it back to them, "Everybody hold on! There's no need for this!"

But Dawson had made his stand and wasn't about to let down until he knew why the big man had come charging at him. He swung his Colt toward Palmer, enough to slow him to a halt and cause him to raise his hands slightly. Then he swung the gun back toward Willie, who backed his horse a few grudging steps backward. The women sat watching breathlessly from the wagon seat. "Somebody start talking," Dawson said in a low, even voice.

Willie started to say something, but Palmer shut him up with a cold stare. Then he said to Dawson, "I'm Sylvester Palmer, stranger. My friend Willie here gets a little out of hand sometimes. He meant nothing by it."

"Could have fooled me," said Dawson, looking the big man up and down as he spoke, keeping his gun level and cocked.

"I know," said Sly Palmer, offering a thin apologetic smile. "He's big and ugly, and he scares the hell out of most folks. But he misunderstood, seeing you riding toward Black's Cut with your own mule and supplies."

Here we go . . . Dawson recalled what Caldwell had told him about buying supplies before getting to Black's Cut. "What business is it of his where I buy supplies?" Dawson asked Palmer as if Willie weren't there. He gave no sign of lowering the big Colt.

"All right, here it is, stranger," said Palmer. "Willie and I work for Giddis Black. He runs everything in Black's Cut."

"So I've heard," said Dawson. "Keep talking." He kept a menacing gaze moving slowly back and forth between them.

Willie said in a thick rumbling voice, "We sell mules in Black's Cut, mister. Supplies too."

"That's good to know," said Dawson. "I'm ready for more supplies. I'll be buying them as soon as I get to town. Once I find my holdings and get set up I'll be needing more, probably an extra mule too. Think your boss will mind selling me what I need, or will I have to bring it all up from Crabtown?"

"He'll be happy to do business with you." Palmer grinned, understanding Dawson. He nodded slightly at the Colt, and Dawson lowered it but kept it in hand, his thumb over the hammer.

Looking relieved, Sly Palmer said in a more sociable tone of voice, "You gathered yourself mighty damn fast with that six-shooter. What's your name, mister? Where you from?"

"I'm Dawson . . . Cray Dawson." He kept his Colt in his hand but backed his horse a step, turned the animal quarterwise to the men, and brought the mule up beside him on the lead rope. "I'm out of Texas, over Somos Santos way."

"Out of Tex— Wait a minute!" Palmer had brushed past the name, then stopped and given him a stunned look as the name caught up to him. "Cray Dawson? The one who rode with Fast Larry Shaw before he died. That one?"

"Yep, *that one*," said Dawson. He was not overly surprised that news of Shaw's death had traveled this far.

"Well now, Willie, boy," said Palmer, "it appears you were about to get yourself killed by a fast gun out of Texas."

"I ain't dead yet," Willie said in a thick, dull voice, giving Dawson a hard stare and a grim expression.

Dawson ignored the big man and said to Palmer, "If we're all through here, I'll be getting on to Black's Cut."

"Yeah, we're through," said Palmer, backing his horse a step. "When you get to town, some of the other boys might want to give you a hard time. But you tell them we talked and you understand how things work."

"I'll do that," said Dawson, also backing his horse a step. Looking past the two men he saw one of the women step down from the wagon and start walking toward him as if she had something she wanted to say. Turning and seeing her, Willie gave his horse a kick, rode alongside the woman, and picked her up roughly, as if she were a rag doll. Seeing her offer no sign of a struggle, Dawson only watched closely with a curious gaze.

"These are a couple of doves works for us," said Palmer, seeing the look on Dawson's face. "We like to air them out on their days off. Makes them easier to live with." He grinned, touched his hat brim, and moved his horse off sidelong to Dawson for a few feet before turning and riding away.

"That was peculiar," Dawson said to his horse, holding both reins and the lead rope in his left hand, and keeping his Colt in his right. He kept watching, seeing the big man drop the woman back into the wagon, then seeing the wagon roll on its way.

From the wagon seat, Clarity risked taking a guarded glance back at the rider, having noted the way he'd handled both Palmer and Willie. But she caught only a quick glimpse of him as the wagon rolled down out of sight on the hilly trail. Beside Clarity, Violet sat rubbing her shoulder and arm where Willie had snatched her up from the ground and held her tightly until he dropped her back into the wagon. "That wasn't a wise thing to do," Clarity whispered sideways to her.

"I don't trust them," Violet whispered in reply. "We're never going back to Black's Cut alive—I just know it. They're going to kill us out here." Her voice quivered with fear.

"I'm afraid you're right," Clarity whispered. "Giddis has decided it's time for us to go." She took on a determined look. "But I am not going down without a fight."

"Fight?" Violet looked at her. "Who are you kidding? We can't fight these animals! We wouldn't stand a chance in hell." She looked at the two men riding fifteen feet ahead of the wagon. "We've both seen Willie snap a man's neck like it's a twig— chicken style as he calls it." She nodded at Palmer's back. "Sly Palmer is no better. He'll do anything Giddis Black tells him to do."

"When the time comes I'm going to fight them," Clarity repeated with finality. "If you're not going to fight, you better be ready to run." She clenched the leather wagon reins in her hands.

A half hour later at a spot where another trail intersected and ran a few yards into a pine woodlands, Palmer dropped back beside the wagon and quickly stepped down from his horse and onto the wagon seat, forcing Clarity aside. "I'll take those," he said, jerking the traces from her hand.

"What—what are you doing?" she asked, looking worried. She moved over against Violet, letting Palmer take charge of the wagon. Beside the wagon, Willie had dropped back and taken the reins to Palmer's horse, grinning down at the frightened women.

"Don't act too surprised, ladies," Palmer said. "I know you both saw this coming a mile away."

"You don't have to do this, Sly!" Clarity said, talking fast as he guided the wagon deeper into the thick pines. "You can let us run away! Giddis doesn't have to know! You'll never see us again, I swear! We both swear, don't we, Violet?" The wagon rolled on, tall stands of wild grass and brush sweeping beneath it along the seldom-used trail.

"That's right," said Violet. "We'll get down from the hills and never be heard from again." She looked around wildly, seeing Willie had stepped down from his saddle and walked along close beside her side of the wagon.

"Now, now, girls," said Palmer, "you've had some good times, made some money. Now it's over. It's time to pay the devil his due."

"No, Sly, listen!" said Violet as Willie's big hand reached down and grabbed her. "We'll never tell anybody what we know, what we've seen!"

Palmer gave her a shove as Willie dragged her from the wagon seat. "No! Please!" she begged.

Palmer immediately reached a hand down and clamped it on Clarity's knee, holding her in place. But even as he did so, she slipped her hand inside her coat pocket and around the razor while Palmer's attention went to Violet and Willie. "Stop fooling around, Willie," Palmer chuckled, seeing the big man prance around, one hand holding Violet by her throat as she struggled.

"Chicken style!" Willie shouted. "*Bloc, bloc, bloc!*" He held his other hand tucked up under his arm, his elbow flapping up and down like a rooster's wing as he made his clucking sound and high-stepped back and forth.

Clarity had looked away, trying to pick her direction of escape. She heard Violet's choking scream and looked back in time to see Willie's big hands twist the helpless woman's head sharply until her scream ended in a sickening snap. *"Bloc, bloc, bloc,"* Willie said again, this time in a quieter tone. He held Violet's suddenly limp body in one hand and shook it back and forth loosely. "Your turn," he said, grinning, staring past Palmer at Clarity. He let Violet's body fall to the ground and took a step toward the wagon.

"In a pig's eye!" Clarity hissed. She sprang to her feet as Palmer turned to shove her over to Willie's large waiting hands. Before Palmer could even comprehend what she'd done, the razor had streaked down across his face, leaving a long streak of blood down his forehead from the left, crossing the bridge of his nose and ending on the right side of his chin.

"Oh God! She's cut me, Willie!" he screamed, feeling the white-hot flash of sharp steel running deep through meat and cartilage. He threw a hand to his face, feeling his warm blood spill freely. But as his hands went to his face, Clarity wasted no time.

"Here's you another, Sly!" she shrieked, sounding hysterical. "For Violet!"

Her next slash went for his throat, but missed by an inch as Willie, having hurried around the wagon, grabbed her and dragged her out. The razor left its trail of fresh blood down Palmer's chest.

"Get your hands off me, you flipping pig!" Clarity shrieked, Willie holding her high in the air as the razor slashed back and forth for his face, missing but keeping him too busy to do the same gruesome handiwork he'd done to Violet.

"Sly, what do I do?" Willie called out. He could barely keep his face away from the sharp slashing steel. "Tell me something!"

"Damn it, kill her, Willie," Palmer shouted, slinging his bloody face back and forth. "I can't see anything!"

Lost without Palmer's guidance, knowing nothing else to do, Willie threw Clarity and her slashing razor as far from him as he could, then quickly looked himself up and down to see if he'd been cut. His eyes bulged wildly as he looked into the deep open gash running the length of his thick inner forearm, from wrist to elbow. "She cut me, too!" he bellowed.

"Willie! Get her, damn it! Kill her!" Palmer cried out. He caught a glimpse of her landing twelve feet away before blood filled his eyes again. He managed to draw his gun with a wet slick hand.

Clarity hurriedly scrambled to her feet and turned, seeing she'd landed near the edge of a steep drop-off and had nowhere to run. "Come, get some more, Willie!" she shouted as Palmer wiped blood from his eyes and tried to aim his Colt. "Dying hurts, doesn't it, you *swives*!" she shouted, slashing the razor back and forth in the air.

Willie stalked forward. "I'll kill you, whore!"

"No, you won't, you rat stool!" said Clarity, looking wildly about, knowing she had only seconds before Willie grabbed her again, or Palmer's Colt exploded. "I'll pick my own way to die!" She backed over the edge of the cliff and slid downward on her belly through dirt and loose rock until she felt the earth disappear.

"Damn whores," Palmer lamented, seeing Clarity disappear with a short scream. "Look at me, Willie. She's cut me something awful!"

"Me too." Willie gripped his forearm, trying to hold the severed meat and tendons together. He walked to the edge of the cliff and looked down. He saw Clarity's wool coat spread out on the rocks a hundred feet below.

"Willie, you've got to get me back to Black's Cut before I bleed to death . . . that damn whore!" Palmer cursed.

"I don't think she's dead," Willie said flatly.

"What the hell do you mean? Of course she's dead," said Palmer. "We both saw her jump."

"Come look and see if that's her down there," said Willie. He stood halfway between Palmer and the edge of the cliff, blood running in long strands from his wounded forearm.

"We've got no time for your foolishness, Willie," said Palmer. "The whores are dead. We've got to get back to town before we both bleed to death."

Chapter 13

Dawson rode into Black's Cut in the midafternoon sunlight, having stopped and grained, watered, and rested both animals shortly after meeting Palmer and Willie on the trail. While the animals rested, he'd spread a blanket on the dirt in the shade of a white oak, and cleaned and checked his Colt, his Winchester, and the short-barreled shotgun he carried shoved into his bedroll.

He'd been prepared for the kind of reception he might receive in Black's Cut after Caldwell had warned him about the place. But, while he'd believed Caldwell, there was nothing like running into the two men on the trail to sharpen his wits and keep him on his toes. Serving the law in Somos Santos had taught him to never ride into a hostile town or situation with tired animals or unattended weaponry. *Not if you can help it . . .* he reminded himself, looking back and forth along the crowded muddy street running the length of Black's Cut. He stopped

his horse and mule for a moment to better take in
the scene before him. Ahead of him on his right stood
an imposing clapboard, log, and stone structure
whose freshly painted sign read BLACK'S BEST CHANCE
SALOON & BROTHEL.

On his left, straight across from the saloon, stood
a building of about the same age and construction
whose sign read BLACK'S CUT HOTEL. A few doors past
the hotel another long sign read BLACK & LANDRY MER-
CANTILE STORE. Out in front of the mercantile stood
two hitch rails filled with pack mules and horses.
Along the boardwalk, wagons stood waiting, their
tailgates down. Miners and clerks filed back and
forth, stacking bags of flour, beans, and feed grain
into the open wagon beds.

"She's a busy place, ain't she, mate?" said a raspy
voice a few feet from him. Dawson looked toward
the voice and saw a short, wiry old man wearing
ragged seaman's clothes and a stocking cap. He
grinned at Dawson around the stem of a large
tobacco-stained briar pipe as his rough hands
reached out and rubbed the mule's muzzle and chin.

"It is, indeed." Dawson noted that the old seaman's left leg was missing, replaced by a thick oaken
peg. "Can you tell me where I'll find the territorial
land office?"

"Locating a claim, are you?" Still stroking the
mule's muzzle the strange-looking little seaman nodded toward the far end of the street where a group
of men and pack animals lounged in front of a log
and earth building where an American flag stood

swaying on a mild breeze. "If you are, you'll be waiting for a long spell."

Dawson gazed at the group of men and asked, "How well do you know the lay of the land?"

The seaman grinned. "If it's a claim filed within the last year and a half, I can just about hike out afoot and lay a hand down on its middle. How *well* does that sound to you?"

"Well enough," said Dawson. He turned slightly in his saddle and pulled the folded mine claim from inside his coat. "I'm Crayton Dawson. The fellow I bought this from said it was filed last fall before the snow set in."

"I'm Cap'n Darvin Arden," said the seaman, touching his stocking cap. "Call me Cap, if you will."

"Pleased, Cap," said Dawson.

Eyeing the folded claim in Dawson's hand he asked, "Who might the original claim holder be?"

"A miner named Jimmy Deebs," said Dawson. "Do you know him?"

"Aye, I do," said Arden, giving Dawson an unpleasant expression. "I wouldn't get my hopes up working a claim I acquired from Jimmy Deebs, if I were you. Deebs made more money buying and reselling claims than he ever made working one."

"He told me as much," said Dawson. "I bought the claim knowing he hadn't found much on it, so I've got no complaints. But I understand it's close to one of the big veins the four Georgians struck back in sixty-four."

"Ha," said Arden, "the only big strike the Georgians ever made was down in Crabtown. Funny how a little blind luck like that can turn a man into an expert, eh?" He gave Dawson a crafty smile, still stroking the mule's muzzle, and asked, "Tell me, Dawson, did no one inform you of Giddis Black? He takes a slice off everybody's loaf, for him and his partner, Landry." He nodded toward the Black & Landry Mercantile Store.

"Let me ask you," said Dawson, "if this Black and Landry are partners, how come Landry's name is only on the mercantile and Black's name is all over town?"

"Landry wants it that way, I've heard," said the old seaman. "He likes staying back, unseen and unheard. They say if you bring him into public light, it's like unleashing a whirlwind." He wagged a finger. "It would serve you well to remember that, mate."

"Obliged." Dawson nodded. "I'll try. Fact is, I met two of Black's men on the trail earlier, names of Palmer and Willie." Dawson glanced again at the sign. "I think we came to an understanding."

"You did?" The old sailor looked surprised. "You came to an understanding with Sly Palmer and Willie Goode?" He studied Dawson closer, looking puzzled by not seeing any wounds or signs of a scuffle. But then a light seemed to come on in his mind as his eyes went across the butt of Dawson's Colt. *"Ah . . ."* he said in revelation. *"Crayton Dawson* it is. You'll have to pardon this old sea dog for not catching the line on the first toss. No offense intended."

"None taken, Cap," said Dawson, almost wishing the old seaman hadn't suddenly recognized his name. "I told Palmer I'd pick up what fresh supplies I need from Black."

"I can see you reasoning with Palmer, especially if he knew who you are. But Willie Goode is a lunatic and a monster. I'm surprised you didn't have a fight on your hands."

"Let's just say he and I came to our own understanding, right from the get-go," said Dawson.

"I hope you shot him dead," said Arden, lowering his tone. "If not, he'll be coming back at you, while your back is turned more than likely."

"It's a chance I'll have to take," said Dawson. "I didn't come looking for trouble."

"But you might find it anyhow," said Arden, "and not just from Willie." He looked around guardedly. "Giddis Junior is on a drinking spree. His father, Giddis Senior, always sends some of his thugs to look after his murdering son. Junior is no better than Willie, maybe a little less touched in the head. He might not care about any understanding you and Sly Palmer have come to."

Tapping a rough finger to his temple, Arden said, "Now that I know who you are, I understand how it is you met two of Black's men and still have your animals, your supplies, and your *hide* as well. But don't sell these thugs short, Dawson," he warned. "Anybody can die."

"You're right," said Dawson. He looked again at the men standing idly in front of the land office.

"Think you can direct me to the claim? If so, I'll get my supplies and be on my way."

"I can do better than direct you," said Arden. "I'll get my own mule and take you there. But I wouldn't chance getting my supplies right now, if I were you," he added. "That's pushing your luck."

"I told Palmer I would," said Dawson. "My word's good, even to a boomtown thug."

Arden shrugged. "All right, then, Crayton Dawson," he said with a slight chuckle, "you can't say I didn't give you proper warning. I'll get my mule and meet you at the mercantile." He started to turn away, but then stopped in afterthought and said, "Might we be taking along a strong bottle of rye . . . for the sake of our spirits and my long ride back?"

"Sure, we'll do that," Dawson agreed. He nudged his horse forward onto the heavily trafficked street.

Standing at the counter of the mercantile store, Dawson and a nervous young clerk packed his individually bagged staples and feed grain into a large white canvas bag. Dawson paid the clerk in dollar bills and silver coin, said, "Obliged," and swung the canvas bag up over his left shoulder. He walked away calmly, although he'd watched through the front window as three men surrounded Arden when the old sailor rode his sorrel mule up to the hitch rail out front. Arden had stepped down with a worried look on his face, but had never entered the mercantile store. Stopping on the boardwalk, Dawson knew why.

"I'm sorry, mate," said Arden, standing on one foot, his peg leg lying where one of the men had pitched it from the boardwalk into the soft mud along the hitch rail. "They wouldn't let me come warn you."

Beside him stood an evil-eyed young man with black beard-stubble and bushy yellow hair sticking out like straw from beneath a weathered black silk top hat. A dead dried wildflower stood in his hatband. He cut in, saying with a dark whiskey-fueled laugh, "I'm Junior, the rotten sonsabitch who yanked Cap's leg off and threw it in the mud. What kind of crazy bastard you suppose does something like that?" His left hand helped support the unsteady sailor. His right hand held a long Remington pistol down at his side.

"Beats me, *Junior*," said Dawson. "Your problems are your problems. But now that you've got all the attention, what can I do for you?" As he spoke he noted one of the three gunmen standing between him and his pack mule and horse. The third gunman stood beside his mule, holding an ax handle with both hands.

"Oh, he's a really *smooth* customer, boys," said Junior Black, noting Dawson's remark, the way he appeared unimpressed with either Junior or his two allies. Leaving the old sailor to wobble and catch himself on a support post, Junior stepped forward, twirling the big Remington slowly back and forth on his finger.

"If this is about the mule and supplies, I met a couple of your men on the trail. We agreed that I might—"

"Save it, Cap already told me," said Junior, cutting

him off. "But for all I know you and this half a piece of punk wood made that story up." He stopped a few feet from Dawson and looked him up and down, appraising him. "He also said you're some kind of fast gun out of Texas." He gave a skeptical smirk. "What do you say, DeLaurie?" he asked the man holding the ax handle. "Does he look like a rootin'-tootin' fast gun sonsabitch to you?"

"Naw," said Chester DeLaurie, patting the ax handle into the palm of his hand, "except for the sonsabitch part."

"What about you, Newhouse?" said Junior to the other man, a stocky young man with the broad back of a teamster and a face like a bag full of rocks with skin drawn over it.

"Maybe he's another one thinks of himself as Fast Larry Shaw." Curlin Newhouse gave a thin, tight grin. "Let's get on with this, I'm needing another drink."

What was that . . . ? Dawson's interest piqued, but this was no time to get curious. He looked the third man up and down, anticipating how Junior Black had intended this encounter to go.

"Yeah," said Junior, "me too." Turning to Dawson he said in a raised voice, using an official-sounding tone, as if to make a public example of him, "For riding into Black's Cut with animals and supplies you bought some place else, I'm hereby levying a fine of fifty dollars on you."

"A fifty-dollar fine?" said Dawson. "What if I can't pay it?" He could pay the fine if need be; he just wanted to hear what Junior and his pals had planned for him. From the sound of Junior's raised voice, pedestrians drew closer and began to watch.

"If you can't pay the fine, you'll have to forfeit your horse and mule," Junior called out loud enough for the gathering bystanders to hear.

"Either that, or I'll beat them both into the dirt, let you watch me do it." DeLaurie grinned, patting the ax handle a little more intensely.

"Shame on you," said Dawson in a lowered tone, his stare turning cold and unreadable.

"Yeah, *shame on you*, DeLaurie," Junior said in a mocking tone. He turned to the stocky gunman. "Newhouse, gather the animals. This man can't pay his fine."

"No, wait," said Dawson, raising a halting hand, "I can pay it. Just let me get my money out." He swung the canvas bag of supplies down from his shoulder and held it out, saying, "Here, hold this."

Newhouse obliged him instinctively, taking the canvas bag by its neck with both hands before thinking, *Oh no!*

Instantly, the gunman realized his mistake, but by then it was too late. Dawson's Colt had already streaked from its holster. The gun barrel caught the stocky gunman full swing across his left temple, sending him backward. Dawson took the canvas bag back from his hands and turned with it quickly, just in time to feel the ax handle swing against it with a hard thud, hitting sacks of flour and beans instead of his rib cage.

Junior, Remington in hand, stood stunned, frozen in place for a moment, seeing the gun barrel fly backhanded across the bridge of DeLaurie's nose with a terrible sound of gunmetal against crunching cartilage. The sight of it caused him to snap into action, but he had already hesitated too long. As he raised his Remington, the ax handle struck a wicked blow against the back of his hand and sent the gun sliding across the plank boardwalk toward Darvin Arden.

"Hell's fire!" Junior shouted, grabbing his stinging hand and looking up in amazement, as if puzzled by how DeLaurie's ax handle had turned against him.

Seeing the question in Junior's puzzled eyes, Dawson said as he drew the ax handle back for a more powerful swing, "Sleep on it."

But before he could swing the ax handle, Dawson heard a shotgun cock, and a voice called out, "Hold it right there! You're not killing my son!"

With the handle still drawn back, Dawson cut his gaze to the man holding the shotgun. "Easy with that scattergun," he said. "If I meant to kill him, he'd be dead already."

"Says you!" Junior managed to cut in.

"Shut up, boy!" shouted Giddis Black Senior. His shotgun remained aimed at Dawson, ready to fire. But knowing that the spread of buckshot would hit his son as well, he said to Dawson, "Back away from him!"

"No," Dawson responded. "If you're going to shoot, do it now, where I stand. Me and Junior will go down together. Does that suit you, Junior?"

"It doesn't *suit* me!" Darvin Arden said before the young man could reply. All three of the men turned their eyes to the old sailor. Standing unsteadily on his only foot, Arden held the displaced Remington pointed and cocked at Junior. "Lower the shotgun, Giddis," he said, "or by Odin, I'll kill him with his own gun!"

"You're going way too far with me, Cap," Giddis Black said in a menacing tone. "I don't know how we'll ever get along after this."

"Don't threaten me, Giddis," said Arden. "I'm old enough to die." He nodded toward the younger man. "But what about Junior there? Is he?" He squinted, taking aim down the pistol barrel.

"Looks like you're the cock of the walk today, Cap," Giddis said, lowering the shotgun, but giving the old sailor an evil stare. "There now, the gun is down. Lower the Remington and lay it on the planks."

"Not yet, Giddis," said the old sailor, wobbling a bit. He gestured for a young boy in the gathering crowd to hand him his peg leg. Taking it, he looked it over, put his stub of a leg into its leather shell, and strapped it deftly into place. Satisfied that the peg was all right, he gave Dawson a nod.

"Pa, don't let him get away with this," said Junior. "His name is Dawson. He's some kind of fast gunman, otherwise he'd be dead. We never had a chance!" He still held his swelling purple hand.

"You're Crayton Dawson?" Giddis Senior asked, beginning to understand why things had gone the way they did.

Dawson only nodded and said, "I'm going to tell you the same thing I tried to tell your son. I met your men Palmer and Willie Goode on the trail. I told Palmer I'd be resupplying here before going up to my claim. He agreed to it. That was what I'd been doing when your boy and his pals started goading me. I'm not a man who takes much goading, as you can see." He gestured at the two downed gunmen. "Now I'm taking my supplies and I'm leaving. If you doubt my story you can take it up with Palmer when he gets back."

"I will, sir, you can count on it," said Giddis Black. He looked all around, seeing a few of his thugs showing up and hanging back waiting for word from him. But upon judging what might happen to Junior in the midst of a melee, he took a deep breath and allowed calm reasoning to take command. "If you're all through here, take your supplies and leave."

"That's what we're doing," said Dawson, knowing Black had only told him to leave to give the appearance of being the one in charge.

Giddis Senior held a hand toward his men, keeping them in check while Dawson and Darvis Arden stepped into their saddles and rode away. Dawson kept an eye back on the boardwalk where the Blacks stood watching them with grim expressions.

Before Dawson and the old sailor were out of sight, Junior said, "I'll kill him, Pa, I swear to God, him and that little peg-leg bastard both!"

Giddis Senior said to his son under his breath, "You ignorant whelp. You're lucky that man didn't kill you and these two wart heads. He could have done so three times over!"

"Pa, I was only—"

"Shut up," said Senior. "You sicken me! Gather your gun and these fools, and get out of my sight!"

Outside Black's Cut, Dawson and the old sailor had just turned onto another trail leading up in the direction Arden said would take them to Deeb's claim, when they saw Willie Goode driving the wagon into town. "My goodness, now, look at big ole Willie!" said Arden, gesturing toward Willie's thickly wrapped forearm.

"Palmer doesn't look much better," said Dawson, wondering what had happened after he'd left them on the trail. On the wagon seat next to Willie, Palmer sat slumped back, his head a-loll, his face covered with wet bloody strips of torn shirt cloth. He held a bloody handful of the same cloth to his stomach. Halting, Dawson said to Arden, "If you're in no hurry to get back, I'd like to ride back along the trail and see what became of the two women."

"After what's happened between me and the Blacks," the old sailor chuckled, "I'm in no hurry to *ever* go back there."

As the wagon rolled by, the two slipped back onto the trail behind it and rode away in the opposite direction. "I have a hunch that riding with you, Cray Dawson, is going to be the most fun I've had on dry land." Arden laughed, putting his heels to his sorrel mule.

Chapter 14

Clarity Jones had slid and rolled and come out of her wool coat. The front of her dress had been shredded and torn away. The razor had flown from her grip when her hands scratched and dug at loose rock and dirt before she felt her body slipping over the edge of a narrow rock shelf and into an airy world of nothingness. But before her scraped and battered forearms left that last few inches of ground, her fingers hooked like steel claws into a tangle of tough twisted tree roots that hung out of the earth's belly. For a moment she had only swung there in a cool breeze, seeing her coat billow out as it plunged downward. She had screamed, but only once, not being a screamer like some of the whores she had come to know during her brief tenure in *the life*.

Now, sitting on the upper edge of the cliff, smoking a short, slim cigar stub, she looked down at her coat lying below and told herself screaming would not have helped. But now, what to do about keeping herself alive? she wondered.

When she'd finished her smoke, she crushed the cigar stub on a flat rock, stood up, and cupped her tattered dress to her scraped and bruised bosom. She did this not out of modesty, but rather to protect herself from the chilling afternoon air. Looking all around, she saw the flattened stems of wild grass where Willie had dragged Violet's body off into the thicker pine woodlands.

She wasn't sure where she should go from here, but she knew that upon seeing the cutting job she'd given Willie and Sly Palmer, Giddis Black would be sending someone out to make certain she was dead. She sighed and tracked along the bent grass, limping a bit, having lost a shoe in her near calamity. *Well, send them on, then, Giddis . . .* she said to herself as if speaking to Black. She wouldn't be here, not if she could help it.

Ten minutes passed before she reached the edge of a five-foot-high cut bank and looked down at Violet's pale naked corpse lying spread-eagle beside a thin stream of water. She wore nothing but her shoes, her dead eyes staring up at Clarity in horror. Her clothes lay in a discarded pile a few feet away. "Oh no, *Willie*, you wretched *swive*! You *did* her! You rotten, mad, sick, bastard!" she cried aloud, scurrying down the cut bank to Violet's side as if arriving there any quicker would make some sort of difference.

But kneeling at Violet's side, seeing the blackened bulge where her neck had been snapped by Willie's powerful hands, Clarity let the reality of death sink in. "I'm sorry, pet, there's nothing I can do for you." She sniffled, brushed aside a strand of hair from Violet's cold forehead, and closed her eyes. As she crossed Violet's arms on her abdomen and closed her spread legs together, she couldn't help but see there were no signs of Willie having done anything more than undressing the body and perhaps taking himself a good long peek. She found something in the image of that just as repulsing as her first thoughts on the matter. "You sick miserable fiend," she murmured aloud.

She spent the next few minutes taking Violet's shoes from her cold dead feet and stepping into them. She put on Violet's wool coat against the cool afternoon. Then, noting that Violet's clothes had been ripped from her, she dressed the body as best she could and dragged it farther away from the braided stream.

"I'm so sorry for you, dear Violet," she whispered, in place of a prayer; and she raked in loose dirt, rock, and seasoned pine needles and partially covered her, in hopes someone would find her who could do more.

Almost an hour later the long shadows of evening found her walking wearily alongside the trail, the wool coat buttoned fully up the front, steam beginning to waft in her breath. When she first spotted the two riders coming toward her along the trail, she did not attempt to hide. Instead she stood staring at them in stunned silence, her hand going into the coat pocket for a razor that wasn't there.

"Miss Clarity," said Darvin Arden, hopping down

from his mule as Dawson also slipped down from his horse, "are you all right, child?" Seeing her swoon, he caught her by both shoulders to steady her.

At first Dawson saw her hand come out of her coat pocket in a threatening manner, as if she held a knife, he thought. But then she blinked her eyes, gained her focus and senses, and, recognizing the old sailor said, "Cap? Oh, Cap! Something terrible has happened!" She turned her head and stared along the trail behind her. "I'm afraid Black's men are coming to kill me!"

Arden gave Dawson a strange look, then replied gently to the confused woman, "Not from that direction, darling. I'm afraid you've been walking right back toward Black's Cut."

"Oh my God!" said Clarity with a terrified look on her face. "I would have walked right into Giddis Black's arms."

"Not now you won't," said Arden. He guided her to the side of the trail and seated her on a rock. "We'll get you away from here, won't we, Dawson?" He looked to Dawson for support. Dawson nodded.

"Where is the other woman, the one I saw you with earlier?" he asked as he took his canteen from his saddle horn, uncapped it, and handed it to her.

She looked at him closely. "That was you, the one who stood up to Willie and Sly?" Before he could answer she said, "Violet wanted to ask for your help. I wish we had. It might have saved her life." She gave them both a grim, flat stare. "Violet is dead. Willie snapped her neck like a—"

"Like a chicken's," said Arden, finishing her words for her.

"Yes, like a chicken's," she said in a softer tone, one in which she made no attempt at hiding her regret. She took a sip from the canteen, then added, "She and I used to laugh at that term, *chicken style*, as if it were funny or cute the way he would threaten us gals with it. What fools we were, Violet and me. We thought we were Black's special girls. What did we know?"

Dawson and Arden stood by silently, letting her get things off her chest. She sipped the water again, then handed the canteen back to Dawson and wiped the wool coat sleeve across her wet dirt-streaked mouth. "Giddis wanted us both dead because we had seen too much—the way he robbed people, the way he had men tortured, killed." She looked at Arden, then at Dawson. "Giddis is sick in his head. He keeps a man on a chain, you know?"

"Yes, I know," said Arden. "But let's not worry about any of that right now. Let's get you up and out of here before some of Black's men *do* come riding up on us." He gestured toward Dawson and said to her, "This is Cray Dawson. He just showed both Giddis and Junior up as cowards in front of the town. They might be coming for him too."

She looked at Dawson and seemed impressed. "You did that?"

"Well," said Dawson, modestly, "we had a run-in. I won't go so far as to say I made them look like cowards."

"But I *do* go so far as to say it," said Arden, help-ing Clarity to her feet. "And I wager that's how Giddis feels about it now that he's had time to mull it over and let it get stuck in his craw." He offered a tight smile and said firmly, "All the more reason for us to get ourselves moving, eh? Once we move into the higher canyons, we'll be hard to find."

"We can divide up the load of supplies between all three animals and make room for you on the pack mule," Dawson said to the woman who stood shiv-ering in spite of her wool coat. "That is, if you don't mind riding without a saddle."

"Won't that take up time?" she asked.

"No, not too long," said Dawson.

"I mean, can I just ride with you for a while?" she asked with a stiff shrug. "Until we get more distance between us and Black's Cut? To tell you the truth, I'm so sore all over I'm not sure I can ride a bare-back mule."

"Pardon me, ma'am," said Dawson, "that wasn't very considerate of me. You take the horse, it's a much better ride."

"I won't take your horse from you, Mr. Dawson," Clarity said. Then giving him a level gaze she said, "But I am so cold, I would welcome riding double with you for a ways . . . until I start feeling a little warmer and less sore?" She had unbuttoned the coat while she spoke and exposed enough of herself to show him how scraped and cut and bruised she'd gotten from sliding over the edge of the cliff.

Dawson felt a little embarrassed but said, "Yes,

ma'am, I understand. You ride with me for as long as you like."

Arden looked on as his newly found friend raised Clarity carefully up onto the saddle, then stepped up behind her and enfolded her into his arms. He watched Dawson turn the horse gently, mindful of the woman's tender condition. Smiling to himself, the old seaman stepped atop his mule and gave it a light whack with his boot heel and sent it off along the trail behind them.

As the two rode on, Dawson said quietly into Clarity's ear, "Ma'am, we saw Willie and Palmer along the trail on our way back from Black's Cut. They were both in pretty sore shape themselves. That's why we decided to come looking for you and your friend, see what had happened to you."

"Oh, really?" Clarity said without turning toward his voice.

"Yes, ma'am," said Dawson. "Palmer looked like he'd walked face-first into a she wildcat."

"Maybe he did," she said, admitting nothing. "What about that murdering degenerate, Willie?" she asked, her English accent showing itself briefly.

"His whole forearm was bleeding through some thick cloth wrapping," said Dawson. "He looked pale from losing blood, they both did."

"Good, then, I hope they both die from it," she said calmly.

"Yes, ma'am," said Dawson, not wanting to push her into talking about it if she didn't want to.

They rode on.

When they arrived at the spot where Clarity had dragged Violet away from the water and covered her, the three hitched the animals to a shorter pine sapling and stood for a moment looking down the cut bank and the half-covered body. "Can we—can we bury her?" Clarity asked, standing huddled in Violet's coat. "I left here hoping someday someone would. I didn't expect to be coming right back here, myself."

"Yes, we'll bury her here," said Dawson. He stepped over to the pack mule and slid a brand-new shovel from within a load of supplies. When he returned with it, they climbed down the five-foot cut bank and searched around for what looked like a dryer grave spot twenty yards farther uphill from the water's edge.

While Arden lay watching the trail for any sign of riders, Dawson dug a grave in a softer stretch of earth on the sloping hillside. When he'd finished, he and Arden wrapped the dead woman in a blanket from Dawson's supplies and buried her. Afterward, with an eye on the trail behind them, in the long dim shadows of evening, they rode on, taking the higher trail that Arden knew would lead them to Deeb's claim.

Rather than risk the glow of a fire being seen, they made a dark camp in a nest of rocks on a steep hillside. The next morning Dawson awakened with the woman snuggled against him. *For warmth,* he told himself, repeating her words from the day before. But he had no intention of moving her away from him. Instead, he laid his arm over her and breathed in the smell of her hair on his cheek and felt her push herself even tighter against him.

In a silver morning haze, the woman arose and looked at him with a soft smile and said modestly, "Thank you, Mr. Dawson. I'm not used to such kindness." Then she moved away quietly, adjusting her hair with her fingertips.

With only a handful of cold jerked elk for breakfast, the three set out on foot, leading the animals up the dangerously sloping hillside and onto a narrow trail that reached deeper into wide rough terrain. At midmorning, having remounted the animals, they stopped at the crest of a rise where a long rounded edge of stone protruded through gravelly earth and a bed of sparse wild grass.

"There you see her, Dawson," said Arden. "Your new home, here in the high gold country." The old seaman stood in his stirrups on one leg, his peg leg serving as balance, and pointed at a weathered-gray shack. "I hope she's what suits you."

"It suits me, Cap," Dawson replied. He nudged the horse forward. Clarity rode behind him now, her arms around his waist. She had made no further mention of riding the mule, and neither had Dawson.

Circling down around a narrow path leading to the shack, the three dismounted, Dawson stepping down first, then assisting the woman to the ground. "It looks like it's been a while since anybody's been here," he remarked, seeing the front door standing open a few inches, a few dried leaves and pine needles lying in a thick layer of dust.

"Aye," said Arden, "and even longer before that since the place had a good cleaning." With his peg leg he kicked an empty tin can, one of many lying strewn about in the dirt.

Twenty yards away, half covered by brush, timber, and debris, Dawson spotted the jagged entrance to the mine shaft. "I'll start cleaning and fixing things up later today." He walked to the pack mule as he spoke and began loosening ropes and load straps. "Right now I've got to take my first look inside my gold mine."

Arden had taken his briar pipe from his coat pocket and started to fill it. But upon hearing Dawson, he put the pipe away and said, "Maybe I'll just go right along with you, if you have no objections."

"Come right along, Cap," said Dawson. He took out a small oil lantern from the loosened bundle of supplies he'd laid on the ground. "You can tell me if that hole in the hillside shows any promise."

"Can—can I come too?" Clarity asked hesitantly, as the two turned toward the mine entrance.

"It's bad luck, a woman in a mine," Arden whispered just between himself and Dawson.

But Dawson turned as if not hearing him and said to Clarity, "Come along, let's all look this place over together."

She hurried in beside Dawson and slipped her arm around his waist. As if having heard what Arden had said, she whispered, "I won't bring you bad luck. I'll bring you only good luck, I promise."

Dawson put his arm around her shoulders. "*Good* luck is the kind I need."

Chapter 15

———

Giddis Black stood at the edge of the circling glow of firelight and watched the two Ute women do their handiwork on Sly Palmer's face. One held the severed flesh together between her thumbs and fingers while the other ran the needle through the upper layer of skin and drew the black thread tight behind it. Curlin Newhouse stood at the head of the cot where Palmer lay groaning to keep from screaming in pain. Newhouse held him steady by both ears while the Ute women continued, against his mindless pleading.

"I can't stand this infernal whining," Giddis Senior growled. He swallowed a long drink of whiskey, then lowered the bottle from his mouth and blotted his lips on his coat sleeve. "Why don't you shut up and take it like a man, Palmer? You make us all look bad."

"Yeah, take a look at my head," said Newhouse, keeping his firm grip on Palmer's ears. "You don't hear me bellyaching about it." Where Dawson had cracked him with the pistol barrel his temple had swollen to the size of a goose egg and blackened to the color of spoiled fruit.

Standing beside his father, Junior, his swollen hand resting in a sling, shook his head and said, "Pa, you've got to let me go after this Cray Dawson. We've got to kill him if we ever want to hold our heads up around here." He gestured with his good hand around the room. Willie sat slumped at a table, his forearm stitched from wrist to elbow, lying on a bloodstained cloth, seeping thin trickles of blood between knots. Across the table sat Chester DeLaurie, his broken nose purple, packed with strips of cloth, his eyes swollen almost shut.

Giddis Senior looked the men over, shook his head in disgust, then said to his son, "If you're trying hard to convince me that you're a complete idiot, you can relax. I see it in every word you've said since Dawson left town." Now it was he who gestured toward the same wounded faces. "Until more of my men get back into town, who exactly do you suppose I send after him?"

"I can go," Willie cut in, looking up from his thick forearm. "My arm's feeling better." He opened and closed his hand to show his improvement. "See? I can ride, shoot."

"Yeah, Willie, you are the true star in my crown," said Giddis in sarcasm. He watched Willie grin, either not knowing or not caring that he'd been mocked. Shaking his head, Giddis walked closer to the table and asked him pointedly, "Are you certain those whores are dead?"

"Yep, I'm certain," said Willie. "I broke Violet's neck, chicken style." His grin widened into that of an evil jack-o'-lantern. "And I shoved Clarity off a cliff."

Giddis stared hard at him for a silent moment, then asked, "A very *high* cliff, was it?"

"Yep, a high cliff," said Willie, nodding his big shaggy head.

"And you saw her land . . . saw her dead on the rocks?" Giddis persisted, having demanded to hear the story repeated since Palmer and Willie returned to Black's Cut, both of them badly cut and bleeding.

"Yeah, she is dead," Willie declared. He had told it enough that he actually thought he'd seen her body below, her coat spread open, her skull crushed and oozing blood.

"If you are lying to me, Willie, God help you," Giddis said in a threatening tone, raising a cigar between his fingers for emphasis.

"Pa, send Willie and me," said Junior. "We can handle Dawson!" He gave Chester DeLaurie a frown for not joining in persuading Giddis Senior.

"And me," said DeLaurie, his voice sounding nasal and full of pain.

"See, Pa. Chester wants to go too," said Junior.

"Nobody's going anywhere until I say so! Now shut up about it!" Giddis shouted, banging his fist down on the tabletop, causing a tin plate of leftover meat to fly off the table and fall to the dirty plank floor. Giddis kicked at the meat and shouted at a

young girl from the brothel who stood by waiting to
assist the Ute women if they needed anything. "Villy!
Get this table cleared! Take this food out of here and
feed it to the bear!"

"Yes, Giddis," the girl said. She stooped quickly
and snatched up the scrapes of meat and bone and
dropped them back into the dirty plate. "And the
man, too?" she asked meekly.

"Naw, to hell with the man," said Giddis. "Didn't
you feed him yesterday, or the day before?"

"Yes, Giddis, I fed the man yesterday," Villy replied in a trembling voice, always one to wither
under Giddis's harsh gaze.

"*Well* then," said Giddis, as if she should know
better than to have to ask about feeding the man two
days in a row, "feed the poor bear today, *child!* Do
not feed the man until tomorrow."

"Yes, Giddis," said Villy as she gathered the rest
of the scrapes from plates sitting all around the long
table. "I'll see to it right away."

She turned to leave and felt Giddis's hand clamp
firmly on her arm. "Have I made myself clear on
that, Villy? If I find you are slipping food to the man,
I will be very cross with you. Do you understand
me?"

"Yes, Giddis, I understand," the frightened girl
said, her eyes growing wide with fear. "I will only
feed the bear, not the man."

"Look at me, child," Giddis said, tapping a finger
to his forehead. "Keep reminding yourself. Don't
feed the man, don't feed the man." He watched her

back through the door with a plate in her hand and pull it shut behind herself. "My God, why do I feel like I'm always talking to a bunch of imbeciles?" Giddis asked the ceiling with his hands spread.

Outside, Villy hurried along toward the old log jail behind the row of buildings, saying aloud to herself over and over, "Don't feed the man. Don't feed the man." But once she'd gotten out of Giddis's sight and looked back over her shoulder, she let out a tense frightened breath and stopped reciting. "Bastard," she hissed.

Glancing all around she palmed a handful of meat scrapes and a half-eaten piece of bread from the high-piled plate and shoved the food down into her dress pocket. She grinned and said to herself, "I *will* feed the man. I *will* feed the man."

At the door to the jail, she knocked and was met by Morse Tucker, aka the Jailer, who swung the door open just enough to allow her to squeeze in, having to rub slightly against him as she did so. "Who are you feeding today, girl, the man or the bear?" Tucker asked roughly, leaning his face down close to hers, his eyes wandering up and down her as he spoke.

"The bear today, sir." Villy's voice sounded frightened again.

"Yeah, I knew," said Tucker, still close, still looking her over. "I'm just checking on you."

"Excuse me, please." Villy slipped from beneath his leering eyes and over to where a large ten-by-ten iron cage sat next to a single cell, in the darkness against the rear wall.

"Uppity baby whore," Tucker growled to himself. He walked over, picked up a shotgun and a bag of tobacco from a littered desk. "Watch that bear," he warned Villy, then stepped outside the door onto the rickety front porch.

In the bear's cage, Villy saw the dark hulking grizzly swing back and forth restlessly, a big logging chain rattling against the iron floor. She could hear the deep hoarse breathing. The strong odor of bear urine and excrement caused her eyes to burn.

Hurrying, she stooped down and shoved the tin plate under an open feeding slot at floor level. Then she stepped back and froze as the big animal charged forward, stopping only as the chain ran out a few inches from the other side of the iron bars. For a moment the big brute stood raised on his hind legs and pawed at the iron cage, only the tips of his thick claws being able to reach the iron bars and rake down them.

The bear let out an ugly snarl into Villy's face, then fell ravenously upon the food on the floor. Villy looked cautiously toward the front door as she slipped sideways a step and saw the haggard bearded face staring out of the darkness in the cell. "Villy?" the voice said in a weak rasp. "Can you help me?"

"Shhh," she said, slipping the bread and meat from her dress pocket and through the bars into dirty trembling hands. "Don't let Tucker catch you with it, he'll tell Giddis!"

"No, I won't let him," the man said, talking

through a mouthful of food as he ate hungrily. "God bless you, darling. Can you get me out of here? Can you slip me a gun? A knife? Anything?"

"No," said Villy, "I can't. This is all I can do for you! I'll bring you some food whenever it's safe." She stepped back from his cage and looked over her shoulder toward the door, while in the bear's cage the big grizzly had already devoured the food scraps and stood licking the iron floor and digging his claws at it as if more food lay hidden there. "That's all I can do, please!"

"Wait," said the weak voice, the man having downed his food almost as quickly as the bear. "Tell me what has happened out there! I saw through the window. Palmer and Willie Goode came riding in covered with blood! Who did that to them?"

"A lot has gone on," Villy whispered. "Clarity and Violet have disappeared. They cut Palmer and Willie all to pieces!"

"Those two," the man said, recalling how Violet and Clarity had doped him and set him up for Giddis Black.

"Hey, they were my friends," said Villy.

"I know," he said. "But go on, tell me more."

"A gunman came to town and broke DeLaurie's nose. He cracked Junior's hand and Curlin's forehead!"

"Who—who is this gunman?" the man asked.

"Dawson, or something like that," said Villy. "I'm not sure."

"Oh, Jesus!" the man whispered. He gripped the bars with both hands, getting excited. "Listen to me,

Villy! You've got to get to this man! Tell him I'm in here! Tell him what's happened to me!" He stared at her wild-eyed, shaking the iron bars in his hands. "Will you do that for me, Villy, *please*?"

"Shh, calm down," she warned him. "I can't tell him, he's already gone! Besides, what makes you think he'll do anything for you?"

"He's a friend of mine, Villy," he said. "He's the best friend—no, he's the *only* friend I've got! You've got to go find him . . . Please tell him about me, before I starve to death in here, or end up in the stomach of that bear!"

"A friend of yours? A big gunman like that?" Villy said, sounding doubtful. "I bet."

"Listen to me, Villy," the man pleaded, "don't you know who I am? Didn't they tell you, Violet and Clarity?"

"Oh yes, they told me all right," she said. "They told me you were out of your mind and thought you're Fast Larry Shaw, the fastest gun alive."

"I *am* Lawrence Shaw, Villy!" He gripped the bars even tighter. "I swear to you I *am Shaw!* Go find Dawson and bring him here! You'll see, I *am* Shaw!"

She shook her head slowly, saying, "I don't know who you are, mister, but we all know that Lawrence Shaw is dead. He was killed outside Crabtown. The town had a big funeral for him and everything."

"That *wasn't me!*" he said. "I had all that planned!"

"Of course it wasn't you," said Villy. "I can see that much." She stepped back and shook her head. "I'm believing you really are touched in the head."

"No, wait, listen!" he pleaded.

But just as Villy stepped over a few inches away from the iron cell, the door swung open and Tucker walked in, finishing a rolled smoke he held between his finger and thumb. "Hey! I said stay back from that bear!" he shouted. "Are you simpleminded?"

"Sorry!" said Villy, jumping back away from the bear's cage as the animal let out a loud bawl and swiped a paw toward the iron bars.

Looking past her, Tucker noted the man in a dark clump on the floor. "Is he dead over there?"

"I—I don't know," Villy stammered, looking toward the downed man as if he'd not moved all the time she'd been there.

"Oh, you don't know," said Tucker. He chuckled and gave her a look as he circled back behind his desk, sat down, and lowered his hands out of sight. "You've got the cutest little voice I ever heard. Are you ever going to work at the brothel, or just keep cleaning up and toting food around?"

"I'll be working there soon," said Villy. "Giddis says he's saving me for himself first. I've never done you-know-what before."

"Oh, I see," said the Jailer. "Well, I can't blame him for that one bit. It makes me ache just seeing you walk in and out of here. Now you come right over here, little darling. Are your little hands awful greasy from handling that elk meat?"

"I can't," said Villy, hurrying toward the front door and grasping the handle. "I got to get back."

"I ain't going to hurt nothing of yours, girl."

Tucker half stood from his chair behind the cluttered desk. "Come over here," he coaxed. "There's things you need to learn right now."

"I've got to go," Villy said, hearing the clink of his belt buckle coming undone. She hurried out, giving a look over her shoulder, past the big grizzly on its chain, toward the dark cell where the man lay in a ragged ball on the floor.

"Baby whore," Tucker chuckled. When the door had closed behind her, he stood the rest of the way up from the desk and walked around to the darkened cell, rebuckling his belt as he spoke to the dark ragged figure. "Maybe you're asleep, maybe you're not, madman. But if it weren't for you I wouldn't be stuck here smelling bear shit day in and day out. Why don't you be a good boy, tell me where that ten thousand dollars of Giddis's is?"

After a silence, the weak voice said, "The money is all that's keeping me alive, Jailer."

Tucker grinned to himself. "You've got enough sense to know that, don't you? But that ain't going to keep you alive forever! Sooner or later Giddis is going to get tired of asking. When he does I'll take delight in hacking off pieces of you and letting you watch me feed them to the bear." He gave a dark laugh and kicked the bars. The man only lay in the same spot in silence, but the bear, startled by the sound, charged forward with a loud snarl, rising up and swiping its claws across the bars, sending Tucker backward so fast he stumbled and fell to the hard plank floor. "Sonsabitches!" he shouted.

Chapter 16

He should not have allowed this to happen, Dawson chastised himself. In the silvery glow of early sunlight through the window, he looked down at Clarity's sleeping face. She lay with an arm over his side of the bed as if he were still there. *We are both grownups,* he remembered her saying the night he'd told her he had someone waiting for him near Crabtown. But now, picturing her that first night, the way she had drawn back the cover, seeing her lying there naked, willing, inviting him in . . .

All right, maybe he hadn't really promised Madeline Mercer anything, but she'd said she would be waiting for him and he hadn't asked her not to. That was enough to make him feel low, as if somehow he was betraying both women. *Jesus* . . . He turned away from the bed, pulled aside the blanket curtain they had hung for privacy, and walked past the bedroll where Arden lay sleeping near the stone hearth.

In minutes Dawson had stoked and raised a fire

from a banked bed of glowing embers, and had boiled a fresh pot of coffee. Sitting alone at the table he ate a short breakfast of leftover hoecake and strips of jerked elk. He stood up and left quietly, the way he'd been doing the past two weeks, leaving Clarity and the old seaman to awaken to the smell of fresh coffee.

For the past two weeks, while Dawson had dug at the walls of the mine with pick and shovel, Darvin Arden and Clarity Jones had been busy, cleaning, scrubbing, shooting snakes, and hauling away debris. But at last the little two-room shack on the rocky hillside had begun to look livable, Dawson thought, standing at the entrance to the mine shaft looking back at the lantern glow in the front window. He wished he'd made as much progress with his mining.

To his disappointment, the Deeb claim had not been a newer find, as the date on the deed indicated, but rather one of the older mines from the early sixties that had been legally filed only a few years after it had gone through a string of new owners. Had there been gold taken from this mine? Of course there had, he told himself. Why else would the shaft reach so far into the hillside? Was there still gold in there somewhere? Yes, he was certain of it. But how deep? How much farther?

Dawson knew that the answer to his question lay not in distances measured by feet and yards, but in the backbreaking labor of *time*. How many days, weeks, months, even years? he asked himself, looking up the steep hillside, seeing it disappear upward into the silvery morning mist. How many years did it take to make a lifetime? he asked himself. His answer was simple. *All of them*, he replied, lighting an oil lantern, adjusting the cover, and stepping into the mine, leading his mule behind him.

Finding an offshoot of the main shaft thirty feet back, he moved along it in the glow of light until he'd located the spot where he'd been digging the night before. He hung the lantern on an iron peg that had been driven into the rock by some former owner. Then he turned the mule and backed it closer to a three-by-four-foot wooden sled-wagon and hitched ropes from the wagon to the mule's collar.

For the next half hour Dawson swung the pick against the wall of solid rock until an assortment of smaller broken rock lay piled up around his feet. "First load of the morning," he said idly to the mule. Leaning his pick against the wall, he lifted the larger rocks by hand and loaded them into the sled.

With the shovel he scooped up the smaller rocks and loose dirt, picked up the long rope leads, and gave the mule a loose slap on its rump. "Now it's your turn," he said to the animal, following along behind the sled load of rock.

Outside the mine, at a steep sloping hillside twenty feet away, he kneeled beside the sled, picked up each rock in turn, and inspected it for color. Those with the slightest variation in color or trace of yellow, he set aside, to be broken into smaller pieces and reexamined. The rest he disregarded as worthless and tossed out down the hill into the tons of similar rocks lying below.

He saw nothing of note or value in the load, or in the following loads he hauled out and examined throughout the morning. But by the time he'd stopped and walked to the shack for a noon meal, he had set aside only a few rocks he felt worthy of any further examination. So far his work at the mine had been slow and unpromising. But this was what miners did, he reminded himself, standing up from the table and stretching his stiff shoulders.

"I'll be through repairing the back windows before long," said the old seaman. "Can you use some help with the digging?"

"I can always use help with the digging," Dawson replied. He left the shack, walked back to where he'd left the mule, and started his routine all over again. By the time evening shadows began to stretch long across the hillsides and deep canyons, he had set aside a good number of rocks to be broken up and reexamined the following day.

After he'd finished the last load of the day, he had begun piling what he referred to as the *keepers* onto the sled when Clarity walked up beside him in the evening light. "Supper's ready," she said. "Did you find any color today?"

"No," Dawson said flatly, "not today, not yesterday, not the day before."

"Cap says it takes time," she offered.

"He's right about that," Dawson replied, not wanting to sound cross with her. It wasn't her fault that he'd found no gold, no promising vein of any significant color. What did he know about the prospecting or the mining of gold? He rose to his feet, damp with the day's sweat and slapping dirt from his knees. He started to say more, but before he could he noted the single rider step his horse into view from within a stand of pine.

"Uh-oh, he looks familiar," Clarity said in a whisper, even though the rider was still thirty yards away.

"Go tell Cap we've got company," Dawson said.

"Should I get the shotgun?" she asked.

Without taking his eye off the rider, Dawson said, "Yes, keep it in sight, don't cock it. I've got my Colt."

He heard her hurry away to the shack. He heard the front door open, and less than a minute later he heard it close, followed by Clarity's footsteps running back across the rocky ground. She stopped a step behind him and moved slightly to the side. Dawson stared at the approaching rider, recognizing him now as the space between them grew shorter.

"Ouch," said a gruff voice, the man gesturing toward Clarity's bare feet. "I'd hate to see this lovely lady get herself a stone bruise, running like that." He stopped his horse a few yards away and continued, saying, "Dawson, every time I see you I get the strongest notion that you don't like bounty hunters."

"Evening, Holley," said Dawson. He held both hands loosely at his sides. "What brings you this way?" Clarity holding the shotgun was just a diversion. In the deep hip pocket of his canvas trousers, Dawson kept his Colt, a bandanna shoved down over its butt to keep it hidden and free of dirt.

"Same thing as last time we met," said Brue Holley. "I'm still looking around, keeping my ears open, hoping to get an idea who really killed Fast Larry Shaw." He grinned behind his mustache. "I'm in pursuit of other wanted men too. But I still want the reputation of killing the man who killed Fast Larry."

"Good luck, then," said Dawson, not wanting to talk about it any more than they already had back in Crabtown. "I'm working my claim, as you can see." He gestured with his free hand, then let it fall back to his side.

"Yeah, I see." Holley looked all around. "I have to say, finding you up here is a surprise. I expect you came up through Black's Cut instead of the way I rode up. I never saw your prints till I picked them up last evening before dark."

"Yes," said Dawson, "we picked up supplies in Black's Cut, then moved on." He didn't want to tell the bounty hunter what had happened in Black's Cut.

"Oh?" said Holley. "Did you meet my friend Giddis Black and his associates?"

His friend . . . ? Dawson tried to keep from looking surprised. "No," he said coolly, "I never got the pleasure. Maybe next time through, when I go for more supplies."

Holley studied his eyes for a moment as if trying to discern things unspoken. He looked curiously at the woman, then at the shack, then back at Dawson and said, "Who is that holding me in his rifle sights?"

"Just a fellow prospector," Dawson said, "trying to figure out if you're a friend or foe."

"Oh, and which am I?" Holley asked.

"You're neither," Dawson said with no expression. "How does that suit you?"

"Suits me fine." Holley backed his horse a few steps before turning it back toward the pines. "I'm spending a day or two camped down on the other side of the pines, before I head into Black's Cut. So, if you see a campfire, don't be concerned, it's only mine." Grinning, he added, "Stop by and see me when you get back to town." He touched his hat brim and smiled down at Clarity. "You too, of course, *Miss Clarity*," he added, with emphasis, making sure Dawson knew that he and the woman were not strangers.

The two stood watching in silence until the bounty hunter rode back into the shelter of the pines along the sloping hillside. "How well do you know him?" Dawson asked.

"How well do you think?" Clarity replied, giving him a look.

"I'm not butting into your business," said Dawson. "I just want to know where you stand with the man."

"I'm a whore, Cray," Clarity said, humbly. "That's where I stand with any man."

"I'm sorry," said Dawson, "I meant nothing by it."

"Neither did I," said Clarity.

Finally, Arden walked out of the shack, limped up beside Dawson, and said, "I've seen that one before. Giddis Black sent that bounty hunter looking for us, you can bet on it."

"No." Dawson shook his head. "He's on his way to Black's Cut, hasn't been there yet . . . hasn't heard what happened."

"Aye," said Arden, "then I'm wrong. He hasn't told Giddis *yet*."

"You didn't miss it by much, Cap," said Dawson. "As soon as he gets to Black's Cut and hears what happened, he'll tell Giddis where we are. He'll probably offer to bring us in to him, for a fee."

Clarity said quietly, "He knows something is wrong. He knows you're lying about not meeting Giddis Black."

"Why do you say that?" Dawson asked.

"Because he knows I wouldn't be out here with you unless Giddis either approved of it, or else I've run away."

"Either way he'll take the news to Giddis Black first thing," said Dawson.

"Yes," Clarity replied, giving him a calm but serious look. "If Giddis didn't know where to look before, he'll sure know it now.

"Then you've got to kill him, before he gets to Black's Cut," she added matter-of-factly.

Dawson and Arden looked at her. "That's murder, child," said Arden.

"So?" She looked at the old seaman in surprise. "What do you call what Giddis will do to you if he finds you? What do you call what his men did to poor Violet, what he intended to have done to me? Once Holley gets to town, trouble is coming our way." She turned with the shotgun and walked away toward the shack, shaking her head.

"I'm afraid she's right, Dawson," the old seaman said. He looked all around with a sigh and said, "In a place as large as this, you would think a man could find peace for himself."

"I expect some of us aren't meant to find peace," Dawson replied grimly. He unhitched the mule from the rock sled, leaving the sled where it stood. He picked up the lead ropes to the mule and gave the animal a light slap on the rump. "I'll get the mule fed and watered. We'll talk over supper, figure out what to do next."

Arden said in a lowered voice, "I believe the one he wants worst of all is Clarity. I know the two of yas have grown close, but for her sake maybe it's best one of us takes her as far as Crabtown and gets her out of Giddis Black's reach."

"I think you're right," said Dawson. "Let's see if she'll go along with it."

The two split off into separate directions, Dawson walking the mule up to the small lean-to shelter while the old seaman limped the rest of the way up to the shack. Outside the lean-to, Dawson grained the mule and rubbed it down. Leading the tired animal to its stall he set an oaken bucket full of water in front of it and stood while it drank its fill.

When the mule raised its dripping muzzle and

slung its head, Dawson picked up the bucket, stepped out of the stall, and closed the stall door behind him. He'd turned and hung the empty bucket on a peg when he realized he had not seen his horse standing in its stall at the far end of the lean-to.

When he'd hurried to the horse's stall and looked in, making sure it was empty, he cursed under his breath, then turned and started toward the shack. Halfway there, he saw Arden step out onto the porch, a lantern in his hand, and look toward him. "My horse is missing! Have you seen Clarity?" he shouted, on his way.

"No," said Arden. "She's not inside. I was coming to see if she's out here with you."

"Damn it, Clarity," Dawson whispered, stopping, looking off in the direction where Brue Holley said he'd made a camp. "I hope you're not about to get yourself killed."

Chapter 17

After dark, Brue Holley sat in clear sight, stirring a stick in his campfire and watching sparks leap upward through the licking flames. His Winchester lay across his lap. Three feet back from the fire his bedroll lay spread out on the ground, awaiting him. When he heard the first faint sound of a horse's hooves, he tensed a bit and listened intently until he heard the woman's voice call his name out softly.

He only grinned and waited until she called out again, saying, "Brue? It's me, Clarity." A silent pause followed, and then she called out playfully, "You knew I'd be coming out here. Aren't you going to be a gentleman and invite me in?"

"That all depends. Are you alone, the way I intended you to be?" Holly replied, his hand still on his rifle, his thumb still over the hammer. "I don't want any company except you, little darling."

"Yes, of course I'm alone," said Clarity, "just like always."

Holley chuckled to himself, then said, "Well, did you come here to make my bells ring? You always could make my bells ring, one way or another."

"Oh, you bet I'm going to *ring your bells* all right," Clarity said, stepping down from Dawson's horse at the edge of the circling firelight. "It's all I've thought of since I saw you earlier."

Holly stood up, grinning. He laid his rifle aside and stood with his hand on his gun butt. "Then what are you waiting for, woman? Get yourself in here, let's take a good look at you."

Clarity stepped closer into the firelight, her wool coat wrapped around her. "Huh-uh," said Holly, wagging a long rough finger at her. "That's not how I want to see you. I want to see *all* of you. Step out of your garments right there, before you come any closer. I don't want to see nothing on you but nipples and fur."

"My goodness, Holley!" Clarity stopped and put a hand on her hip as if in exasperation. "You act like you don't trust me."

Holley's grin faded. "Oh, I trust you, my little English fox. But I trust you more naked than I do with pockets." His hand rested on the gun butt standing on his hip. "Now, let me see some skin, or get on away from here."

Clarity gave a pouting look. "When you told us where you were camped, I thought you were saying it so I'd come visit you. Now I get here and you're acting like I'm up to no good."

"Save the act," said Holley, his hand tightening on

the Colt. "I'm not joking. Take off that coat, then your dress."

"Very well, then," said Clarity, seeing him on the verge of drawing his black-handled Remington, "but you've taken all the surprise out of my visit." She opened the coat and dropped it to the ground.

"My Gawd!" Brue said, his breath suddenly turning shallow. Clarity had worn nothing under the coat. She stood naked and pale, firelight glimmering on her fine cream-colored skin.

"Can I come closer now?" she asked teasingly, already moving forward toward him. "I need some big warm hands all over me."

"Oh *yes*, you come right ahead," Holley said, loosening his gun belt and draping it in close reach over his saddle lying on the ground. "I didn't mean to doubt you, little lady," he said as she stepped past him, lay down on the bedroll, and looked up at him as he peeled off his boots and pitched them aside.

"I should hope not," she said, "after all the times we've done this." She gave an impatient smile and said, "Are you going to make me wait all night for it? I came here because I need to feel a man between my thighs." She cupped a breast and watched him hurriedly pull off his trousers and drop them in the dirt.

"Oh? Dawson wasn't good enough for you?" Holley said, crouching down over her, laying a rough hand on the tender flesh beneath her navel.

She gave a slight sigh of ecstasy and closed a hand over his, guiding it upward. "No, not after seeing you today, not after remembering how good it's always been between us."

"I'll be telling Giddis I seen you out here with Crayton Dawson soon as I get to Black's Cut," he said, on his knees between her legs, ready to lie down atop her. "So if this is supposed to keep my mouth shut, it better be the best I ever had." He grinned down at her.

"This is all I came here for," she whispered as if in deep longing, her free hand reaching down and squeezing him tightly. "Am I going to get what I want, or not?" Her hand slid off him and down between her thighs to her soft folds of flesh, lingering there for a moment while her free hand held him away from her.

"Oh yeah, you're sure enough going to get it," said Holley. He felt her hand move away from his chest to allow him entrance. Lying down atop her, he hurried, reaching and groping, eager now, his blood rushing, his breathing quickened. He made a hard lunge into her and felt her legs go up around him. She let out a gasp as he lunged again.

But as he began to take her, he felt a white-hot burn streak deep along the side of his throat beneath his ear. "Damn it!" he said, slapping a hand to his neck without stopping his hard steady thrusting inside her. But he did stop thrusting as he felt the warm stickiness of blood all over his hand. "I'm bleeding," he said in surprise.

Without answering, Clarity tightened her legs around him and rolled him onto his side, taking him farther away from the holstered Colt lying on the saddle at the head of the bedroll.

"Damn! Turn me loose! I'm bleeding," Holley said, not yet understanding what had happened to him. Then suddenly it came to him, and he struggled with her knees until she unlocked them and scurried from beneath him. She grabbed the Remington and yanked it from the holster just before his blood-slick hand could get to it. "You cut me, you English whore!" he bellowed, seeing the gout of blood spew from his throat with each beat of his heart.

"Yes, I've killed you, Holley," she said calmly, standing over him, splattered with his blood, the Remington in her hand pointed down at him. "Now be a good chap and lie still. It will all be over soon." Her voice took on a soothing condoling quality.

"Gawddamn you! I'll kill you!" Holley tried to shout. Yet he knew that his greatest effort had only produced a diminished effect. He made his hardest grab for the gun in her hand, but the move was only a weak and awkward groping in the air.

"No, no, it's you who've been killed," Clarity corrected him, talking to him as if he were an injured child. She only had to take a short calm step backward to avoid him. His bloody fingers left four long red streaks down her shin. "There, you see," she said, "there's nothing you can do. Lie still, it will be much easier for you."

"Of all . . . damn things . . ." Holley melted onto the bedroll on all fours, blood pouring steadily but lessening. In a moment his arms collapsed, dropping

his front half to the blood-soaked blanket, but leaving
his hairy rear end still raised and glimmering in
the firelight.

"There, all done," Clarity said, lowering the gun.
She stooped and picked up the bloody straight razor
she'd taken from Dawson's personal belongings before leaving the shack. Using her thumb and finger
she laid the razor over by the coffeepot. Her eyes
went to Holley's face as he made a last gurgling
coughing sound. But then, seeing his wide blank eyes
staring out across the ground, his cheek pressed to
the wet blanket, she let out a breath, stood up, and
walked to where her coat lay in the dirt.

As she bent down to pick up the coat, she heard
the sound of hooves breaking through the brush
toward the campsite, and stood up quickly, holding
the coat bundled in front of her. "Cra—Cray!" she
said, startled, seeing Dawson step into the firelight,
gun in hand, leading Arden's sorrel mule behind
him.

"Oh no," Dawson said, looking past Clarity and
at Holley's naked body, his rear end still up. "That's
what I was afraid of." He turned toward Clarity,
seeing the gun in her hand, and said without pointing his Colt at her, "Lay the gun on the ground."

"Sure." She shrugged. "I wasn't aiming it at you.
I only grabbed it to keep him from getting to it and
killing me." She let the gun fall to the ground and
held the bundled coat in front of her. "Your razor is
lying over there," she said, as if to be helpful.

"You didn't have to do this, Clarity," Dawson said,

his Colt slumping in his hand. "We would have talked this thing out and done something."

"Oh? What, pray tell?" she asked coolly. "We know what he would do once he got to Black's Cut. He told me as much before he died." She pointed toward Dawson's horse standing to the side in the firelight. "May I get my clothes? It's dreadful cold, like this." She nodded down at her nakedness.

"Yes, get your clothes on," Dawson said. Seeing the blood-streaked finger trails down her leg as she walked toward the horse, he asked, "Were you . . . I mean the two of you . . . ?"

"Yes, we were," she said matter-of-factly, "but only for a moment, just until I got him where I wanted him. It was necessary."

Dawson just stared at her in silence. She dropped the coat, opened the saddlebags, and took out her dress and undergarments. She took the canteen from the saddle horn, uncapped it, and began washing blood from her legs. "We both knew this had to be done, Cray," she said, looking at him with soft gentle eyes as she dressed herself. "Please don't think ill of me."

Looking over at his bloody razor, Dawson shook his head and said, "Clarity, I don't know what to say. You cut Palmer and Willie."

"Yes, after they killed poor Violet and were going to kill me next," she said with resolve.

"Now this bounty hunter," Dawson said, gesturing toward Holley's raised rear end.

"Yes, who would have gladly handed us all three

over to Giddis Black," Clarity said in her defense, "and who would have gladly ridden back and killed us all three in our sleep if Giddis asked him to—"

Dawson raised a hand toward her, cutting her off. "I know you cut Palmer and Willie in self-defense," he said. "And I can't blame you for killing Holley. It's just—just going to take me a minute to get used to what you've done here." As he spoke, he stepped over, reached out with his raised boot, and gave Holley's naked behind a nudge, sending him over onto his side.

"I know you're a gunman, Cray," Clarity said. "Is what I do with a razor any different than what you do with a gun?"

"No, it's not," Dawson said without having to hesitate or consider the question. "But I try to avoid trouble as much as I can. I only use my gun when I have to. Even then it's not something I'm proud of."

"Listen to you," Clarity said, bemused. "Do you think I go around every day, just slicing and slashing anyone I get the urge to?"

"That's not what I meant," said Dawson, realizing he'd said the wrong thing.

"Don't you think I *try* to avoid doing something like this? This is ghastly, and it's not something I'm proud of doing." Having dressed as she talked, she'd moved close to him and pressed herself against his chest. "Please hold me, Cray," she whispered. His arms went around her. "No, I'm not proud of myself," she whispered, shaking her head. "But he would have come back, or Giddis's men would have

come back. Either way, that would have been the
end of us together, and I don't want us to end." She
paused, snuggling against him. "I'll kill anybody
who tries to come between us."

Jesus . . . Dawson looked at the blood sprayed all
over the ground, the blanket, the saddle. He looked
at the pale bloodless corpse with the side of its throat
gashed open. He wanted to say something, but this
was not the time or the place. He thought of Madeline Mercer, alone, awaiting his return. He'd mentioned to Clarity that he had someone waiting for
him. He'd mentioned that she was a widow who
lived off a trail leading into Crabtown. He had not
said her name. But now he regretted mentioning her
at all.

"Come on," Dawson said softly, pulling gently
away from her. "Let's get Holley out of sight. We
need to straighten things up and get out of here."

Chapter 18

When Dawson and Clarity had pulled the bounty hunter's trousers onto his limp body, Dawson tied a rope from his ankles to the sorrel mule's saddle and dragged the body deep into a stand of pine. He folded the man's arms on his chest, closed his startled eyes, and laid his wide-brimmed hat over his pale bloodless face.

Hat in hand, Dawson stood restlessly over Holley for a moment, as if trying to think of the right words. Finally, he looked up at the dark starry sky at a loss and shook his head. "Lord, I don't know what to say about this one," he murmured.

Back at the campsite, Clarity had wiped the razor on the bloody blanket and dragged the blanket out of sight into thick surrounding brush. She wiped off the saddle with Holley's riding duster. Then she tossed the saddle onto Holley's horse and prepared the animal for the trail. She gathered the coffeepot and everything else lying about, wrapped them into the duster, and carried it out into the brush as well. "And that's that," she said to herself, satisfied. She shoved Holley's Winchester down into the saddle boot and hid his big black-handled six-shooter up under her coat.

"We're all ready to go," she said, standing beside the fire when Dawson returned with the mule. She stepped over to him, stuck the folded razor down into his shirt pocket, and patted his chest. "Don't forget to give it a good washing before you use it again."

"I won't," said Dawson, looking down at his pocket. He gave the camp a good once-over, noting Holley's rifle in the saddle boot, yet realizing that the bounty hunter's big Remington was nowhere to be seen. But without mentioning it he turned to Clarity and said, "Mount up. I'll kill the fire and be right behind you."

Before turning to step up into the saddle, she asked with a serious expression, "You're not going to stay angry with me, are you?"

"No," Dawson said sincerely, "I'm not angry with you. I suppose you did what we all knew had to be done."

She smiled. "Good, I don't want you to be angry. I want to make you happy, Cray . . . happier than you've ever been."

Dawson only nodded, not knowing what to say. He watched her step into the saddle and turn the horse to the trail. Then he put out the fire, stepped into his saddle, and followed her, leading Arden's mule behind him.

They rode in grim silence back to the mine shack, where upon seeing them in the moonlight, Arden came limping at a trot, a lantern glowing in his hand. "It's about damn time the two of yas returned," he called out, sounding cross with worry. "Are you both all right? I heard no gunfire." He looked curiously at Holley's horse, the bounty hunter's rifle in the saddle boot.

"We're all right," Dawson said. He stepped down from his saddle and helped Clarity down from hers. "There wasn't a shot fired," he added. Nodding toward the shack, he said to Clarity, "Why don't you go inside and get some rest? Cap and I will see to the animals."

"I killed him, Cap," Clarity said flatly.

"*You* killed him?" The old seaman looked back and forth between them.

"Yes, I killed him," said Clarity. "I'm telling you myself, so no one else will have to." She looked at Cray, then turned and walked toward the shack.

No sooner had she walked out of hearing range, than Arden said quietly, rubbing the muzzle of Holly's horse, "No matter who killed him, I'll rest easier knowing the swine is dead." He took on a look of uncertainty and asked, "He is dead, isn't he? You're sure of it?"

"Yes, I'm sure of it," said Dawson. "If you'd seen the gash in his throat . . ." He shook his head, letting his words trail.

"Aye," said Arden as if in reflection. "I've always thought this gal would be a wildcat if a body pushed her too hard. You can bet that Palmer and Willie weren't the first ones she ever commenced slicing on. She must've kept her past a secret even from Giddis and his men."

Dawson thought about it, then said, "If Palmer and Willie weren't the first ones she ever cut, I wonder if Holley was the first one she ever killed."

"I wouldn't have any idea," said Arden, rubbing his beard-stubbled chin as they turned the animals and led them toward the lean-to. "Does that trouble you, knowing the woman you're sharing a bed with is capable of killing?"

Dawson thought about the folded razor in his shirt pocket, and about the big Colt standing holstered on his hip. "I suppose it shouldn't, but yes, it does trouble me, some."

"Is the silent fury of the cold steel any less civilized than the blast of a gunshot?" Arden asked.

"I don't know what it is," said Dawson, thinking about the men who had fallen to the dirt in his gun sights. "Maybe it's just the way she went about it." He pictured Holley's naked behind stuck up in the air, his gaping mouth and startled eyes lying on the blood-soaked blanket.

"Oh? And how did she go about it?" Arden asked.

"Never mind," said Dawson. "If she wants to tell you, she will. It's not my place to talk about it."

But as if Dawson's comment alone was enough to evoke an image of how Clarity had set up the bounty hunter before killing him, Arden said, "Ah, I see. A man can spend a restless night, realizing how easy it is for the woman beside him to end his song with a simple flick of the wrist."

"Yes." Dawson looked up at the eastern sky where a thin wreath of silver dawn crept upward among hill and mountain peaks. "I believe I've just had such a night."

Arden grinned knowingly, dropping his sorrel mule's saddle and pushing the animal into its stall. "Aye," he said, "and the night's not over yet."

"It is for me," said Dawson, loosening the cinch on his horse and swinging the saddle from its back.

When they'd finished with the animals and walked to the shack, Dawson didn't undress and go to bed, where Clarity lay asleep in his other shirt. Instead, he looked at the pan of pinkish bloody water she'd used to wash herself. After a moment he picked it up, walked it out onto the porch, and slung it away. When he walked back inside, he stood looking into the low flames of the open hearth, then said to Arden, who lay on his bedroll propped on an elbow smoking his pipe, "It's almost time for me to get to the diggings. I think I'll start early."

"Might I finish with my briar and go with you?" Arden asked, almost knowing the answer before it came from Dawson.

"No, you get some shut-eye," Dawson replied. "I need to do some digging alone this morning."

Clarity awakened later than usual after having spent much of the night on horseback. Standing from the bed, she pulled the loose shirt around her and looked at the small nightstand, noting that the pan of wash water had been moved. She looked all around and, seeing that both Dawson and Arden were not in the shack, she stooped down and ran her hand under the bed, making sure the Remington she'd taken from the bounty hunter was still there where she'd put it.

Her fingers touched the gun butt. Satisfied, she stood, walked to the small front window, and looked out toward the mine entrance, then over to the spill where Dawson stood picking through a sled load of rocks, separating the keepers from the pile. All right, she told herself, seeing him toss a glance up toward the shack, last night had been rough. But this was a new day. It was time for her to walk down and see where they stood. She combed her fingers through her hair. *Here goes . . .*

Outside, emptying the sled, Dawson saw Clarity step down from the porch and walk toward him, her folded arms holding the shirt closed across her breasts. He had started to take the mule and the sled back to the mine, but he waited for her to reach him before nudging the mule forward with a tap of the rope. "Morning," he said, not wanting to seem affected by what had happened the night before.

"Morning," she said. She knew better from the way he only looked at her in passing, as if not wanting his eyes to reveal his thoughts.

"My goodness," she said, holding the shirt closed tightly against the coolness of morning, "I practically slept the day through, didn't I?"

Dawson, unable to think of any comment that would sound right given what had happened to cause her to be up so late at night, said nothing.

To prevent an awkward silence, she looked all around and asked, "Where's Cap?"

"He took the animals over the hill to graze," said Dawson. "He'll be back soon."

"No hurry." She smiled. Unfolding her arms, she slipped her right arm under his, hooked it over his forearm, and walked alongside him. Like a young couple on a church social outing, Dawson told himself. Not at all like some couple who had dragged a dead man into the pine woodlands after this smiling young woman had killed him in the midst of a sexual act.

Uncomfortable with that thought, Dawson looked down at her, seeing her breasts partly exposed, jiggling gently with each step they took behind the mule. "You need your coat on. You'll take sick out here like this."

She snuggled against his arm. "It feels good against you."

A few yards into the mine where daylight ran out, Dawson stopped the mule and pulled away from her long enough to take the lantern from its peg and light it. When he turned back toward the lead ropes, Clarity stood between him and the mule. "Are things going to be good between us again?"

Dawson let out a breath, put his arms around her, and held her close. "Yes. Let's let things settle down. I told you there's someone waiting for me."

"Yes, but isn't that something you men tell all of us working doves?" She looked deep into his eyes.

"No," said Dawson, "it's the truth. I only told you about her to keep things honest between you and me. I didn't want to mislead you."

"Whoever she is, I want to take her place," Clarity said.

"I can't talk about somebody taking her place," Dawson said. "I care a lot for this woman." Stepping back from her, he buttoned the loose-fitting shirt all the way up to the collar.

"Then let's not talk about it now," she said. "Not everything happens at once. Some things take time."

Noting how calm and reasonable she appeared today, Dawson felt a little better. "You're right," he said, handing her the lantern. "Here, light the way for us. Maybe today we'll get lucky."

"You mean I can stay while you work?" she asked, sounding surprised. "I won't bring you bad luck, a woman being in a mine? Remember what Cap said?"

"I remember." Dawson smiled, coaxing the mule and sled along to the place where he'd been picking away at the wall. "But then you said you'd bring me *only good luck*, remember?"

"Yes, that's right, I did say that," she said, standing back and hanging the lantern on a peg. "All right, then, good luck it is." She stood back out of the way and leaned against the opposite wall in the lantern light. She watched him go to work, taking up the pick and swinging it hard time and again until a pile of rock lay surrounding his feet.

When he lowered the pick and stepped back, wiping sweat from his forehead, he said, "There's something I've meant to ask you . . ."

"Yes, go ahead," she said.

He leaned on the pick handle and said, "In Black's Cut, a couple of Junior's thugs named DeLaurie and Newhouse mentioned a man Giddis keeps on a chain. One of them said the man thinks he's Fast Larry. Who is this person Giddis keeps on a chain?"

"Oh, you mean the *mad gunman*," said Clarity. "He's just some poor insane bugger who beat Giddis Black pretty badly at poker. Giddis had one of the girls dope his drink and knock him out. For the past month he's been kept chained to a post in the old log jail. Giddis can't seem to decide whether to hand him over to Willie Goode, or put him into a bear fight, which is another one of Giddis's favorite pastimes."

"A bear fight." Dawson winced.

Returning from grazing the animals and walking into the mine behind them, Arden cut in, saying as he puffed on his briar pipe, "It's more like a bear *feeding* than it is a *fight*. Believe me, I saw one when I first arrived in Black's Cut. I never want to see another one."

"Where does he get the bear?" Dawson asked.

"He has his own. It's a young boar grizzly he keeps half doped and half starved. Keeps it in the cell right next to the mad gunman, just to keep him scared out of his wits, I suppose.

"Giddis Junior and his thugs can't wait until they get to see another man ripped apart by a crazed boar grizzly. They're all fiends!"

"Why does the mad gunman think he's Lawrence Shaw?" Dawson asked, dreading, yet preparing himself to hear the answer he expected.

"That's something Clarity can best tell you about," said Arden, giving her a look.

But Clarity looked a little ashamed and said, "All right, maybe we did a bad thing, Violet and me. Giddis saw the way this man handled a gun and decided he was too dangerous. After the mad gunman won ten thousand dollars from Giddis at poker, Giddis had Violet and me set him up. We took him to bed, doped him up, and handcuffed him to the iron head rails. When he came to and realized what we'd done, he started raving, threatening, claiming he was Fast Larry Shaw, and telling us what he would do if we didn't set him free."

Dawson started feeling tenseness in his chest. "But nobody believed him because you all knew that Lawrence Shaw had been killed down in Crabtown, right?" he asked, wishing he was wrong but getting a powerful hunch that he wasn't.

"Sure, exactly," said Clarity. "So, making all those wild claims got him dubbed the *mad gunman*, and only made Giddis want to torture and torment him more."

Dawson let out a breath and said to Cap, "Are the animals well grazed?"

"Oh yes, very well," Cap replied. He saw the look on Dawson's face and asked, "What's wrong, pard? You look as if someone has kicked you in the belly."

"That's about what it feels like," Dawson said. He looked around in the darkness. "Cap, it looks like you'll be working the claim without me the next few days. I've got to take a ride."

"Where are we going?" Clarity asked, stepping forward with the worried look a woman gets when she feels she's being left behind.

"Not *we*, Clarity," Dawson said, rolling down his shirtsleeves. "I'll be making this ride alone."

PART 3

Chapter 19

From the end of the long catwalk on the roof of Black's Best Chance Saloon & Brothel, Giddis Black stood at ease smoking his cigar in the fading evening sunlight. He looked down onto the muddy street like some feudal lord appraising his kingdom. Behind him, Giddis Junior stood looking all around too. But the young Giddis Black took no appraisal of the muddy kingdom below, nor its inhabitants as they ventured in and out of sight. It went without saying that this was all his, by virtue of being his father's son.

"So, what do you say, Pa?" he asked, tired of waiting on his father's decision. "If we run into Brue Holley along the trail, we'll just tell him everything that happened and start him looking along with us. It'll save him riding all the way here, then riding all the way out again."

"You might be right," Giddis Senior said grudgingly. He watched as the young girl, Villy, carried a tray of covered food from the restaurant to the old log jail building. "But can I trust you and your pals to keep a civil tongue around Holley?" He watched Morse Tucker open the door for her. He smiled to himself, seeing the Jailer make a grab for Villy's behind, and seeing her manage to slip nimbly past him. "Brue Holley is a man with a low boiling point, like myself. He takes offense easily and will not tolerate fools."

Beneath them, inside the saloon, the voice of a tinny-sounding piano rattled out through an open window and resounded along the street.

"Don't worry, Pa, I'll see to it everybody's on their best behavior," said Junior, who had also watched Villy walking toward the jail. He'd never seen her from this high an angle. "We meet Holley, we'll tell him you want him to help us look for Dawson and that little peg-legged turd, Cap Arden."

Senior shook his head. "Damn, you've already screwed it up," he said in disgust. "You don't tell a man like Holley that *I want him to help you* hunt down Dawson. That would be an insult to him!"

"All right, I see," Junior said quickly, hoping to stop any further discussion on the matter. "I won't say that you want him to help us." He knew that regardless of what he agreed to, once he rode out of Black's Cut he would do as he damned well pleased. "I'll tell him you want us to help him hunt Dawson any way we can. Make him think he's in charge." Junior grinned.

"If Holley is riding with you, I have no doubt who

will be in charge," Senior said, knowing his son was absorbing little of what he'd been trying to tell him.

"What does that mean?" Junior asked, looking offended by the remark.

"Nothing," Giddis Senior sighed. He reminded himself that Junior had at least come upon a good idea, riding out and meeting Holley along the trail . . . that could save some time. Giddis really needed to get his hands on Dawson and Arden and show the people of Black's Cut that he would not be made a fool of. "How's the hand?" he asked to change the subject.

"Good as new," said Junior, "maybe better." He wiggled his gloved fingers. "See?"

Giddis Senior nodded, and asked in a monotone voice, "And Newhouse's head?"

"He's good," said Junior. "He's rearing to go."

"And DeLaurie's nose?"

"His eyes are both purple underneath, but his nose is healing along pretty good."

"Take Roy Erby and Billy Buffet along," he said, reminding himself what quick work Dawson had already made of these three.

"Why, Pa?" Junior spread his hands. "Me and the boys have a grudge to settle. I want this straight up and fair, just him against us three."

Senior looked disgusted. He was not about to try and explain anything. "Take them along and shut up about it! They're both good men in a fight."

As Junior stomped away, Giddis Senior turned his attention back to the street in time to see Villy walk quickly out of the log jail. The young girl looked angry and scared; she straightened the bodice of her dress in front where Tucker had groped at her on her way out. "It's time I make a woman out of you, Villy," Giddis murmured, turning and walking back to the trapdoor. "Then, if Tucker wants some of you, he'll just have to pay for it, like everybody else will."

As Giddis stepped down out of sight through the trapdoor, Dawson watched from within the shelter of a tall pine tree on a hillside over a hundred yards away. He'd seen Junior come and go in the waning evening light, and he'd scanned the street and seen the young woman take the tray of covered food to the log jail—the place Clarity and Arden had told him about. He needed to see and find out more. And he would, *tonight,* he told himself, collapsing the telescope lens between his hands and climbing down.

Inside the log jail, Morse Tucker took a long stiff leather strap down from a peg on the wall and walked over to the cell where the man sat staring out at him through the iron bars. "Now, what did you say to me?" he asked in a menacing voice.

A raspy voice replied matter-of-factly, "I said why don't you leave her alone, you foul-smelling son of a bitch?"

"Oh, I see," said Tucker. He held the strap between both hands and popped it like a whip. "You know what? Tonight just might be the night I beat your worthless ass to death myself, and feed you to this hairy monster."

"Giddis wouldn't like that at all, you killing me," the man said.

"Yeah, well—"

In the iron cage, the bear arose to the sound of the leather strap and let out a long threatening bawl, cutting him off.

"Shut up, you flea-bitten, fly-blowing—" Tucker swung the strap savagely, the end of it going between the bars and lashing down on the bear's muzzle as he lunged at the end of his chain.

The bear went crazy. He bawled louder and longer, squirming and rolling back and forth on the cage floor, his paws rubbing his pain-stricken muzzle. The iron cage rattled and rocked back and forth violently with his powerful rage.

"Sweet Jehoshaphat, Tucker!" Giddis Black shouted as he swung the front door open and stepped inside. "Shut that squalling beast up! It sounds like you're buggering him in here!"

"He won't stop! What can I do?" Tucker asked above the bear's roar.

Giddis gestured toward the desk where two biscuits and a pile of beef stew lay in a deep tin plate. "Feed him something, damn it!"

"That's my supper!" Tucker bemoaned, yet he still hurried over, scooped up a handful of hot stew, hurried back, and slung it through the cage bars. "Damn, now I've burnt my hand."

The bear quickly forgot his pain and hurried all around, grunting, lapping bits of meat and stew gravy from the iron cage floor. Giddis walked past Tucker shaking his head, and stared into the darkened cage where two eyes bored back at him. "Good evening, Mad Gunman," he said, with an air of civility. "Are you ready to give me back my ten thousand and put this unpleasantness behind you?"

The long scraggly hair and beard moved back and forth slowly. The man said, "I would be an idiot if I gave up that money, Giddis. It's my only ace left in the hole."

"Ha," said Giddis, "a true poker player to the end, you are." He raised his cigar between his fingers and wagged it slowly. "But this thing has gone on just about long enough. I'll have that money or I will chop off parts of you and let you watch the bear have you for dinner."

"It'll be the most expensive dinner you ever served, Giddis," the mad gunman replied.

"Don't test me on this," said Giddis, "because serve it I will." He stared at the dirt-crusted face in contemplation for a moment, finally saying, "Just for the sake of conversation, I'm going to ask you this once again." He tried to study the man's eyes as he asked, "Who are you . . . I mean, *really?*"

The man only stared, offering no reply.

"What? No answer?" said Giddis. "After all those days, all those beatings Tucker has given you for your claiming to be Fast Larry Shaw? Now you've abandoned the idea altogether?" He looked puzzled.

"I'm leaving here soon, one way or the other," said the man, with resolve.

"Indeed you are, Mad Gunman," said Giddis. "I thought you might tell us what name to carve on a marker, if there's enough of you left to bury."

This was getting close to the end of the game, the mad gunman thought, realizing that had he convinced Giddis that he was Lawrence Shaw, there had been too many beatings, too much bad blood between them for Giddis to allow him to live. All Giddis wanted was the ten thousand dollars. Villy had told him about Dawson and what had happened in town. Giddis was starting to look bad, a gunman putting three of his men out of action—one of them his own son. Now killing a man without getting his money back from him. That would look weak, even to his own men.

"What's the difference who I am?" he said. "Do your worst. It's not me you'll be feeding the bear, it's your ten thousand dollars."

"In that case, I'll pay someone to play a sad mournful fiddle while we both watch *your* foot and *my* money go down his gullet," Giddis said, turning his head slightly and blowing a stream of smoke into the bear's cage.

"That's no worse than some of the ways I've imagined I might go," said the man. In the bear's cage the big animal paced back and forth on the end of his chain, his muzzle lowered to the floor, sniffing, grunting, leaving a trail of saliva.

Giddis grinned and puffed the cigar. "Good. Then

you won't be disappointed. *I* won't be disappointed. And the bear—well, let's just say he's always pleased to take potluck."

Tucker stood behind the desk holding a wet rag to his hand, having picked up the hot stew with his cupped fingers. He watched Giddis turn and walk toward the front door. "Can you send somebody over to relieve me for just a little while tonight, Giddis? I got a young lady I want to visit."

Giddis turned and looked at him as if giving it serious consideration. He pictured Villy leaving in a hurry to keep Tucker's hands off her. After a moment, he smiled cruelly and said, "No, I don't think so, not tonight, Jailer. I don't trust anybody around here as much as I trust you." Gesturing with a nod toward the pacing bear, he said, "Keep that big monster quiet, whatever it takes."

"What about this sumbitch?" Tucker said, staring at the mad gunman. "I was fixing to skin him with this strap before you come along."

"Skin away, then," said Giddis. "But don't you kill him, or I'll be skinning you. For ten thousand dollars I at least want the pleasure of watching him get smaller with every bite."

"I'll be damned," Tucker said to the closed door after Giddis stepped out and slammed it shut behind him.

In the darkened cell, the mad gunman chuckled under his breath.

"What have you got to laugh about, you filthy knobby-kneed sumbitch?" said Tucker. He snatched the leather strap and walked back toward the cell door. "I'm going to beat you till you beg me to kill you."

Behind the log jail in the darkness, Dawson moved at a crouch through a stretch of weeds littered with whiskey bottles, rats, and rotting garbage. When he'd stopped for a moment, he heard the sound of leather strap against human skin. He winced, but continued forward in the darkness. When he'd run low and quickly across the alley and slid down against the back of the building, he heard the low bawling of the bear, and the voice of the Jailer cursing with each swing of the strap.

"I ain't . . . stopping till . . . you beg me to," said the halting winded voice inside the log jail.

"Then . . . you take a rest . . . let's start all over," came a painful reply. "I've got . . . all night."

Was that him? Was that Shaw's voice? It sounded familiar, didn't it? Dawson asked himself, listening intently.

"To hell . . . with you," said the Jailer. "You ain't worth it. Let the bear . . . have you tomorrow. I need me a drink."

Dawson heard footsteps across the cage floor, followed by the opening and the closing of the iron door, then the opening and closing of a desk drawer. He listened, hearing that raspy voice again, saying with a dark chuckle, "You're worn out . . . and I'm still laughing at you . . . *ha, ha.*"

That was Shaw, no doubt about it, Dawson told

himself. The voice sounded weak, as if the man was ill, barely able to speak. But yes, that was him all right, he was certain. Still he waited, needing to get a look at his face. Sliding down into weeds along the wall, he sat in the darkness as still as a stone.

A full half hour passed before a complete silence fell over the log jail. Dawson stood up quietly and pulled himself up to the small iron-barred window. The terrible odor from inside caused him to bat his eyes and have to breathe through his mouth. Silence gave way to a low, steady snore coming from the bear's cage. Across the room, through the bars, he saw Tucker's sleeping form leaned back in a chair, his mouth agape toward the ceiling, a bottle of whiskey standing on the desk in front of him. *Here goes*, Dawson said to himself.

"Shaw, is that you?" he whispered, praying not to awaken the bear or the jailer. "It's me, Dawson."

He heard no reply at first. Just a sudden startled scrape on the floor told him he'd been heard. But then he heard a scooting sound across the floor and the slight muffled clink of the ankle chain. "Shhh," a voice said, as grimy fingertips appeared on the inside window ledge and a grimier sunken face appeared right behind them, wide-eyed and near starvation. "My God, Dawson . . . it is you," the dirty tortured face whispered through the iron bars. "Give—give me a gun."

"I'll get you out, Shaw. That's why I'm here," said Dawson, seeing through the dirt and scratches and pus-filled sores that it was indeed his friend Lawrence Shaw.

"No. Jus—just give me a gun," Shaw said, his voice trembling. A thin hand reached out as if to grasp a gun butt. "Please! Please!"

"Quiet down," Dawson whispered, hearing Shaw grow louder as he spoke. "I'm coming around. Be ready to go."

"No! Please! Give me a gun," Shaw pleaded.

But Dawson, realizing his friend was talking out of his head, said no more. Instead, he dropped silently from the window ledge, slipped around the building, and crouched down again in the darkness beside the front porch. He looked both ways along the street and toward Black's Best Chance Saloon & Brothel. Then he slipped onto the porch and over to the front door.

Chapter 20

From inside his cell, Lawrence Shaw watched the door creak open softly, and saw Dawson step inside and close it behind himself. As Dawson stepped over to the desk where Tucker sat sprawled back in his chair, Shaw arose slowly and moved to the cell door. He held his ankle chain in his hand to keep it from dragging on the plank floor. Staring with great anticipation, he waited until Dawson drew his Colt, raised it, and brought the barrel down hard atop Tucker's head.

Tucker's limp figure lolled sideways with the blow's impact. "Dawson, give me his gun!" Shaw whispered, seeing Dawson reach down, take Tucker's Colt from his holster, and shove it down behind his belt.

But Dawson went about his business. "Where's the cell key?"

"On the peg," Shaw whispered, pointing out through the bars. "And he keeps the key to this ankle chain in the top right drawer!" He cut a glance toward the bear, who had staggered up onto all fours and stood swinging his big head back and forth in curiosity. "Don't move too fast, this animal will start bawling to wake the dead!"

Silently, keeping himself from getting into a hurry and agitating the bear, Dawson slid the drawer open and took out a single key. With the ankle key in hand, he took the cell key from a wall peg and stepped over behind the knocked-out jailer's chair. He leaned the chair farther back, and dragged Tucker, chair and all, over to the cell door.

"All right, now give me a gun!" Shaw hissed, staring hard and cold at Tucker's face.

Seeing the look on Shaw's face and knowing his friend was not himself from torture and starvation, Dawson stuck the key into the cell and said, "Not right now. Let's get you out of here first."

"Cray, damn it," Shaw insisted in a weak and rasping voice, "give me a gun!"

But Dawson didn't seem to hear him as he kept an eye on the bear and opened the cell door slowly. "Here, hold this," he whispered to Shaw, handing him the key to the cell door. Stooping down he opened the ankle cuff and laid it quietly on the plank floor, not wanting to alarm the bear. Standing, he helped Shaw walk out of the cell. "I brought a spare horse, in case it was you in here."

"Who told you about me? Was it Villy?" Shaw asked.

"No, I don't know a *Villy*," said Dawson, not

wanting to tell him just now that one of the women who had set him up was also the one who told Dawson about him.

"Oh? How did you know?" Shaw asked, eyeing the spare gun in Dawson's belt. He rubbed his grimy hands up and down his dirty trousers.

"It's a long story, pard," said Dawson. He turned away, getting the gun out of Shaw's sight, removing the temptation of him snatching it. "Let's go." He stepped out of the cell and started to drag Tucker's chair back inside.

But Shaw said, "No, wait! Why won't you give me a gun?"

"You look weak and done in," said Dawson. "I don't want you flying off the handle and shooting this man, bringing the whole town down on us."

Shaw shook his head as if dismissing such an idea. "Go get the horses and bring them around to the side," he said, nodding down at Tucker. "I'll gag him and cuff his arms through the bars, so he can't yell out when he wakes up."

Dawson gave him a questioning look. "Are you all right to do that? You *do* look weak and—"

"I *am* weak and done in, so what?" said Shaw, cutting him short. "I still know what I'm doing, if that's got you worried." He gave Dawson a look. "Now give me his gun and go get the horses."

"Hurry up, I'll be waiting," said Dawson. He turned and walked to the front door. On his way, he reached out, picked up Tucker's rifle leaning against the side of the desk, and kept going.

Shaw only stared for a moment, then shook his head and turned to where the knocked-out jailer began to come to with a moan. "Wake up, Tucker, you low-living gut-sucking dog," he growled, reaching down and untying Tucker's bandanna from around his neck.

"He should have given me your gun," he whispered. He tied the bandanna around the jailer's mouth, gagging him. He jerked Tucker's trouser belt from around his waist, pulled his arms behind the chair back, and tied his hands together tight. "Since he didn't, I'll just have to make do." He reached over and lifted the bolt on the bear's cage.

"Uhmmm. *Uhhmm!*" said the jailer, coming to. He slung his head wildly as Shaw dragged him backward in his chair and lined it up with the bear's open cage door. *"Huh-un! Huhh-un!"* Tucker pleaded, still shaking his head.

"Here we go, Jailer, dinner is served, compliments of the *mad gunman!*" Shaw leaned the chair back and slid it forward as hard as he could in his weakened condition. At the edge of the cage door the chair legs snagged on the iron threshold and toppled forward just as the bear made a sudden charge and reared up at the end of his chain. Tucker came up to his feet, the chair dangling from his tied hands, his own weight hurling him into the bear's open arms where his bandanna came down, only to be replaced by a mouthful of foul greasy fur.

Outside, holding the spare horse that had belonged to Brue Holley, Dawson heard the terrible muffled

cry of a man being mauled by a starving bear. *"Jesus,
Shaw!"* he said aloud, looking around in the darkness, hoping no one else heard the sound. No sooner
had the sound started than the front door opened
and Shaw hurried out as best he could. Running
weakly and barefoot over to the edge of the porch,
he climbed onto the saddle with Dawson grabbing
his bony shoulder and giving him a pull.

"That didn't take long, now, did it?" he said, out
of breath. The horse beneath him spun in place, almost throwing him from his saddle. Dawson grabbed
the animal by its bridle and settled it. From the open
door of the log jail came an awful sound of crunching, slurping, and tearing.

"Shaw, you didn't!" said Dawson.

"You wouldn't give me a gun," Shaw replied,
gathering the horse beneath him. Hearing the sound
of running boots coming from the direction of the
saloon and brothel, Shaw said in a strengthening
voice, "One more thing! Follow me!"

"Shaw, wait!" Dawson shouted. "We've got to get
out of here!"

Shaw jerked sharply on his horse's reins and
looked back at him. "I came to this town with boots
on. I'm not leaving barefoot." He held his hand back
to Dawson, palm up, and said, "Fill it."

Dawson took the gun from behind his belt and laid
it into his waiting hand. "If you're going to do some
revenge killing, I want you to know, one of the
women who set you up is dead . . . the other one
lives with me."

"What? She's *living* with you?" Shaw stared as if in disbelief.

Running boots grew closer. Shaw's and Dawson's horses fidgeted and crow-hopped, eager to go. "We'll talk about it later!" Dawson said.

Shaw put his horse up into a run, Dawson right behind him, staying in the back alleys until they reached the rear door of the saloon. Dawson said wryly, "This figures," as Shaw jumped from his saddle.

"Hold my horse, keep me covered!" Shaw said, out of breath, his long tangled hair and beard flying in every direction.

"What are you doing?" Dawson called out, trying to keep his voice down. He watched Shaw run to the second of four tall wooden privies standing in a row behind the saloon. Opening the door, jerking a drunk out of it, and giving the man a shove, Shaw ran inside and came out only seconds later carrying a thick leather wallet.

"Who the hell you think you are?" the drunk shouted, still struggling to his feet, tugging to pull up his downed trousers.

"Sorry, ole hoss," said Shaw, hurrying past him and back to his waiting horse while he riffled through the thick cash inside the wallet. "All here," he said. But instead of climbing back into his saddle, he looked up at Dawson and said, "Just one more thing. I'll be right back." He took out the Colt, checked it, made certain it was loaded, then turned and walked into the saloon through the rear door.

Knowing nothing he said would stop him, Dawson slipped his rifle from the saddle boot and stepped down, holding both horses. "You're covered," he said.

"What's going on out there?" Villy asked Giddis Senior, the two of them hearing the sound of voices and running boots rumbling along the boardwalk toward the log jail.

"Damn it, I don't know," said Giddis. "But you stay right here and keep your mind on what we're doing. We're off to a good start here." He grinned and grabbed his shirt and coat from the chair beside the bed. Throwing his shirt on, carrying his coat, he gave a suspicious look toward the closed door. "No way . . ." he murmured. Then he turned from the door and stepped out the window onto a small balcony.

Villy walked to the window, raising the front of her nightshirt enough to cover her exposed breasts. She looked out in time to see Giddis slide down a support post to the street. He moved along at a trot toward the log jail, some of his men falling in around him. Behind her, the sound of the door bursting open caused her to turn toward it with a gasp.

"Where is he, Villy?" Shaw asked, stepping inside. Tucker's gun was in his hand, cocked and ready.

Startled, she pointed out the window and stood aside as Shaw hurried over and looked down. He only caught a glimpse of Giddis as the saloon owner turned out of sight toward the log jail. "You'll have to keep . . ." Shaw said quietly. Turning to Villy he looked her up and down, seeing that he had arrived before anything had happened between the two. "Grab some clothes, you're getting out of this business before you start."

"But, but I can't!" she said. "How will I live? I have no one! Giddis bought me from an orphanage and paid my way here from Missouri."

He fished the thick wallet from inside his soiled and smelly shirt. "Giddis's ten thousand will buy you a brand-new start. The rest is up to you."

"But *why?*" She couldn't understand. "I don't even know you . . . except for you being in the jail, and me slipping food to you."

"Yes, you slipped food to me and that's what kept me alive, Villy," said Shaw, forcing himself to sound impatient. "The *mad gunman* never forgets a good turn. Now, come on, let's get out of here."

"Oh God, I can't tell you how glad I am that I don't have to *do this*, with him," she said, hurrying now, realizing this was really happening. "I mean, if I had to I would, you know, because an orphan girl has to do what's demanded of her. But I have to say, I really thank God, and *you*, that this is—"

"*Please*, come on," Shaw said, cutting her off. He jerked her coat from the chair back and slung it around her. "You can thank God and me later."

She stalled, looking worried. "You don't mean I'm going to have to . . . ?"

"No," said Shaw, grabbing her and making her move on out the door and into the hallway. "You don't have to do anything with me . . . or anybody else, until someday when you decide that *you* want to. Sound fair enough?"

"Yes, fair enough," she sighed, moving along to the far end of the hallway, through a door leading down to the rear alley.

"Who is she?" asked Dawson, as soon as the two stepped outside the saloon and headed to Shaw's horse.

"This young lady is going with us," Shaw said firmly, leading Villy to Dawson's horse, "and she'll have to ride with you. I smell too much like a bear."

"All right, I've got her! Let's go!" said Dawson, getting edgy. He could hear the sound of angry men's voices from the direction of the jail, and he knew that at any minute those men would come looking for them. He leaned in his saddle, hooked an arm around Villy, and raised her up behind him.

Climbing into his saddle, Shaw gestured up the alley and said, "Follow me to the mercantile. I'm not leaving here like some saddle tramp. I'm getting some boots, a hat and coat. Giddis Black owes them to me."

"You're out of your mind!" Dawson said, cutting a glance toward the log jail where the bear bawled loud and long above the sound of shocked and angry voices. But then Dawson realized that instead of the jail, the sound of the bear came from the hillsides south of town.

"What about Giddis?" Villy asked Shaw, her arms

around Dawson's waist, holding on. "Him and his men will come to kill you!"

Shaw gave them both a flat stare, batted his bare heels to the horse's sides, and sent it bolting along the dark alley. "Hang on tight, ma'am," said Dawson, sending his horse along behind Shaw. "I think that's what he's hoping for."

Chapter 21

━━━━

Inside the log jail, Giddis's men stood staring at the few bloody rags and remains of Morse Tucker slung all about the empty cage. In a wild frenzy the bear had broken its chain and charged out of the cage and through the men as they'd entered the log jail. One of the men, Tommy Corbin, managed to get off a shot. But the bullet had not even slowed the bear down. All that remained of the big brute was the chain that had snapped at its thick leather collar.

"What are you waiting for?" Giddis shouted at two miners standing nearby, gawking wide-eyed. "Get the poor bastard out of there!" To his own men he shouted, "Find that lunatic mad gunman and kill him!"

"What about your money?" asked Sly Palmer, the vicious cuts on his face still healing, red and puffy.

"Forget about the money!" shouted Giddis. "I want him dead! Look what he did to the Jailer!"

His men turned to follow him out the door, but

before Giddis reached it, his bartender ran in from the saloon and said, "Giddis! Hurry! The store is on fire!"

"Which store, you fool?" Giddis bellowed, his cigar flying from his lips.

"The mercantile!" said the bartender. He looked wildly around at the others and said, "You better grab buckets and come quick! It's blazing high!"

"Damn it! What next?" Giddis shouted, stomping from the log jail toward the main street, only one suspender looped up over his shoulder.

"Uh-oh," said Sly Palmer.

Giddis and his men all stopped abruptly as they turned onto the main street and saw the dark silhouette facing them, thirty yards away. All of the men but Palmer and Willie stepped back around the corner, out of sight. Behind the figure flames licked high from the doors and windows of the Black & Landry Mercantile Store. "Is that Mad Gunman?" Palmer asked. His hand slipped down and cupped the butt of his holstered Colt.

"Damn right it is," said Black, his voice turning low and menacing. "The fool has come seeking mortal retribution."

"Have we got any?" Willie asked in earnest, his mouth agape.

Without taking his eyes off the silhouette, Giddis said, "Oh yes, Willie, indeed we do." He shoved Willie back to the others, who stood out of sight drawing guns and preparing themselves for a fight. Then Giddis reached his left hand over, pushed Sly Palmer's hand off his gun butt, and lifted the Colt. "Let me borrow this for a couple of minutes," he said. Switching the gun to his right hand, he took a step forward.

"But, boss—" Palmer tried to protest.

"Hush now," said Giddis, "I'll bring you back the mad gunman's ears." He called out to the lone figure, "You should never have stopped, you imbecile! Now I'll have to kill you myself, instead of feeding you to the bear!"

"Giddis, damn it, please!" said Palmer.

"Shut up, go get yourself a rifle!" said Giddis. He stepped sideways and forward, putting himself in the middle of the street. "All right, Mad Gunman, let's get right to it. Show me what you've got!"

"It's *not loaded*, Giddis!" Palmer said, trying to keep his voice down.

Palmer's words caused Giddis's expression to turn flat and grim. He stopped as if frozen in place. "Who in hell carries an unloaded gun?" he said, standing with the Colt cocked and half raised, ready for a fight. He felt his hand go weak and let the worthless pistol slump to his side.

"I was fixin' to load it," Palmer whispered.

"Thank God I'm still out of range," Giddis said, taking a cautious step backward. But no sooner had he said it than he saw the mad gunman reach behind his back. "Merciful God!" Giddis whispered as a rifle swung up from behind the mad gunman's back and rested against his shoulder. Giddis let out an exasperated breath and said with finality, "There goes that."

Palmer winched and leaped sidelong to the ground as the single rifle shot hit Giddis squarely in the chest and knocked him backward ten feet. He hit the dirt, past the corner of the building where the men stood staring, stunned for the moment.

"Get him, boys! Kill him!" shouted Palmer, crawling quickly to Giddis's side. Giddis's hand trembled and clawed aimlessly at the air above him. "Hang on, boss. I'll get the doc!" Palmer cried out, seeing the bloody gaping hole in Giddis's chest.

"Wait!" Giddis moaned, gripping Palmer's sleeve.

"What is it? What can I do for you?" Palmer asked, leaning in close enough to hear him. The men ran past them, firing and shouting toward the spot where the mad gunman had stood.

"Load . . . the gun," Giddis said with much effort.

Palmer picked the gun up from the dirt and started to do as Giddis asked. But he stopped upon opening the cylinder and gave his boss a strange look, saying, "Oh no. It *was* loaded after all. See?" He held the gun butt toward Giddis's face.

Giddis's trembling hand reached up, clicked the cylinder shut, and closed tightly around the gun butt.

Up the middle of the street the rest of the men had stopped and looked all around, realizing the mad gunman was gone. But they turned quickly at the sound of the pistol shot, in time to see Palmer fly backward and hit the ground. "Giddis shot Palmer," Willie said, as if in awe. The men watched Palmer's pistol fall from Giddis's hand, followed by his hand falling limply to the ground.

A bucket brigade of townsmen, miners, and whores had formed and started passing buckets of all size and shape from one pair of hands to another, dousing the flames but still having little effect on the raging inferno. Giddis's men had turned and run back to where Palmer lay dead, the front top of his forehead missing. In the dirt beside him, a few feet away lay Giddis, his breathing labored and faint.

"He's alive!" said a hardcase named Brady Fogle. "Get him up and over to Doc's!"

As the men raised Giddis between them, Willie Goode's eyes widened as he looked out through the flame-lit darkness. "Oh no, look who's coming here!" As he spoke he raised a trembling Colt from his holster and cocked it clumsily.

"What the—" said Fogle, dropping one of Giddis's legs and drawing his big Dance Brother's revolver. "This sumbitch is loco!" He and Willie aimed at the big lanky underfed bear as it came charging out of the darkness, bawling savagely. The men carrying Giddis ran toward the doctor's office, Giddis's left foot dragging the ground.

Shot after shot roared from their pistols, kicking up dirt at the bear's running paws and whistling past his big head. Finally, just before Willie and Fogle broke into a retreat, the big monster swung around in a wide circle and disappeared back into the darkness. "Whoa!" said Fogle, his Dance Brother's still up, smoking in his hand. He walked forward with caution. "I don't enjoy this sort of adventure. That bear has been captive so long, he keeps coming back. Must think this is home!"

"I don't like this either," said Willie Goode, walking along beside him, his pistol also smoking. "Think we hit him?"

Looking down at a blood trail leading all the way back in the direction the bear came from, he said, "I don't know if we hit him, or Corbin's shot hit earlier. But he's wounded, and madder than hell over it, I'm guessing."

"Let's go," said Willie, "before he comes back and eats us like he did Tucker."

Fogle backed away with him, giving him a side-long glance and a dark chuckle. "Hell, Willie, I thought you was the one wanting to *fight* that bear. I was going to wager a dollar or two on you."

"That was Giddis's idea, not mine," said Willie, his thick fingers restless around the gun butt. "Seeing what happened to the Jailer, I'm thinking it wasn't such a good idea. I could get et, like Tucker."

"Don't think about getting yourself et by a bear," Fogle said. He looked up the street past the burning mercantile store. "Think about getting yourself out of the way when Hyde Landry finds out you've let the mad gunman burn his store down." He saw the dark shapes of two horses cross the street and drift away into the deeper darkness, one of them carrying two riders. But he kept silent.

"I never *let* a damn thing," said Willie, also looking up toward the raging flames, but not in time to see Shaw, Dawson, and the young woman ride away.

*   *   *

Stopping, looking back at the flames, Shaw let out a breath and carved another large bite off the cured ham he'd lifted from a wall peg in the mercantile store. In his lap lay small bags of dried apples, dried peaches, a can of peas, a can of beans, and a handful of horehound candy sticks. "I wish I'd burned the whole damn town," he said, chewing hungrily. He wore a new shirt, a new pair of trousers, new boots, and a tall Montana-crowned hat. Around his waist he wore a new tied-down holster with a new Colt standing in it. He'd doused himself with a bottle of lilac water until he could bathe somewhere in a creek along the trail.

"It was time to go," said Dawson, hoping he wouldn't change his mind and go charging back for more revenge.

"Yeah, I know," said Shaw. Looking over at Villy, seeing her eyes riveted on the sticks of candy, he smiled. "Here, for you, my angel of mercy." He handed her a stick of candy, then took another bite of ham. Nodding in satisfaction at the high-rolling flames while Villy gratefully stuck the piece of candy in her mouth, he turned the horse and headed for the trail.

In the doctor's treatment room, Giddis Senior lay stretched out on a surgery table. Blood from his naked back ran to a narrow gutter that ran the length of the table and dripped out a drain hole into a bucket on the floor. "At least the bullet went clean through him," said Dr. Irvin Russel, the town physician. Beside the table stood a bright oil lantern on a wide tray lined with surgical tools. To the side stood a half dozen of Giddis's gunmen and thugs.

"Is he going to live, Doc?" asked a man named Carl "Big-nose" Burnett.

"Don't ask me," the doctor snapped in reply. "All I do is spend days and nights doing all the handiwork. God's the one decides whether or not it'll keep a man living." He gave the man a sharp stare before turning back to Giddis.

For the past hour the doctor had carefully cleaned and inspected the gaping wound. Wiping his hands on a thin towel he leaned down to Giddis and asked close to his ear, "Where's Junior?"

He watched Giddis's eyes as he listened closely for a reply. But Giddis only rolled his eyes and moaned. The doctor had not yet dressed the wound, but rather left it open front and back, allowing it to drain itself of impurities and clothing fragments before he began closing it. He waited for a moment, then asked Giddis again, a little louder this time, still watching his eyes, "I said, where's your boy, Junior?"

"He sent Junior and some others riding out, looking for the man who busted everybody up a while back," said Fogle, standing bedside with Willie and the others.

"I didn't ask you, I asked him," the doctor said sharply. "I'm trying to see what shape his mind's in."

"His mind ain't where he got shot," Willie said in a thick voice.

"What's the use?" the doctor murmured under his
breath and shook his head. "Why would they go
looking for the man that did something like that to
them? Haven't they had enough?"

Fogle gave the doctor a flat stare and said, "Why
don't you tend to the healing, sawbones? We'll decide who's had *enough*, and who ain't."

"Right you are," said the doctor, turning away and
walking to a glass-front medicine cabinet.

When he turned back to Giddis with a small medicine vial and a hypodermic needle in hand, Willie
looked at it and swooned in place. "I can't watch
this," he said. He turned to leave the room, but at
the doorway a strong gloved hand shoved him back.
"Stay put, *idiot*," a gunman named Clifford Ritchie
demanded.

Stepping into the room behind Ritchie, Hyde
Landry stopped and looked down at Giddis with an
icy appraising gaze, then said to the doctor, "Don't
dope him down just yet, Doc. I want to know what
happened to *my* mercantile store."

The doctor stood back as Landry bent down close
to Giddis and said, "Was this the mad gunman, the
one I warned you to get rid of? The one you *had* to
keep alive, for the sole purpose of torturing him?"

"My—my money . . ." Giddis rasped in pain.

"Your ten thousand dollars that you *lost* to the
man in an honest card game?" Without waiting for
a reply, Landry turned to the men standing against
the wall, all of them looking worried and ashamed.

"And you bunch of bummers. When were you going to send somebody over to tell me about this?"

"We—we knew you'd get upset," Willie ventured.

"Upset?" Landry gave a short dark laugh. "You haven't seen upset." He looked at the rest of the men, and said in a low menacing tone, "Every one of you, get a horse and get ready to ride. Bring some lanterns and torches. We're going after this mad gunman. Only we're not going to act like fools and threaten to feed him to a bear. We're going to kill him where he stands."

"Not trying to be out of line, Mr. Landry," said Fogle, taking a step forward with a hand raised. "We was just talking, about how this man claimed to be Fast Larry Shaw when he was first jailed? Well, we've thought about it, and from the looks of things we think he just *might* be."

"Just *might* be, huh?" said Landry. He and Clifford Ritchie gave one another a short smug grin. "Notice that while he was bear meat, he was nothing but a bummer, a madman. Now that he's shot Giddis and burned down my store, he *might* be Fast Larry Shaw."

"I know for a fact that Fast Larry Shaw is dead," said Clifford. "My cousin saw his body in Crabtown a while back. He had a fly walking on his ear." He looked from face to face and added, "Besides, I almost wish it was Fast Larry. I'd enjoy shooting him full of holes."

"Fastest gun alive?" said Landry. "Let me tell all

of you something from the get-go. That fastest-gun-
alive talk has never been nothing but some more
overblown Texas bullshit. Everything that comes out
of Texas is bigger, bolder, *faster!*"

"Begging your pardon, Mr. Landry," said Fogle in
a meek tone, "but there are some fast guns out of
Texas. That much ain't no bullshit. I've known
some."

Landry stepped over close, put his arm over
Fogle's shoulder, and drew his head in close, more
like a headlock than a gesture of comradery. "Listen
to me, Fogle," he said. "You go get your horse, and
do like I tell you. I promise you when we drag his
dead ass back here, I'll hang him upside down from
the livery post, let you shoot his pecker off. How's
that?" He squeezed the crook of his arm harder
around Fogle's neck until Fogle said, "Yes, sir, I'm
with you all the way!"

"Good," said Landry, turning him loose with a dis-
missive shove. "Now everybody get moving. Whoever this mad gunman is, he's going to hell, soon as
we catch up to him."

Chapter 22

Shaw, Dawson, and the young woman rode most of the night on high dangerous trails in only the light of a quarter moon. They stopped every hour or so to rest the horses and listen for sounds of riders on their trail. Hearing none by the time they'd reached a turn-off toward Dawson's claim, they stopped and sat, the two horses' reins in hand, in the darkness beneath a cliff overhang. Shaw ate dried peaches and washed them down with water from Dawson's canteen.

"Wish I'd thought and gone to the saloon before we left," he said to the dark silhouettes sitting near him. "A bottle of rye would taste awfully good about now."

"I'll settle for the water," Dawson said, reaching out for the canteen, having to touch Shaw's arm to let him know he was there.

Shaw put the canteen in his hand, and before taking a drink Dawson passed it along to Villy, touching it to her forearm to guide her to it. She took the canteen, sipped from it, and passed it back. Dawson sipped, then passed it back to Shaw. "Water's probably best for now," said Shaw, swishing it around. "Just because we haven't heard them doesn't mean they're not on our trail."

"Somebody might be," said Dawson, "but it won't be Giddis Black."

"No," said Shaw. "I'm pretty sure I killed him, in spite of the darkness and the flames making it hard to aim. I saw him go down. If he didn't die right then, I'm betting he's dead by now."

"Who does that leave in charge? Junior?" Dawson asked.

"Probably Palmer," said Shaw, having no idea Giddis had killed Palmer in the street. "Giddis doesn't trust Junior very far, I learned from listening and keeping quiet."

"Mr. Landry is who'll be in charge," Villy offered in a shy tone.

"Yeah, if he's in town," said Shaw, eating another dried peach. To Dawson he said, "Hyde Landry is Black's partner, in case you don't already know."

"I've heard of him," said Dawson. "Clarity and Cap say he's the one in charge behind the scene."

"He's in town," Villy offered quietly. "I saw him going into his room at the Best Chance with two of the girls. Giddis kept me hidden from him, afraid he'd want me. If he had, Giddis would have had to turn me over to him." She sighed. "Then Giddis wouldn't get to be the first to *you-know-what* me."

The two Texas gunmen sat in an awkward silence

for a moment. Finally, Shaw said, "Well, that's all behind you now. When things settle down, we'll find a coach stop or relay station and get you out of here so far, they'll never know where to look."

"Do you have a family anywhere?" Dawson asked.

"An aunt in Louisville, I heard my mother mention from time to time before she died of the pox," the young girl said. "If I can get there, I'll find her."

"Louisville . . ." said Shaw, contemplating. "That's a peaceful, pretty place. As soon as we get you some transportation, I'll hand this money over to you."

Villy sat quiet, making no reply.

After another silence, Shaw said to Dawson, "Clarity Jones." He shook his head in the darkness. "I can't imagine you ever hooking up with her."

"Cap and I found her along the trail," said Dawson. "Willie and Palmer had killed Violet, and—"

His words were cut short by a gasp from Villy. "Oh no! Violet is dead?" she said, already sounding tearful.

"I'm sorry, Villy," Dawson said, regretting having mentioned it in front of her. "Yes, Violet is dead," he continued in a more considerate tone. "But Clarity is alive and well. You'll be seeing her when we get to my claim."

"Her and Violet were good to me when Giddis bought me and had me sent here," she continued tearfully. "They were going to be my friends, like big sisters. They were going to *teach me* the business."

Shaw sighed. "Well, luckily you won't need to learn the business now."

"I know," said Villy, "but if I was going to have to learn it, it would be best to learn from friends like them, wouldn't it, in case I ever had to?"

Shaw fell silent. Dawson smiled to himself, knowing the girl had a way of thinking like Clarity, or Violet, or any dove in the business.

Finally Shaw changed the subject, saying to Dawson, "If it hadn't been for Villy here, I would have died in that stinking cell. She kept me from starving to death."

"It was Clarity who told me about you being there," said Dawson. "She admitted that she and Violet were the ones who set you up, doped you, so Giddis could take you prisoner."

"I would have killed them both had I gotten my hands on them," Shaw said. "Now I find out that Violet is dead." He shook his head again in the darkness. "And you and Clarity are living together. It's a strange world we live in, pard."

"Yes, strange," said Dawson, not yet ready to tell him about the widow Mercer. "But I suppose some strangeness can be expected when you go around making folks think you're dead."

"That might have been a mistake," said Shaw. "Talk about strange. I didn't realize how much I depended on being who I am until after everybody started thinking I was dead. I wanted to slip away and be like everybody else. Now I realize that being like everybody is all right unless you're not used to it." He chuckled and took a bite of ham.

"You should have seen the crowd that turned out to see the body of Fast Larry Shaw," Dawson said.

"A large turnout, huh?" Shaw asked.

But before Dawson could answer, Villy said, "Wait!" hearing him mention the name Fast Larry Shaw. "You mean, you *are* Fast Larry Shaw, like you tried telling me? Like you tried telling everybody?"

"Can you keep it a secret?" Shaw asked her.

"Keep it a secret?" she asked. "You've tried your best to make me believe you're Shaw."

Sounding a little embarrassed, Shaw said, "Yes, but that was when I thought it might save my life, not that it helped any. Now that Black's Cut is behind me, I want to go back to being dead."

"All right," said Villy, not sounding sure she understood his reasoning. "I'll keep your secret. To me you'll always be the mad gunman anyway."

"To me too," Dawson said wryly, "after all this."

"Don't start on me, Dawson," Shaw said with a dark chuckle. "You don't know what it's like to wake up every morning on a cold floor, smelling bear piss, thinking any day you're going to get fed to that bear and end up in a pile of its droppings."

"What's that?" Villy cut in, her dark silhouette pointing out toward a half dozen flickering lights along a winding distant trail.

"That's them," said Dawson, standing and dusting the seat of his trousers with one hand, his other holding his horse's reins. "It's good that we saw them from here."

"Yep," said Shaw, "and now it's time to go." He stared out at the lights and said, "We've got two things to wonder about. How smart are they at tracking, and how much water can we follow and cross between here and your place?"

"They're not too smart at tracking," said Dawson, "or they wouldn't be showing us their lights."

"Yep, good point," said Shaw. "Now, what about the water?"

"There's lots of runoff slews, two creeks if we want to use them, and lots of hard rock shelf if we want to come out of the water and leave no tracks."

"This is my kind of country, pard," said Shaw. "Lead the way."

Dawson stepped into his saddle and lifted Villy up easily behind him. In minutes the two horses had slipped away like ghosts into the dark night.

A thousand yards away, Giddis Junior heard a sound that caused him to stand in his stirrups and look all around. "What was that?" he said in a harsh whisper. Gathered around him on their horses sat DeLaurie, Newhouse, Billy Buffet, and Roy Erby. They all rose in their stirrups as well.

"Whoa, look at this!" said Buffet, calling their attention to the flickering lights as Landry and his men winded into sight on the trail below them.

"That's got to be them," Junior said in a harsh whisper, snatching his rifle from his saddle boot.

"Easy, Junior," said Erby, also in a lowered tone. "If it's them, how'd they get behind us?"

"Yeah, and *why* did they get behind us?" said Buffet.

"I don't know, damn it, but that's them!" Junior jerked his horse around angrily and said, "All of you follow me, we're riding down before they pass us."

"Wait, Junior!" Buffet pleaded, struggling to keep his voice lowered. But it did no good. Junior and DeLaurie had already hurried off the trail onto the steep sloping hillside.

"They've killed themselves," Buffet said to Newhouse and Erby. The three hurried their horses forward fifty yards, following the trail down to a cutback. At the cutback they turned and rode along the lower trail.

At the head of the riders on the lower trail, Landry and Ritchie were the first to hear the sound of horses' hooves moving down toward them from a steep hillside covered with dried brush and loose rock. Ritchie started to draw his Colt, but seeing him in the glow of torch and lantern light, Landry said in a lowered voice, "Hold it, Clifford. The only person stupid enough to be riding up there in the dark is Junior."

Ritchie looked back at the line of torches and lanterns lighting the trail, and said, "Everybody kill your light and sit still."

Sitting in silence moments later along the darkened trail, Landry and his men heard a loud yell, and the wild nickering and whinnying of horses. "Here they come," Landry said sidelong to Ritchie.

Down the hillside came the thrashing, rumbling sound of man and animal breaking through brush, and tumbling and sliding through loose rock. "Damn!" said Ritchie, staring in the darkness as Giddis Junior and DeLaurie came spilling, horses and all, onto the trail in front of them.

"Hold your fire!" Landry called out, for both the men behind him and the men riding toward them from the cutback. "Junior, it's me, Landry!"

On the trail in front of him, Landry heard the horses' hooves checked down to a walk. Buffet called out, "Landry, it's me, Billy Buffet! What are you doing out here?"

"Light the lanterns," Landry said to Ritchie. Then to Buffet he called out, "Come help us scrape Junior off the trail."

Landry's riders relit their lanterns and torchlights, revealing Junior and DeLaurie sprawled on the trail, their horses struggling onto all fours and shaking themselves. Stepping down from their saddles, Ritchie and Landry walked forward and stared down at Giddis Junior without offering him a hand. "How did you know it was me?" Junior asked, spitting dirt and wiping a hand across his lip.

"Just a lucky guess," Landry said flatly. Beside him, Ritchie stifled a laugh. Six feet away DeLaurie moaned and struggled to his feet, his eyes and nose still purple from his encounter with Cray Dawson.

Junior rose to his feet, slapping bits of brush and dust from himself. "What are you doing out here, Landry?" he asked. As he spoke, Buffet and the three other men came into the light, their horses at a walk.

"The mad gunman escaped from the jail and shot your pa, Junior," Landry said bluntly.

"Pa, *shot!*" Junior looked stunned. "Is he *alive?*"

"He's alive," said Landry, "but who can say for how long? The doctor didn't sound too hopeful to me. If you want to ride back and check on him, that'll be all right by me."

To Landry's disappointment, Junior said, "No, so long as I know he's alive. It's best I stay out here with you and hunt down the mad gunman."

"I knew that's what you'd say," said Landry, without revealing his disappointment. "Gather your men and all of you ride back there," he said, jerking his head toward the rear.

Junior looked back, not liking the idea of riding behind Landry, or anybody else. Taking on a stronger tone he looked Landry up and down and said, "If my pa dies, do you realize where that puts me?"

Landry knew the answer Junior wanted to hear, but he wasn't about to give it to him. Instead he gave a flat grin and said, "As far as I'm concerned, it puts you at the bottom of a big hill you just fell down from."

Chapter 23

———

Shortly after sunup, Dawson, with Villy's arms around his waist, led Shaw to the shack where Cap stood over at the entrance to the mine, the lead ropes to the pack mule in hand. Seeing the three approach him, he laid the lead ropes down on the box sled, took out his briar pipe, and loaded it. By the time the two horses had drawn nearer, he stood puffing smoke and blowing it onto a passing breeze.

"I'm glad to see you made a safe return," he called out to Dawson. Looking at Villy and recognizing her, then at Shaw, and recognizing him as the mad gunman, he said, "And my lands, look at you two." He smiled and said, "If we keep bringing everybody here from Black's Cut, we'll soon have no need to ever go to town."

"Morning, Cap," said Dawson, touching his hat brim. He looked all around the front of the shack and the lean-to and asked the old seaman, "Where's Clarity?"

"Gone," said Cap. He pointed toward the lean-to. "Took my good riding sorrel and slipped away in the night . . . me right there sleeping by the fire. Didn't hear a sound out of her." As he told them, his hand idly went to his throat and rubbed the loose skin there. "I don't know what to make of that woman."

Dawson looked concerned. "Which direction did she go in?" he asked, already getting a bad feeling about it.

"The sorrel's tracks led off that way." He pointed his pipe stem in a southerly direction.

"The trail to Crabtown," Dawson murmured aloud to himself.

"Yep," said Cap, hearing him. "Earlier that day she'd asked me how far it was to Crabtown. I asked her why she wanted to know. She said she might be going there to pay a woman a visit."

"I've got to go," said Dawson, all of a sudden knowing that Madeline Mercer was in danger.

"Go?" said Cap. "You just got here."

"I know." He turned to Shaw, and said, "I wasn't going to tell you about the widow Mercer until later on. But I'm afraid Clarity is headed that way to kill her."

"Madeline?" Shaw looked surprised. "What does Clarity Jones know about Madeline Mercer?"

Dawson took a deep breath. "I told her how much I care for Madeline Mercer, that's what she knows." He gave a firm nod. "There, I said it."

"You sure did," said Shaw, with a bewildered

shrug, still looking surprised. "But how do you even know Madeline?"

"When I left Crabtown, Caldwell asked me to check on her, make sure she was all right, after coming to see your body, then going back to her big empty house alone."

"His body?" Cap asked, also puzzled. "Who is this fellow?"

"This is Fast Larry Shaw, Cap," said Dawson.

"No, I'm *not*," Shaw cut in quickly.

"No, he's not," Dawson said, correcting himself, Villy saying the same words in unison with him.

"Fast Larry Shaw is dead," Villy completed for them both.

"Right," said Dawson, "but this man claimed to be Shaw when Giddis held him prisoner, so I—" He stopped short, not wanting to lie anymore. "Look, who this is doesn't matter. It's a long story. Right now I've got to get on the trail and get to Crabtown."

"I'm riding with you," Shaw said.

"Good," said Dawson. "I'll tell you everything while we ride."

"I can't wait to hear it," Shaw said, giving him a critical look. He said to Villy before she could step down from behind Dawson, "You're going with us. We'll still get you to some transportation and get you out of here."

Dawson said to Arden, "What about you, Cap? You can't stay here. Giddis Junior hasn't forgotten you held a gun on him."

"Aye, you're right." Arden considered it for a moment, then said, "But I like it up here, and if it's all the same with you, I think I'll just stay put. I've found some color last evening. I've got a good feeling about this mine."

"But it's in my name," said Dawson.

"That doesn't matter to me," said Arden. "If I strike it rich, I'll come look you up. You can give me a finder's fee."

"How about fifty-fifty?" said Dawson, reaching a gloved hand down to him.

"More than generous," said Arden, reaching up and shaking hands on the agreement.

"You keep a real careful eye on these trails. Make sure you disappear for a while if you see any of Black's men."

"Don't fear for me, mate," said Arden, stepping back as they started to turn their horses to the trail. "I've weathered bigger storms than the one Giddis Black can blow my way."

Clarity freshened up in the back room, with a pan of water and a washcloth, and put on her new riding trousers and riding coat with a fur-lined collar. She left her dress, wool lady's coat, and undergarments lying over a chair back and walked out to the counter of the trading post. She looked dispassionately at the body of the trading post owner lying sprawled backward across the counter, his trousers down around his ankles.

"You're a jackrabbit, you are," she said to the body in a soft tone, watching blood drip thickly from both sides of his sliced throat. His dead eyes stared at the ceiling as if in terror that any second that ceiling would fall. She reached out and flipped open the saddlebags she'd carried in from the mule. Reaching inside, she pulled out the big Remington with both hands, checked it, and carried it to the open window. "All right," she murmured quietly to herself, "let's get an idea how to best do this."

She rested the gun butt on the window ledge, then bent down and sighted along the barrel toward the owner's brother, who stood in a corral thirty yards away, hurriedly preparing a horse for the trail for her. With difficulty she cocked the hammer back and squinted down the sights, lining the front sight up between the V at the rear of the barrel. She centered the sight on his back and held her hands steady for a moment.

"No, this won't do," she told herself, relaxing as she let out a tightly held breath. In the corral, the owner's brother looked toward the building every few seconds, anxious for his turn; but Clarity realized that with the glare of sunlight he couldn't see in— she hadn't been able to when she looked the place over on her way in off the trail.

She held the Remington up higher, steadying it against the side of the window frame, still cocked, and sighted it again. After a moment she said, "Blast it all," lowered the gun, and looked at it in her hands. Well, she reminded herself, she had to get prepared to do something. He would be here any minute. She turned a studious look back over her shoulder at the counter.

In the corral, Ben Stoval, the owner's brother, finished with the horse and gave a tug on its reins, leading it toward the hitch rail out in front of the building. He knew he should have looked the sorrel mule over a little closer, but damn, he could do that anytime, he told himself. His turn was coming, he thought, grinning, pushing his dry ragged hair to the side.

He spun the horse's reins at the hitch rail and paced back and forth, his hands shoved deep in his trouser pockets. After a few paces, he called out toward the open door, "Abraham, the horse is ready."

Getting no reply, he continued pacing and scratching his lowered head, then stopped and called out again, "Abe? I say, brother Abe. This horse is ready and waiting. Can I come on in . . . take my turn? I don't want to be overlooked in this trade."

From inside, Clarity called out, "Get on in here, mister. I'm not forgetting you."

"Hot damn," said Ben. "Here I come!" He'd hopped three wooden steps onto the edge of a plank porch when the blast of a shotgun lifted him and hurled him backward ten feet into the dust.

"Yes, this will do nicely," Clarity said aloud to herself as she stepped out with the smoking shotgun in her hand and looked down at Ben Stoval. Most of his chest and face were missing. She reached her left hand up and rubbed her right shoulder where she felt the kick of the shotgun. "A bit powerful," she said, "but it does get the job done." She studied the effect of the shotgun blast while the horse at the hitch rail shied sidelong and muttered in fear.

"Here now," she said, stepping over and rubbing the horse's muzzle, "let's have none of that. I wouldn't hurt you, you dear creature." She looked back at the body on the ground and considered something for a moment. Then she walked inside and came back out carrying the chair she had thrown her clothes over.

She measured her steps from where she had stood inside the front window, across the wide front porch to where the body lay on the ground, coming up with a distance of nine paces. She'd have to keep that figure in mind, she thought.

Setting the chair in the dirt, she stooped down and took Ben Stoval under the arms and lifted up with all her might. With much struggling she finally managed to wrestle the limp body up onto the straight-backed chair and lean it in a way that it held itself in place. "All right," she said aloud, dusting her hands and catching her breath, "now down to work." Looking all around, she decided with satisfaction that she would never have a better chance than this.

Inside the trading post she laid the shotgun on the counter and took a Winchester repeating rifle from a wall display. It was a rifle just like the one she'd taken from Holley but left at the mining shack. She loaded it and levered a round into the chamber the way she had seen men do as they prepared their horses for the trail. She walked to the front window and rested it on the sill.

After three shots, the body and chair fell backward. Clarity sighed and walked to the tool rack where she took down a coil of rope and two shovels. Outside she righted the body back onto the chair and tied it tightly in place. Then she propped the two shovels behind the chair and went back to the front window.

An hour, and a box of rifle bullets later, she fanned smoke from around her with a hat she'd taken from a rack, kicked through the strewn brass shells at her feet, and walked to the pan of water in the back room. This time, freshening up meant washing her face and hands, and wiping the wet cloth at dabs of blood her coat had taken on from handling the bloody body.

Wearing the new Stetson hat and carrying the shotgun, the rifle, and plenty of ammunition for both, she rode away from the trading post without looking back until she reached a high point in the trail toward Crabtown. Then she only looked back toward the trading post long enough to call back over her shoulder, "*Swives!*" Then, turning, she rode off in the evening sunlight.

Two hours later, she made a dark camp alongside a nameless creek. She spent the night hidden in a stand of spruce and cedar, sleeping with her back against a tree, the horse's reins in her hands. In the morning, well after dawn, she awakened to the piercing sound of metal against metal and ventured from the woods to see a stage driver and his guard repairing a wheel less than twenty yards away. When the guard saw her lead the horse out of the woods toward them, he quickly nudged the driver to get his attention.

"Well, I'll be stumped, James," the driver said, turning and rising from the coach wheel. He stared along with his guard, seeing Clarity comb her fingers through her hair and place her new Stetson back atop her head. "Is she one of the girls from Black's Best Chance?"

"I don't know, Dillman," said the guard, his shotgun leaning against the side of the big stagecoach. "But she sure looks better than anything I've ever come upon along this run."

"Morning, ma'am," said Vernon Dillman, wiping black axle grease from his hand onto a dirty rag. Seeing the sleepy look still on her face, he added, "I hope we didn't disturb you none?"

Clarity only shook her head. She didn't speak until she stopped and stood ten feet away. The two men heard a trace of her British accent as she said, "Good morning, gentlemen. I hope you can give a poor lost dove some direction."

Dove . . . ? Dillman's hat came quickly off his head; so did James Yarrow's. "My goodness, darling. That's what I *live* to do," Dillman said.

But Yarrow, in spite of his youth and his fondness for women, remained on his job protecting the stage. He looked her up and down, but in doing so checked the woods behind her and took an instinctive sidelong step over to his shotgun. "Ma'am, if you don't mind me asking, where did you get such a fine-looking horse?"

"Easy, James," said Dillman with a nervous laugh. Then to Clarity he said, "Excuse my young friend here. I'm afraid he's been too long in the wind up here. It can make a body—"

"I traded a mule for it to a fellow yesterday," Clarity replied, sensing that he knew something about the animal's origins. "He told me he bought it from a trading post back there somewhere." She pointed a dainty finger back toward the trail.

"There, you see, James?" said Dillman. "The lass took the horse in trade. Now be done with it."

But the guard would have none of it. Instead of being done with it, he asked pointedly, appraising the horse as he spoke, "What did you give to boot for the difference?"

"What do you think?" Clarity said evenly, a slight smile coming to her lips.

"By the stars above," said Dillman, getting excited at their sudden prospects out here in the wilds. "Little lady, can I interest you in a quick—"

"Sorry," said Clarity, "not this morning. But the next time you're in Black's Cut, you can have a turn on the house."

"My, but isn't that so kind of you!" said Dillman. "Now, what kind of directions are you needing this morning?"

Chapter 24

———

Along the trail, Dawson and Shaw talked while Villy slept against Dawson's back. By the time they had reached a point looking down and across a stretch of land toward the trading post, Shaw knew all about Dawson and Madeline Mercer. Shaw had no ill feelings. "The fact is," he'd said, "I don't think the woman cared all that much for me. If she did she never showed it, I mean in any way that—"

"Careful what you say, Shaw," Dawson said evenly, cutting in before Shaw went any further. "I happen to care a lot for the woman."

"I understand," said Shaw, "and that being the case, you ought to know I wouldn't say something against her." He considered his words for a moment, then said, "I suppose it's enough to say that she and I wasn't meant to be."

Dawson nodded, looking at the distant figure sitting alone out in front of the trading post. "As your recent death goes to prove."

"If I'd had any designs on the woman, I'd have told her," said Shaw. "But I saw it wasn't going nowhere, her and me and that mountain of money her husband left her." As he said that, he turned a flat stare to Dawson.

"I never cared about her money," Dawson said. He started to elaborate, but something about the solitary figure sitting in the straight-backed chair facing the trading post gave him pause to change the subject. "Something doesn't look right over there."

"Yeah, you're right," Shaw agreed, seeing the lone figure sitting stone still, hatless in the afternoon sun. Stopping their horses, Shaw looked all around, then looking off into the western sky he said, "Looks like we're not the only one's thinking something is amiss." Two buzzards circled high in the air, still checking the feeding area before circling down to it.

The two rode down to the trading post, keeping an eye on the figure in the chair and the open front door, until they got close enough to tell the difference between dark blood on the ground and afternoon shadows. Awakening behind Dawson, Villy asked, "What's going on?"

"Nothing you're going to want to see," said Dawson. "There's a dead man sitting up ahead on the right, so just look the other way." He nodded at the corpse fifteen yards away as they drew closer.

"All right," said Villy, turning her head away and resting it on Dawson's back. Yet, as soon as both horses stopped, she couldn't resist turning and staring at the mangled corpse.

"Oh God!" she gasped. Dawson felt her scramble wildly down from behind him. She ran a few feet away and began upheaving the thin meal they had eaten at noon.

"I told her not to look," said Dawson. The two swung down from their saddles and stood back looking at all the buckshot and bullet holes in the bloody ragged shirt.

Seeing the two long-handled shovels propped against the chair back, Shaw offered, "Looks like somebody thought they needed target practice."

Looking first at the dark thick blood, then staring up at the sun for a moment, Shaw said, "This was yesterday, most likely this time of evening. It takes buzzards a while."

"Yeah, I know," said Dawson. Looking toward the corral he said, "There's Cap's sorrel mule." Turning, he walked onto the porch and in through the open front door. Seeing the corpse sprawled back across the counter, he deftly drew his Colt and held it poised and ready. "I still have a hard time thinking Clarity can do something like this," he said. Turning, he walked to the window and looked down at the countless number of empty cartridges lying strewn on the floor.

Shaw, also with gun in hand, walked across the floor and looked first at the corpse's slit throat, then into the room where Clarity had washed herself. "I don't," he said firmly. He turned, facing Dawson with Clarity's pantaloons hanging from his gun barrel. "Look familiar?"

"Ummph," said Dawson in a gesture of regret. Holstering his Colt he looked all around. "I suspect she's grown capable of doing just about anything."

With a bemused look, Shaw said, "Let's not forget she set me up to be starved to death or fed to a bear. Guess what weapon she used then." Without waiting for a reply he continued. "She's been *capable* for a long while. All she's been doing is finding herself some better weaponry along the way. Now she knows that a shotgun and a rifle go farther than a straight razor."

"I was a fool to ever let myself . . ." His words trailed.

Shaw only nodded in agreement.

Outside, Villy called out, "There's a stagecoach coming."

Through the window, Dawson saw the driver and guard above a cloud of dust. "Let's get some shovels," he said. "We'll get the driver and his shotgun rider to bury them. We've got no time, if we mean to catch Clarity before she finds out where Madeline Mercer lives."

"Good, I hate burying anyway," Shaw murmured, walking toward the door.

Outside, the two stood facing the coach as it rocked to a halt. Seeing both men standing with four shovels lying at their feet and their gun hands free and ready, the driver called out, "No need in having your bark on, boys, we know you had no hand in this. We saw you riding in from a long ways back."

Shaw and Dawson relaxed a little. Shaw motioned

toward the mangled corpse, with bits of bone and flesh splattered about on the ground. "I expect you two know this man?"

"Sure do," said the driver, standing from his seat and stepping down from the side of the coach. "From what's left of him I believe he's Ben Stoval." The guard watched and waited, shotgun in hand, until the driver stood firmly on the ground. "His brother, Abe Stoval, owns this place," the driver continued, stretching his back as he looked all around.

"There's another man inside," said Shaw, "probably the brother you're talking about."

"I'll be blasted," said the driver. "The Stovals are good men, the both of them."

"Then you and your guard won't mind burying them, before the buzzards swing in," Shaw said, reaching out with his new boot and kicking one of the shovels on the ground.

"What's wrong, you can't help bury them?" asked James, still in his seat atop the coach.

"We're after the woman who killed them," Dawson said. "We're trying to stop her before she kills again."

"A woman?" Dillman looked shocked. "You don't mean the dove who works in Black's Cut!"

"You've seen her?" Dawson asked quickly.

"We sure did," said James, getting more interested, and less suspicious. "She's riding a horse that I just *knew* was ill-gotten." He gave the driver an I-told-you-so look, and said, "Dillman here gave her directions this morning before she rode off."

"Directions to where?" Dawson asked quickly.

"To the Mercer spread, off the trail before Crab-town," said the guard.

"We've got to go," said Dawson.

"Where does this stage go from here?" Shaw asked.

Dillman said, "We swap rigs here with a coach that runs back to Black's Cut and points north. Then we take their mail and cargo back to where we started, southeast all the way to Winston, sometimes as far as Townston."

"Is there a railhead in Winston?" Shaw asked.

"Yep," said Dillman, "trains run in and out as long as the weather allows."

"I want you to take on a passenger," said Shaw. "I'm paying her fare."

"You mean the child—the young lady, that is?" Dillman asked, correcting himself, looking closely at Villy, who sat with a stick of candy in her mouth.

"No, you were right the first time," said Shaw. "She's a *child*." Giving the stage driver a look of warning, he added, "All the way to Winston you keep telling yourself over and over that *she's a child*. Do you understand me?"

"I sure do, mister. I have children of my own," said Dillman.

"Good." Shaw eyed him sternly as he reached into his shirt pocket for stage fare. "Then you can appreciate my concern."

Before the first light of day had spread wide and wreathed the horizon, Clarity stepped down from the horse and tied its reins to a fence post behind the stock barn. She waited, watched, and listened; and when a lamplight grew to brightness in the rear window of the indoor kitchen, she moved forward as silent as a cat, rifle in hand.

Inside, Madeline Mercer carried fresh coffee into the dining room in a china serving pot she'd filled from the metal coffeepot atop the small cookstove. She poured herself a cup of coffee and sat down to the ink, pen, and writing paper she had laid out earlier for herself. This was the morning she would force herself to write a letter to Cary Dawson and leave it with Jedson Caldwell in Crabtown.

My dearest, darling Crayton, she said to herself, rehearsing her words even as she began writing them down. She stopped for a moment and thought further on how to tell him that she had left the ranch, but that she would be longingly awaiting his return to her in her mansion in—

"No, that won't do," she murmured aloud in the large empty room, cutting herself off. She went back with the pen and scribbled through what she had written down. Then she crumpled the sheet of stationery, tossed it aside, and took a fresh sheet and spread it in front of her.

Crayton, my dearest, she wrote. *Pledging to you once again with all of my heart, that nothing will ever come between us, I travel forthwith to my estate in New York where I await your return with*

Stopping only long enough to consider her words for a moment, she sipped her morning coffee and began writing in earnest. By the time she had finished, she had poured and finished another cup. Finally, she sighed, signed the letter across the bottom, sprayed it with a small bottle of perfume, and folded it neatly.

Outside, at the lower corner of the dining room window, Clarity stood atop a wooden crate she carried with her from against the side of the barn, and peeped in carefully. She saw Madeline Mercer folding the letter. She watched her pick up an envelope. But before Madeline slipped the folded letter inside the envelope, both women's attention went toward the sound of a wagon as it creaked and rumbled up to the house.

From the wagon seat, Acting Deputy Madden Peru thought he'd seen something or someone look around the front corner of the house. But upon sitting for a few seconds without seeing any other movement, he dismissed the matter, climbed down, and tied the wagon at the iron hitch rail. Still, his senses were piqued as he walked to the front door and rapped on it with the ornate iron knocker.

Hidden around the corner of the house, Clarity listened as the door opened and Madeline Mercer said, "Good morning, Deputy. I was expecting Jedson Caldwell. Is everything all right?"

"Yes, ma'am," said Peru, taking off his hat. "Sheriff Caldwell is meeting with the territorial judge this morning. He asked me to come escort you to town. I hope that is all right . . . ?"

Clarity wasted no time. While the two were speaking, she hurried around to the back door and slipped inside quietly, her rifle levered, ready to cock and fire. She stood against the kitchen wall for the next few minutes hearing them talk back and forth, while Madeline put on her coat and hat, and walked out to the wagon. Behind her, Peru walked out carrying two large leather travel cases. In the front foyer two more heavy cases still sat waiting on the floor.

Seeing him walk back up toward the house, Clarity hurried past the leather cases and into the parlor room where a large window faced the front yard. At the front gate sat the wagon. Beside the wagon Madeline Mercer stood looking out over her land. This would have to do, Clarity told herself, knowing this would be a much farther shot than she had practiced for.

She stood against the parlor wall until she'd heard Peru come and go from the foyer. Then, seeing him walk along the pathway to the wagon with the large travel cases in hand, she eased the window up and kneeled down, leveling the rifle out across the window ledge.

Do it now! she demanded of herself, knowing that this might be her last chance.

"Oh, one more moment, please, Deputy," said Madeline, seeing Peru place the last large leather case on the wagon bed. "I'm afraid I forgot something."

"Yes, ma'am, no hurry," said Peru. He leaned back against the side of the wagon as she turned and walked along the path to the house.

Even better, Clarity told herself. Madeline was

walking back to her, alone! She quickly searched herself for the folded straight razor, excited by the prospect of keeping this simple and silent after all. But in her excitement as she started to draw the razor from inside her coat, the rifle wobbled unsteadily on the window ledge. As she grabbed it, the barrel went sideways and banged noisily against the side of the window frame.

Seeing a rifle pointed at Madeline, Peru shouted, "Ma'am, get down."

Hearing him caused Clarity to panic. *No time for the razor!*

Madeline had stopped, frozen in place, first at the sound of Peru's words, then at the sight of the rifle barrel pointed at her. Finally, she found the voice to scream, *"Deputy!"*

Hurry! a voice cried out in Clarity's head. Snatching the rifle, she dropped back to one knee at the window ledge, cocked it, and fired. But as she pulled the trigger, she felt the sharp sting of a bullet hit her high in the shoulder, twist her around, and send her backward onto the polished wooden floor. Her rifle flew from her hands. She scrambled to her feet and rushed toward the back door, feeling blood pumping from the wound. The black-handled Remington fell from under her coat, onto the floor behind her.

"Stay *down!*" Peru shouted at Madeline, running past her, shoving her sidelong to the ground before bounding into the house. Inside the front door, his Colt cocked and ready, he saw the blood trail through the house. He saw the Remington. To the left in the parlor, he saw the rifle. He caught a glimpse of the tall Stetson fly from atop Clarity's head as the kitchen door swung open and she raced outside toward the barn.

A woman? he asked himself, seeing her hair coming undone more and more as she ran.

His answer became conclusive when Clarity stopped and steadied herself against the barn wall. He saw her breasts as the leather coat lay open, blood running down the front of it. Keeping his gun on her, he said, "Ma'am! Stay where you are. Keep your hands up."

"I'm shot!" Clarity said, gasping, as if she'd just realized it that second. She spread her hands and staggered in place. "Don't shoot me, please!" she pleaded.

Peru stood with a hand raised toward her. "Stay put," he said again, stepping closer, spreading her coat open more, to see if she might have another gun stuck down in her waist.

"I'm unarmed," she gasped. "I'm all through. Please, just help me."

Stepping to the side, Peru turned and saw Madeline Mercer walking toward them. The discarded Remington looked huge in her delicate hand. "Everything's all right, ma'am," said Peru. "I've got to get her bandaged and get her to town. She's bleeding bad."

Behind him, Clarity's right hand went into her coat

and found the razor. She jerked it out and flipped it open. Peru didn't see it; Madeline did. What Peru saw was Madeline raise the Remington with both hands, cock it, and let out a scream. *"Noooo!"*

Peru felt the razor go across the shoulder of his coat as the gun exploded in Madeline's hands, causing her to step backward and steady herself from the recoil. Turning quickly and looking down, Peru saw the razor fall from Clarity's hand. He turned slowly to face Madeline Mercer. "Ma'am, you just saved my life."

"No, Deputy," said Madeline, "you saved *my* life." Stepping forward, she looked down with him at the dead woman on the ground. Then both turned their eyes to the vicious slice that had gone through his thick coat sleeve and managed to nick his upper arm.

"I think we might have saved one another's life," Peru said, offering some middle ground.

Madeline found herself staring into his eyes, as if now she saw him in a whole new light. "Let's go inside and take a look at this shoulder."

"It's nothing, ma'am," said Peru, but only half-heartedly.

"Don't argue with me, Deputy," Madeline said softly. She reached out and took his hand, the Remington hanging loosely at her side. She pulled him along gently yet firmly. "And please call me Madeline."

Inside the house, Peru sat at a table in the kitchen, shirtless, while Madeline cleaned and dressed the cut across his upper arm. Tying strips of cloth around the bandage to hold it in place, she said finally, "There, all done. Good as new."

Standing, putting on one of her late husband's clean white shirts, Peru said, "I expect this is a lucky day for both of us, Miss Madeline."

"Yes, I feel the same," she said, studying his eyes in the sunlight through the kitchen window.

Peru left the house to wrap Clarity's body in a blanket in order to take her to town. Madeline picked up the envelope lying on the dining room table, wadded it up, and shoved it down in her coat pocket.

Chapter 25

Knowing the sorrel mule would slow them down, Dawson and Shaw turned the animal loose. They did not wait for the stage driver and his guard to finish burying the Stovals. But by the time they had reached the place where the trail rounded out of sight of the trading post, they looked back and saw the two climbing up onto the stage seat. Villy stood on the step with the stage door open, waving like any child would do.

"Yes, Villy, good-bye," Shaw said, as if the girl could hear him from such a distance. "Now *please* get inside the damn stage before they take off." He shook his head and said to Dawson, "I love that kid for what she done. But I worry about her. I don't think it would take five minutes for somebody like Violet or Clarity to bring her right back to becoming a dove."

"I hate to say it," Dawson replied, "but everything about her says 'dove in the making.' " Turning their horses back to the trail, he asked, "How old is she anyway?"

"She said she *thinks* she'll be sixteen this fall," Shaw replied. "Lot of orphanages don't keep real good records. Some like to push the age up a year or two if they think it will help get somebody to take the girl in."

"Yeah, somebody like Giddis Black," said Dawson, gigging his horse up into a faster gait. "Maybe with the money you gave her she can build herself a life somewhere, never have to think about being a dove again."

"I'd like to think so," Shaw said. "That's all I can do."

They rode on, pushing the horses hard, only stopping for short rests and to water the animals from converging streams as they crossed narrow stretches of deep-lying canyons and flatlands. During the late afternoon, they stopped at the crest of a low rise, seeing the Mercer house in the near distance. "I'll stay back and keep her from seeing me," said Shaw. "If it's okay for me to ride in, give me a wave." Looking at the quickly falling sun, he added, "If it's dark, wave a torch. I'll do the same if Landry and any of Black's men come riding down on us."

"She wouldn't even recognize you unless you stood a foot away," said Dawson, noting the thick dark beard hiding his face, the shaggy hair hanging beneath his hat brim.

"All the same, I'll stay back here," said Shaw. He

lifted a boot and crossed his leg over his lap, letting Dawson know he'd made up his mind.

"I'm beginning to think Madeline had a lot to do with you faking your death," said Dawson, already turning his horse toward the Mercer house.

"Think what you will." Shaw reached back and pulled the remains of the ham from his saddlebags.

"I can't believe I came up here looking for peace and quiet," Dawson murmured under his breath.

A thin purple darkness had set in by the time he reached the hitch rail, stepped down, and spun his reins. A lamp should already have been lit, he reminded himself, noting the darkened windows. He looked down at the wagon tracks in the dirt, then walked the path to the front door and rapped soundly on it with the iron door knocker.

After two more tries with no response, he turned the door handle and found it locked. Walking around to the parlor window and finding it locked as well, he peered in with the last wispy trace of daylight over his shoulder and saw enough to tell him something had gone on inside. A smear of blood and an overturned corner of a rug was all he needed to see. He drew his Colt, cracked the glass with its barrel, and reached in and unlocked the window.

"Madeline? It's me, Cray Dawson," he called out into the large silent house, not wanting to get himself shot as he stepped forward, seeing the next splotch of blood. "Are you here?" He stepped over into the adjoining foyer. "Can you hear me?" With his Colt drawn and ready to cock, he followed his gun barrel and the blood trail into the hallway and toward the back door.

Moments later, seeing the torchlight wave back and forth, Shaw perked up in his saddle, put the ham away, and rode down to the house. Stopping at the hitch rail he found Dawson standing with the quickly made torch in his hand and a worried look on his face. "What did you find out here?" As he asked his eyes searched across the front of the house.

"I don't know," said Dawson, "but Clarity's been here. I found my razor in the dirt back by the barn. There's blood, both inside the house and out." He gestured at the ground in the glow of torchlight. "Somebody left here in a wagon, not long ago from the looks of it . . . today, yesterday at the most."

"Blood, huh?" Shaw looked out along the direction of the wagon tracks. "You looked the house over good?"

"Yes, real good," said Dawson, knowing Shaw was asking if he might have overlooked a body in a closet or under a stairwell. "It's empty."

"The barn?"

"I've looked everywhere," said Dawson. He stared at Shaw with a grim knowing expression.

"Let's not go thinking the worst until we have reason to," said Shaw.

"We've got to follow these tracks," said Dawson, holding the torch.

"I've got a feeling they'll lead us to Crabtown," Shaw said.

"We'll ride all night," said Dawson.

"Kill the torch, though," said Shaw, gazing off along the high trail they had ridden down from an hour earlier.

"We can use it to follow the wagon tracks," Dawson said.

"And they can use it to follow us," Shaw replied coolly, gesturing toward the tiny glittering beads of lantern and torch light winding down the high trail.

"God, I hope she's all right," Dawson said in a half-prayerful tone. He rubbed the torch back and forth on the ground to put it out, then stamped on the smoldering end of it. Looking at the distant lights on the high trail, he said, "Maybe that's not even Landry's and Black's men."

"Maybe it's not," said Shaw, "but let's not count on it."

When they'd first arrived in Crabtown, Madden Peru rolled the wagon up to the hitch rail out in front of the sheriff's office and said to Madeline Mercer before stepping down and dropping the tailgate, "I hope you and me will see one another real soon, Miss Madeline."

"We will. I'll see to it we do," she said. "But only if you promise to start calling me by my first name. I am a widowed woman." She smiled. "Not a miss, or a ma'am. I am Madeline. All right, Madden?" She

lightly touched her fingertips to his forearm, realizing
for the first time the great similarities in their names.
"Madeline and Madden," she said playfully, testing
the sound of the names together. "Or, Madden and
Madeline," she said. "Wouldn't it just be something
if you and I grew close? Our names, I mean."

Peru swallowed, suddenly feeling a bit shy. "Yes, it
would at that," he said. Seeing Caldwell step out of
the office and come toward the wagon, he'd stepped
down and hurried around to the passenger side, in
order to help Madeline down before Caldwell could
walk around and take the opportunity from him. . . .

That had only been yesterday evening, Peru reminded himself. But once he and the young widow
had looked deeply into one another's eyes, last night
over dinner, things had moved along quickly. *Oh
yes* . . . He smiled to himself, rocking backward and
forward on his heels, gazing out across the morning sky.

"What are you so happy about this morning?"
Caldwell asked, walking up beside him without
Peru noticing.

Upon Peru's hearing Caldwell, his smile disappeared as if it might reveal his thoughts. "Nothing,"
he said instinctively. "That is, nothing out of the ordinary," he corrected himself. "I mean, sometimes a
man can just be happy, can't he?" He shrugged. "It's
not that I have anything to not be happy abou—"

"Forget it, Deputy," said Caldwell, cutting him off.
In a guarded tone he said, "I saw you and the widow
Mercer at the restaurant last night, remember?"

Peru stiffened a bit. "Yes, of course I remember, I hadn't lost my senses. We enjoyed one another's company. Is there something wrong with that?"

"No, nothing at all," said Caldwell, not mentioning that he had also watched the two of them slip away from one another out in front of the hotel, only to see Peru return later and look all around before walking inside. "The fact is, I'm glad to see you and the widow both find someone you care for."

"Who says we care for one another?" said Peru. "Can't two people have a nice meal together without it meaning there's something between them?"

"Sorry," said Caldwell, seeing the deputy turn a little bristly. "I didn't mean to imply anything untoward." Not long after seeing Peru enter the hotel, Caldwell had watched the lamp go out in the widow's window overlooking the dirt street. "I only meant that, after all the poor woman has gone through, it's good to see her enjoying herself. All right?" He gave Peru a questioning look.

"Yeah, it's all right." Peru relaxed and even smiled thinly. "Just between you and me, I believe her and me could care a lot for one another, given the chance."

"Well now, that's good to hear," said Caldwell, unaware of what had happened between Madeline and Cray Dawson when he'd sent Dawson by to look in on her. "I strongly believe every man deserves a chance at finding himself a good woman and settling down."

"What do we have here?" Peru asked quietly, not really hearing his last few words.

He and Caldwell both looked off at the two riders coming toward town from the north in a rise of dust. "Someday I hope to find a good woman myself," Caldwell added absently, the riders having drawn his attention from such matters.

His eyes on the riders, Peru asked, "Did you find out who the dead woman is?"

"Oh yes, I did," said Caldwell, also staring intently at the two riders. "Turns out she's a dove from Black's Cut. A couple of miners and a tin-goods peddler all three recognized her."

"Why do you suppose she tried to kill Madeline— I mean, the widow Mercer?" Peru said, catching himself before sounding too familiar with her.

"Who knows?" said Caldwell, shaking his head, but still watching the riders draw nearer. "Some of these doves are crazy to begin with. Then they dope themselves up and make it worse. She might have been running away from Giddis Black, just wanted to rob the widow and move on. You happened by and foiled her plan."

"Well, I'm glad I got there when I did," said Peru, letting out a breath. "I feel like it was all meant to be that way, me and the widow coming together right then."

"Hey, that looks like Dawson," said Caldwell. Without further comment, he stepped down from the boardwalk and stood waiting as Dawson rode up and turned his horse sidelong to him in the street. Looking past Dawson to the edge of town, Caldwell saw the thin rider with the full thick beard stop and pull his horse to the side. *Shaw . . .* he said to himself.

Dawson nodded, as if seeing Caldwell's thoughts. "I just came from the Mercer spread," Dawson said. "I'm afraid something bad has happened out there."

Caldwell held a hand up, stopping him. "You're right, something bad did happen," he said, seeing the worried look on Dawson's face and realizing instantly that there had been something between him and the widow. "Some dove from Black's Cut tried to shoot her. But lucky for her, Deputy Peru was there. He shot the dove before she got the chance."

"Oh? The deputy was there?" Dawson looked at Peru, keeping his suspicion hidden.

"Yes," said Peru. He stepped down beside Caldwell, taking an interest. "What brought you by the Mercer spread?"

Before answering Peru, Dawson saw something in Caldwell's eyes that told him to weigh his words very carefully. So he did. "The dove's name is Clarity Jones," he said. "I followed her to the Mercer spread. She was on the run from Giddis Black's men."

"Oh," said Peru, although Dawson's answer didn't really explain much.

Caldwell cut in, giving Dawson a look that asked him to go along with things. "I said as much, just a moment ago. I said the dove might have run away from Black's Cut. Maybe she meant to rob the widow for getaway money."

"Yeah, that's about the size of it," said Dawson

with a shadow of curiousness crossing his brow. "So . . . the widow is all right, then. That's the main thing." He wanted to get Caldwell alone and ask what was going on. He already had a pretty good idea that it involved Peru and the widow.

"Who's that?" Peru asked, gesturing with a nod toward the edge of town, where Shaw sat slumped in his saddle eating some dried apples from the bag.

"He's the mad gunman, also from Black's Cut. Nobody knows his name. He escaped Giddis Black's jail. He also shot Giddis Black in the street. Might have killed him."

"Broke jail and killed a man, eh?" Peru said.

"Easy, Deputy," Caldwell cautioned him, seeing Peru's gun hand poise at his holster. "Anybody escapes Giddis Black's jail deserves a reward."

Looking at Peru, then at Caldwell, noting the badge on his chest, Dawson asked, "*Sheriff*, can I speak to you inside?" He stepped down from his horse before Caldwell answered.

Caldwell said, "Sure thing." Then to Peru he said calmly, "We'll be right inside."

Peru only nodded, and turned his gaze out toward the mad gunman, who sat atop his horse eating steadily.

Inside the sheriff's office, Dawson asked in a lowered voice, "What's going on? Is there something between the widow and Peru?"

"First, you tell me, is there something between the widow and *you*?" said Caldwell. "I don't want trouble for her. The woman has been through enough."

"Yes, there is something between us, or there *was*, when I left her place to get on to Black's Cut," said Dawson, searching Caldwell's eyes. "Now your turn," he said firmly.

"You mean when I asked you to stop by and look in on her?" Caldwell seemed surprised.

"Yes," said Dawson. "Now what about Peru?"

Caldwell considered the matter for a moment. "Dawson, I'm sorry," he said at length, his expression telling Dawson everything. "She and Peru feel they saved each other's life. If you could only see the way they—"

Dawson turned away, angrily slamming his fist down on the battered oak desk. "Of all the rotten . . ." His words trailed.

"No trouble, Dawson, please," said Caldwell.

Dawson took a deep breath and collected himself. "No trouble. You've got my word." He considered it and said quietly, "One day earlier, it would have been her and me, instead of her and Peru." After a moment, he sighed, accepting his loss. "But then, who would want a woman that he only won by being one day earlier than the next man?"

Caldwell patted his back in condolence. "That's the way to look at it," he said, although he didn't quite understand what Dawson meant. "What's easily won is easily lost, I've always heard."

Dawson gave him a look but let it go. "Does Madeline know he thinks he's the one who killed Shaw?" he asked.

"No, but maybe it will never come up. Since he

pinned on a badge he hasn't said much about killing Shaw."

"That's good," said Dawson.

"Besides, since you left here there's been four other
men who claimed they killed Shaw," he said.

They stopped talking when the door opened and
Madeline Mercer stepped inside. "Oh, Cray, darling,
it is you. I saw you ride in, from my hotel window."
Then it dawned on her what she'd done, and she
knew from the look on his face that he knew as well.
She went forward into his arms, but not in a way
that he would have expected. Her greeting told
him everything.

"Hello, Madeline," Dawson said, holding her in
the same subdued manner in which she had pre-
sented herself to him.

"Where is Peru?" Caldwell asked, stepping over
and looking out the window.

"He's down the street talking to some thin bearded
gentleman," said Madeline, her tearful eyes never
leaving Dawson's. "I slipped in while he's away.
Cray, I—"

"Shhh," said Dawson quietly, stopping her. He
and Caldwell gave one another a look. Caldwell ex-
cused himself and stepped outside. "Madeline," said
Dawson before she could speak again, "I came here
to tell you good-bye. I'm headed off on a long
journey. . . . I didn't want you waiting for me."

As he spoke it dawned on him that this conversation had awaited them at some point in their future,
even if she hadn't taken up with Peru. Dawson knew

he could not have played this hand so cool and pain-lessly, not if he'd loved her as deeply as he'd imagined. This was not him in love with this woman. This was only him *wanting* to be in love with her.

"Oh, I see." Madeline stiffened a bit and stepped back. "Well, it is most civil of you to come tell me. It proves you are the gentleman I knew you to be." She searched his eyes, seeing something there that she could not fathom. "If—if that is why you came here, then I bid you farewell and wish you the very best."

"Thank you, Madeline, for everything," said Dawson, seeing a look of relief in her eyes.

Chapter 26

————

When Madeline left the sheriff's office, Caldwell and Dawson stood in silence until finally Caldwell said, "That was a noble thing for you to do, Dawson. You could have put her in a bad spot, caused her and Peru a lot of misery."

"It came to me while we were talking," Dawson replied quietly. "Had I been as serious about the widow Mercer as I thought I was, I wouldn't have ridden off from her to find a gold mine I'd never seen, that I bought from a man I barely knew."

"Good point," said Caldwell. "So, with that done, I expect you and our friend the mad gunman will be leaving Crabtown?"

"Spoken like a true lawman," Dawson said. "As far as I'm concerned, we're already gone. But to tell you the truth—"

His words stopped short as three rifle shots exploded from the edge of town. "Giddis Black's men?" Caldwell asked, already turning toward the door.

"That would be my *first* guess," said Dawson, right behind him.

Caldwell swung the door open and allowed Dawson to leave first, asking him, "How many?"

"A bunch," said Dawson. He crossed the board-walk, grabbed his reins, and in a second had turned his horse in a flurry of dust and raced away toward Shaw and Peru.

More rifle shots exploded in the distance, coming from the large number of riders who had spread abreast at the sight of Shaw. Townsfolk fled in every direction, taking cover wherever they could. Dawson spotted Shaw and Peru at the edge of town, lying flat on the ground. Shaw had slapped his horse's rump and sent it racing away, out of danger.

"The deputy's hit!" Shaw called out, looking back long enough to see Dawson leap from his saddle, Winchester in hand, and slap his horse on the rump. Rifle shots whistled past them; pistol shots kicked up dirt thirty yards away, still out of range but getting closer as the riders bore down toward the edge of town.

"How bad?" Dawson dropped to one knee and returned rifle fire, causing the riders to spread wider. The heavy fire waned as one of their men flew back-ward from his saddle and rolled away in the dirt. Back to his feet, Dawson ran forward and slid in beside Shaw.

"I'm all right," Peru shouted, blood spreading on the front of his shirt. His left arm hung limp in the dirt.

"Shoulder wound," said Shaw. "Clipped his collar bone and took a chunk of meat off."

"Stuff this in it," said Dawson, jerking the bandanna from around his neck and tossing it to Shaw.

"I'm all right, damn it!" Peru insisted. Shaw poked the bandanna into the bullet hole causing the bleeding to slow down, but not stop.

Dawson fired three more rifle shots in quick succession and said, "Let's go!"

The two dragged Peru to his feet and began running with him between them, back toward the sheriff's office. Running to meet them, Caldwell fired shot after shot from a Spencer rifle, taking another rider from his horse and causing the rest to duck down in their saddles. "Dawson, there's over a dozen men out there!" he shouted as Dawson and Shaw passed him, hurrying along with Peru.

"Then shoot some of them, *Sheriff!*" Dawson shouted in return.

By the time the four of them had gotten to the boardwalk out in front of the sheriff's office, the riders stopped firing and slowed their horses at the edge of town. At the head of the riders, Hyde Landry stood in his stirrups with a raised hand and fanned the ten riders out in both directions. Behind him sat Clifford Ritchie and Giddis Junior, both of their rifles still smoking. "Circle this shit-hole!" Landry bellowed. Toward the sheriff's office he called out, seeing the four slip inside the door and close it, "Nobody leaves here, Sheriff! Not before you hand over the mad gunman!" He paused, listened for a moment, then shouted, "Do you hear me?"

Caldwell looked out the window, but didn't answer as he stuck fresh rounds into his Spencer rifle. "How is he?" he asked over his shoulder.

"He'll be all right," said Dawson. "But we need to get him to the doctor."

"Out the back door," said Caldwell. "Do it quick before they circle us."

Before anyone could make a move, the front door flew open. Madeline Mercer ran in and shrieked, "Oh, Madden! Are you all right?" She pushed Shaw aside, not recognizing him, as she threw herself down to Peru, who sat slumped in the desk chair.

"Take him to the doctor's, Widow Mercer," Caldwell called out.

"Can you help me get there, Madeline?" Peru asked, taking her hand in his.

"Yes, of course, come along," Madeline said, helping him to his feet. On their way to the rear door, she gave Dawson and Shaw a quick glance. Her eyes lingered on Shaw, doing a quick double take. Recognition flickered on her face for a second, but then she seemed to lose it.

"Madeline?" Peru said quietly, awaiting her in the open door.

"Yes, of course," she said, appearing to have snapped out of a deep thought. She helped Peru through the door and closed it behind them, her eyes making one more quick searching glance at Shaw's thin bearded face.

"She'll be wondering about that for a long time to come," Shaw said in almost a whisper when the door closed behind the two.

"The poor woman," said Dawson. He lifted his Colt and checked it. "She deserves better than either one of us."

From the edge of town Landry called out again, "Sheriff! The man you're protecting shot the leader of our town and burned down my mercantile store. You and I are on the same side of the law here. Hand him over. He's a *criminal,* far as Black's Cut is concerned."

Caldwell stood against the wall beside the open front window and called out, "That may be. But the town you just shot up is my jurisdiction. The man you just shot down is a legally sworn *town deputy.* Now, what does that make *you and your men,* as far as Crabtown is concerned?"

"We're real sorry," said Landry. "That was a mistake on our part, Sheriff. I know which man shot him. I'm going to turn that man over to you. But you've got to give me the mad gunman. Deal?"

Spread out around the town perimeter, the men looked at one another. "What the hell'd he mean by that?" Fogle asked Tommy Corbin, the two of them having fired more shots than the others.

"Beats the hell out of me," said Corbin, whose shot had been the one to hit Peru. "Sounds like he's about to trade me over for the mad gunman!"

"No deal," said Caldwell. "The only deal you'll

get here is to come forward, surrender your guns, and file into my cells. I'll see to it you get a fair trial next time the territorial judge rides through."

"This hardheaded sonsabitch," Landry said to Ritchie and Junior. He glared at Junior. "Why did you start shooting to begin with? Nobody told you to!"

"Because I saw the bastard who shot my pa sitting there eating candy, that's why!" Junior said, incensed by such a question.

"This is going to get *real* ugly, *real* quick," Landry growled under his breath, looking back toward the open window of the sheriff's office. "I heard what happened to Sheriff Foley," he called out. "It was a damned shame. But if he was here, he would see my side and hand the mad gunman over."

"Surrender your guns and turn yourselves in," said Caldwell. "If you don't I'll be coming to Black's Cut to drag you back here, faceup or facedown. I don't care which."

Landry gritted his teeth. "Damn it," he growled.

"Rider coming," said Ritchie, drawing attention back along the trail they'd ridden in on, dust still settling slowly on the still morning air.

"Hell, it's Philbert!" Ritchie said in surprise.

"Don't shoot!" the rider called out, raising his hands as he saw all the exposed weaponry glinting in the sunlight.

No sooner had he brought his horse to a halt than Junior grabbed the horse's bridle and shook it, saying to the rider, "You were supposed to stay in Black's Cut, keep an eye on my pa!"

"I did, Junior!" said Philbert Karnes. "That's why I'm here." He gave Landry a nervous look before saying to Junior, "Your pa is dead!"

Junior's face turned white hot with rage. Spittle flew from his lips as he turned in his saddle and screamed in rage toward the sheriff's office, "I'll *kill* you, you son of a bitch!"

"No, Junior," Philbert shouted. "It wasn't the mad gunman that killed your pa! That boar grizzly came back, ripped down the door, and carried him away!"

"The bear . . . ?" Junior stared wide-eyed, stunned. "You mean he ate my pa?" His hand closed tightly around his gun butt. "You let that brute kill my pa?"

"Check yourself down, Junior," Landry warned in an even tone, stepping his horse between the two.

"Mr. Landry," said Philbert, "we did all we could. We hunted all night, following the bear's trail. It was awful. We found pieces of poor Giddis slung everywhere. I hate thinking about it."

"Jesus!" said Junior, tears of grief and rage in his eyes. "The mad gunman turned that bear loose."

Philbert continued, "We heard Giddis scream and squall for nearly an hour while we tried to catch up to the bear. In the end we scraped together some toes and a couple of your pa's ribs . . . for a funeral."

"Yiiiii!" Junior screamed, unable to control himself any longer. He jerked his horse around and started to put the spurs to it, but Clifford Ritchie made a hard swipe with his pistol barrel and sent Junior to the dirt, knocked cold.

Landry called out to the sheriff's office, "To hell

with the law! We'll burn this town to ashes if you don't give him to me."

Caldwell started to answer defiantly, but seeing Shaw shake his head, he stopped and said, "I mean what I said. He broke the law here. I'll take him down for it."

"I understand," said Shaw, a stick of candy in the side of his mouth. "You can do that afterward, if he's still standing. He raised his Colt an inch in his holster, dropped it loosely, and walked to the front door.

"Whoa, what's this?" Landry asked no one in particular, as Shaw stepped down off the boardwalk and started walking straight and steadily toward him. "Looks like the sheriff knew I wasn't bluffing. He's sent the mad gunman right out to me."

"He's wearing a gun," Ritchie remarked, taking the reins to Landry's horse. He held them as Landry stepped down from his saddle and pulled his long coat back behind his holster.

"That was a wise decision on your part, Sheriff," Landry called out.

"That wasn't my decision, Landry. It was his," Caldwell replied.

Landry's confident smile faded a little as Caldwell's words sank in. "See why we all say he's mad?" he said with a laugh. But even his own men took on a more serious and attentive look as Shaw walked closer. "All right, Sheriff, we're square now," Landry said. "You can relax now and go on about your business."

"I'm keeping it fair," Caldwell said as he and Dawson stepped out of the office and down into the street. He walked forward, and stopped a few feet back and out to the side of Shaw. He carried a rifle in one hand, a shotgun in the other. When he reached his chosen position in the street, within shotgun range, he dropped the rifle at his feet and cocked both hammers on the shotgun.

"Wave the men in around us, Clifford," Landry whispered, seeing Dawson had walked a wide circle and now stood flanking him from thirty feet away.

"There's the dirty jake who busted my nose!" said DeLaurie, his voice still a nasal twang. He stepped down from his saddle and shoved his horse away. "I want you, mister!" he said, staring hard at Dawson.

Dawson only nodded his acknowledgment.

"Me too," said Newhouse, down from his horse and tapping the side of his head where Dawson had cracked him with his pistol barrel. On the ground, Junior raised himself up on all fours, his head throbbing. But seeing Dawson, he growled like an angry dog and forced himself onto his feet, facing Dawson first, then turning to Shaw.

"Before I kill you, Mad Gunman," said Landry, taking off his tight black leather riding gloves and sticking them down into his belt, "tell all of us who you are."

Dawson stood in silence, watching Shaw, who said in a quiet tone, "I'm the man who killed you, Landry. That's all you need to know."

Landry's expression turned to stone. "Good

enough for me, but there's some here who've heard you claim to be Fast Larry Shaw."

"I made that claim," said Shaw. "But everybody knows Fast Larry is dead."

"I see," said Landry, watching his eyes, looking for just the right second to make his play. "So, who are you, just some *fast gun* who never quite made it? Was never quite good enough? Somebody fast, but never quite fast enough?" Before he finished his words, his hand went for his gun, knowing that his questions had caught the mad gunman off guard. *Hadn't they . . . ?*

Before the tip of his barrel had cleared his holster, Shaw's shot nailed him. He tumbled backward with pieces of his bloody heart splattering all over Ritchie and Giddis Junior. The two stood staring in frozen disbelief, having not even seen Shaw's gun come up from the holster before Landry went flying backward, dead.

Then Ritchie snapped out of it and shouted, as he drew his gun, "Kill them!"

Caldwell, seeing Newhouse and DeLaurie faced off toward Dawson, sent the first blast of buckshot at Newhouse at the same time as Dawson's Colt came up and sent a bullet through DeLaurie's chest. The two hit the ground at the same time. Shaw's next shot spun Ritchie in a hard circle, and then the second blast from Caldwell's shotgun hit him so hard he flipped backward out of his right boot and landed facedown in the dirt. His gun sailed from his hand, hit the ground, and fired.

Nearby, Fogle folded at the waist when the stray bullet hit him. He went down on buckled knees, and looked all around wide-eyed and bewildered, his gun still in his hand, unfired.

In the midst of the blazing gun battle, Junior fired wildly, shot after shot, hitting nothing. Screaming and cursing in his anger, he ran toward Shaw with his pistol out at arm's length. "I've got you, Mad Gunman. You son of a bit—"

Shaw's shot silenced him and sent him rolling in the dirt. He stopped rolling and lay dead at the feet of Madden Peru, who had seen Caldwell step out of the office with shotgun and rifle and come running. A loose unfinished bandage dangled from Peru's shoulder. "I—I missed it?" he said.

In the midst of the melee, Tommy Corbin had slipped away, grabbed his horse, and shot out along the trail like a dart. Seeing the rider growing smaller, Dawson said to Peru, "Shoot him, if you need to shoot somebody."

Peru drew his pistol quickly and instinctively. But as he raised it to take close aim out over his cocked forearm, he shook his head, lowered the gun, and said, "I can't do it. I won't back-shoot a man without an awfully strong reason." He looked at Caldwell and said, "Sorry," as Corbin vanished into the rising dust behind him.

Caldwell, Dawson, and Shaw all three looked at one another, glad to see Peru's response. "No apologies needed, Deputy," said Caldwell.

But Peru, seeing a slight smile on Dawson's face

and misreading it, said, "I would have been here sooner if I could have. I'm not afraid. I can handle myself."

"We know that, Deputy," said Caldwell, opening the shotgun and letting the empty smoking shells fall to the dirt.

Shaw looked down and began reloading his Colt. Dawson opened the chamber on his Colt, punched out the empties, and did the same, looking at Peru as he did so.

Shaw stepped over, stooped down beside Landry, and slipped the Colt from his holster. "This was my Colt," he said, "the one they took from me in Black's Cut." He examined the Colt as he said, "He would have killed me with my own gun."

"Yes," Dawson said to Shaw, still looking at Peru, "but instead, you killed him with his own gun, the one you took from his store."

Shaw chuckled, "Yeah, come to think of it." He stood up with his old familiar Colt twirling back and forth slickly on his finger, dipping into his holster, then springing back into his hand. "Welcome home," he said to the gun flashing in his hand.

My God! Peru stood staring, speechless, impressed by the quickness, realizing that on his best day, as fast as he was with a gun, he was no match for something like this. It didn't even look real, he thought, seeing a blur of iron flash in and out of this man's hand.

Seeing the look on Peru's face, Caldwell grinned, unable to resist saying to the mad gunman, "In case

you haven't heard, Peru here is the man who killed
Fast Larry Shaw, straight up, one on one."

The Colt stopped cold in Shaw's hand and seemed
to jump down into his holster like some slick, shiny,
well-trained animal. "Oh, you did," he said flatly,
staring at Peru with an unreadable expression. "Tell
me, was he as fast as everybody said?"

Peru looked from face to face, knowing that something important hung on his answer; yet he had no
idea what it was. Finally he nodded and said sincerely, "If it's all the same, I'd just as soon not talk
about killing a man. I've learned that it's not something a man ought to go around talking about."

The three stared at him as the townsmen ventured
forward from hiding. Finally, Shaw said in the same
flat, expressionless voice, "That's probably a good
idea, Deputy." His eyes moved across Dawson and
Caldwell; a trace of a smile moved across his face.
"You never know who might be listening."

Dawson, Caldwell, and Shaw all laughed. At first
it caught Peru by surprise; but then he realized they
weren't laughing at him, but rather finding in common some dark ironic joke that men like these three
shared. Something part of their world, something to
do with the right and wrong of things, and the way
these kinds of men handled it. He wasn't sure what
it was, yet he understood it, he thought. He understood it because he was one of them. Yes, that was
it. He was one of them.

He nodded and laughed along with them, watching Shaw and Dawson turn and walk to where their

horses had joined one another and stood awaiting them. He watched them step into their saddles, tip their hats, and ride away.

"Theirs is not the laughter of fools," Caldwell said, quoting some obscure text, "but the laughter of bold men who allow no wrongs to go unattended." He turned with a sigh and carried his rifle and shotgun back toward his office.

Peru stood watching as the two rode away, south-westerly. As they grew smaller on the horizon, he felt Madeline Mercer's arm slip into his. "Who is that sinister-looking man with the beard?" she asked.

"The mad gunman," he said. "Or at least that's what Caldwell and Dawson called him."

"There's something familiar about him . . ." she said, letting her words trail into contemplation. She thought about it as she watched the two ride out of sight. "Oh well, I suppose I'll never know." They turned arm in arm and walked away toward the doctor's office.